Temple of Legends

The Assassin's Tale

Michael Long

ISBN: 978-1-61296-668-7

PUBLISHED BY BLACK ROSE WRITING

www.blackrosewriting.com

Printed in the United States of America

Suggested retail price $16.95

Temple of Legends is printed in Andalus

First off I want to thank my girlfriend Ashly,
for being by my side this whole time.

My mom and dad for always believing in me.

My brothers Jason and Kevin,
for being the best brothers a person could have.

And the kids. Justin, Olivia, Abel and Hailey
for bringing so much joy to my life.

Temple of Legends

The Assassin's Tale

Chapter 1

Mike was so distracted by his own thoughts that he barely noticed the snow falling all around him, not that it was really surprising though, since it was getting close to the end of the year. But it wasn't winter that was causing his mind to wander but more so the upcoming wedding that he knew he needed to be at, a wedding between the woman he was in love with, and a man who wasn't him.

Candice had been in his life for a very long time, and most of that time they had been together, it was never in the open. They were always hidden behind closed doors or in the shadows, something that he always hated, but at the same time he knew their love had to remain that way, and it took him a very long time to realize that it wasn't fair for either of them to live their lives like that. She deserved to be with someone she could love out in the open, someone she could have a family with, someone who wasn't him.

It was then that he realized he was getting closer and closer to his destination, and he made himself stop and take a few quick breaths of the brisk winter air. He could feel the snowflakes as they landed on the top of his head, something that came with having short dark brown hair.

He could hardly feel the cold at all thanks to his thick dark blue leather armor, something he was very thankful for because he knew the weather was far below freezing this night, and he didn't want the coldness to distract him from the mission at hand.

His right hand made its way to the hilt of his ebony dagger on his belt, and he couldn't help but wrap his fingers around it, he was so used to them being there that they were now nothing more than a part of his body, his very soul even, and with that in mind, he began taking a few more steps towards the cottage he knew wasn't that far away.

"Stop right there or I will be forced to kill you."

Mike barely heard the words, as he stood in front of the small gate blocking his way to the cottage, a place he needed to get to so he could kill the man who lived in it. He couldn't help but let his eyes drift from the front door of the cottage towards the guard who had spoken to him, and it was then that he saw the man holding a small crossbow aimed towards him, but even that didn't keep his sight for long.

He knew this small town very well and had traveled here often in his hundred and twenty-eight years, and even now with the snow falling so quickly and covering the ground with its whiteness, he knew he could make it to any one of the small town's gates with his eyes closed and get away if he needed to.

He once again shifted his gaze but this time towards his feet, and he watched as the falling snowflakes slowly began to cover his dark blue leather boots. He felt a small bit of guilt wash over him at that moment, knowing that very soon the perfectly white snow-covered ground would be stained with blood.

He felt his hands slowly reaching for the hilts of his two daggers once again, and he couldn't help but flex his fingers around them, feeling the smoothness of his dark blue leather gloves on their ebony hilts.

The rest of his leather outfit was the same dark blue color as his boots and gloves and fit to his body perfectly, covering him from his neck to his toes in its harden but very flexible protectiveness. He also brought his two matching ebony swords with him, and even though they were weightless, he could still feel them strapped to his back, within easy reach.

"And why would you want to kill me, kind sir?" Mike found himself asking, as he returned his gaze to the guard and the crossbow, which was still pointing his way.

"You are trespassing on private land, and it is my job to keep people like you off of it," the guard said while trying to keep his voice steady. Clearly he was afraid for his life.

"People like me, kind sir?" Mike said, while taking a few more steps towards the guard. "And who might people like me be?"

"You are one of those immortal assassins sent here from your godforsaken temple, on who knows what kind of sick business," the guard said, as his finger inched closer to the trigger of his crossbow.

"If you truly believe me to be one of them, why would you even bother pointing that silly thing my way in the first place?" Mike asked, pulling his two ebony daggers from their harnesses. "If that were to be true, then it wouldn't really kill me now, would it."

"Maybe it would or maybe it wouldn't. I'm not caring one way or another, as long as you turn around and walk away," the guard said, and then he let out a soft whistle and three other guards came out of the small door of the cottage, all of them armed with a sword.

"I am simply here to kill the lord of this house, nothing more and nothing less," Mike said, gripping the hilts of his daggers even tighter. "My fight is not with you four, so if you wish to live through this day, I ask that you lay down your arms and let me pass."

Mike knew that even the four of them wouldn't stand a chance against him, after all, he had trained for 120 years in the art of killing and fighting, where as he could tell right away that these guards were nothing more than hired novices.

"Like I said before, if you come any closer, I will be forced to kill you," the same guard said again, and this time Mike noticed the crossbow slowly begin to shake in the man's nervous hands.

"Fools you all are for protecting a man who rapes and murders the young, and if you insist on standing in my way, I will kill you quickly and your lives will become nothing more than a waste, and your names will quickly be forgotten," Mike said, taking a few more steps towards the gate in front of him.

Mike could tell right away that the men were not going to back down and let him pass, and he couldn't help but feel a small amount of guilt wash over him. He never had a problem killing people who deserved to die, but killing the innocent ones who tried to protect them never sat well with the assassin, and with that thought fresh in his mind, he took a few more steps closer.

He felt the crossbow bolt strike him just under his ribs and he could feel its metal shaft cut through his armor and bury itself deep into his chest, which would have killed most men but Mike smiled as he felt the pain, knowing he would live through it, and he couldn't help but slightly laugh as he felt the poison of the dart slowly enter his blood stream.

Mike ran towards the gate with a speed no simple man could have managed and made a quick jump over the four-foot high gate, landing with a slight roll. Coming back up to his agile feet in seconds, he slowly began walking towards the closest guard, who was quickly trying to reload the crossbow.

"I guess you chose wrong this day, thinking you could kill me with such a weak weapon," Mike said as he walked right up to the guard, kneeing him the chest.

Mike couldn't help but watch the man lean forward, as all of the air left his lungs. Guilt washed over him once again, as he brought his left hand down towards the back of the man's neck, burying his ebony dagger's blade right down to the hilt. He pulled it out a few seconds later and watched the lifeless man's body drop to the snow-covered ground.

Again his eyes found their way back to the falling snow and then back to the spot the guard now lay very dead by his feet, and he couldn't help but feel a little sadness as the man's warm blood quickly changed the white snow to a deep dark red color.

It was the noise of the three remaining guards that brought Mike to the situation at hand, and he quickly realized that the three of them had made a triangle around him. He smiled again, as he looked upon them with disbelief in their eyes.

"I will give you one more chance to lay down your arms and be on your way," Mike said, while leaning down so he could use the snow to wipe the blood off of the blade of his dagger.

"We have you outnumbered, and unlike our friend you just murdered, we will not be caught off guard," The man standing right in front of Mike said, as he took a few more steps towards him.

Mike looked up towards the man, even as he continued to clean the blood from his dagger, and he couldn't help but smile, yet again. The guard in front of him was now within arm's reach, and yet he had just said he wouldn't be caught off guard. Once again with a speed no simple man could match, Mike launched himself forward, and with his right hand he came around so quick he managed to embed his right dagger straight in the guard's wrist of his sword arm, which forced the man's sword to fall from his limp grip. With a second quick spin, and a slight flick of his left wrist, Mike sliced the man's neck and ended his turn, facing the last two remaining guards, not even looking towards the second dead body falling towards the snowy ground.

He noticed then that the last two remaining guards had taken a few steps away from him, and he realized then that all of this nonsense would be over with soon enough, and he could continue with the business he had come to this small town for.

Mike never liked fighting novices because they always rushed their movements and their attacks. They never planned ahead, and he could always read their plays before they even decided to make them. They always rushed because their life spans were short, like all humans, unlike him who had all the time in the world. After all, he was immortal.

Even as the guard on the left came in with a quick thrust of his sword, Mike knew the best way to block the attack was with his left hand while parrying the attack from the second guard with his right, and so it went on for a few long moments, but in the end he knew he would win because after all, he would never run out of energy or strength and he could already see the two of them beginning to sweat and tire.

Mike watched as the guard on the left went for a downward slash towards his unprotected shoulder. Because he planned on just the attack, with a quick kick to the guard on the right, he was able to sidestep the sword's slash and answer back with three quick dagger stabs to man's now exposed spinal cord before turning back to the last of the guards who was in full flight heading away from the battlefield.

Mike couldn't help but shake his head as he watched the man run away, and he wondered if he would ever stop running or if his fear would keep him going till the end of time. It was then that he turned back towards the main door of the cottage, and started walking towards it and away from the blood stained snow-covered ground.

He turned the small door handle, pushed it gently open, and slowly walked into the cottage not knowing if more guards were hidden inside. Soon he found himself in a very small entry way and very much alone.

Now that he had a moment to himself, he replaced his daggers into their harnesses and reached towards the crossbow bolt, which was still embedded in his chest and leather armor. As he pulled it out, he couldn't help but wince ever so slightly from the pain.

It didn't take him long to figure out that the lower floor was empty of people, and he slowly began walking up the only staircase in the small cottage. Again he was surprised by the lack of guards inside the house, and he quickly found himself facing the only doorway on the upper level.

A quick turn of the doorknob let Mike know the door was locked but an even quicker kick from his leather boot sent the door and most of the frame flying into the room. With a smile on his face, he walked in, and it was then that he noticed a single man sitting on a red recliner looking towards the fireplace on the far side of the room.

"So the assassin finally came a calling," the man said as he turned his sights from the fire towards Mike for the first time. "What took you so long?"

"I got busy killing your guards and all," Mike said while walking towards the other chair by the fireplace and sitting in it. After all, he didn't fear this old man.

It was then that Mike looked the man over fully and was surprised to find him in his late fifties with white shoulder length hair and a matching goatee. He was nicely dressed in a fine black and green silk suit, and a pair of leather dress-shoes, but he was also slightly overweight, and Mike didn't think he would have to struggle too hard to kill the old man.

"Did you kill them all?" the old man asked, looking back towards the fireplace and poking the logs with his golden cane, a cane Mike knew he used to beat the young girls to death with after he was finished with them.

"No, one of them ran away while I was busy killing the others," Mike said, watching the tip of the golden cane begin to glow a bright red color as the fire heated it up.

"Was it the young one?" the old man asked with sadness in his voice. "The one with brown hair and hazel eyes, is he the one who ran away?"

"Yes I believe it was him. The others had blonde hair and fought and died for a foolish cause," Mike said while spinning the poisoned crossbow bolt around in the palm of his hand.

"Awe, that one was my son, and thank you for sparing his life," the old man said as tears began to flow down his pale cheeks.

"He will continue to live as long as he doesn't come back for revenge," Mike said, while quickly reaching across and stabbing the old man in the leg with the poisoned bolt, hoping it had enough poison left in it to kill him, slowly and painfully, because the old man didn't deserve a quick death.

The old man flinched in pain as the bolt jabbed into his left leg but was able to manage a quick swing of his golden cane but it wasn't quick enough. Mike caught it midair with his right hand, and he could feel the heat of it trying to burn its way through his leather glove, another quick jerk of his wrist sent the cane flying across the room.

"Did she send you hear to find me?" the old man asked as he pulled the crossbow bolt from his leg. "Was she the one who ordered my death?"

"It doesn't matter now, you are already dead." Mike stated, standing up from the chair and turning away from the old man.

"How do you know there was enough poison left on the bolt to kill me?" the old man asked, watching Mike head back towards the door.

"Your eyes are already turning a shade of black and your ears are bleeding," Mike said, turning to face the old man for the last time. "So if I had to guess, I would say you have about an hour of great pain heading your way before your body will begin to shut down, and only after that will you die."

"How long have you been one of them, boy?" the man asked, for his final question.

"I have been training as an assassin for a hundred and twenty years now," Mike said, walking towards the door. "They took me in when I was eight years old and gave me a life to live, killing men and women the likes of you."

"Give it time assassin, and you too will see that you have become no better than us," The old man said, trying his best to fight back a fit of coughing. "You are just hiding your evil behind that blue armor of yours."

Mike was already out of the room before the old man finished talking, but his heightened sense of sound allowed him to hear all of it anyways, and a part of him couldn't help but stop for a second at the man's final words, but with one final shrug of his shoulders he headed out of the small cottage and back into the snow.

It was then that he realized he needed to make his way back home, something he was trying his best not to do, something he dreaded very much. He didn't know if he was going to be able to hold himself together long enough to make it through the wedding, let alone the months that would follow it, and with one last look up towards the fast falling snow, he forced his feet to move forward.

Chapter 2

Mike awoke from let another full night of sleep, and even though he was in a hurry to return to the temple, he couldn't find the willpower to get himself up and out of the comfortable bed he was currently lying in. He could never figure it out, but for some reason it seemed like all of the inn's seemed to have the nicest of beds.

It had been two weeks since he left the small town and he was about half way home, but he figured he had earned a few days off so he could enjoy some much needed rest and peace. He didn't know if he could handle seeing Candice now, not so close to her wedding day, even the thought of it made his stomach turn as he laid on his back staring at the ceiling.

Candice was the head of all of the assassins and the leader of the priestess's of the grand and holy Temple of Legends and also the one who handed out the list of people who deserved to die, and for the better half of Mike's long life, the women he loved. But like all things, their love was forbidden by the order, and in the position of power that Candice was in there were many out there looking for a reason to overthrow her or to simply kill her and move up the ranks.

After all, she was rated as high as the gods, some would say, in this world where Mike was no more than a powerful pawn in the god's grand design. Because of that he had ended it with her, and told her that it would be best is she found a noblemen or a bishop to marry, a person who would be acceptable in everyone's eyes, everyone's but Mike's.

So even though it was his words that drove her towards her soon to be husband, it still brought sadness to his heart. But he knew he too would one day move on, after all, living forever should heal even the wounds of the heart.

Mike was brought out of his thoughts of Candice when a rough knock sounded at his door followed by a kick or two before the door swung open, and a giant of a man walked in dressed fully in a bulky blue and silver suit of armor and a matching fully enclosed helmet. His right hand was resting on the hilt of his jagged but perfectly crystal clear sword, and he had a silver shield resting on his left arm.

Followed behind the man in the suit of armor was a tall but slender female wearing only a pair of cotton pants that fit to her long legs and butt tightly and a small brown button up jacket with only two of the buttons done up across her breast but revealing everything else from her cleavage up and everything else under her breast, including her many different tattoos, which seemed to cover most of her naked flesh.

It was her forest green eyes which stood out the most because her pupils were in the shape of two small leafs, one in each eye, and of course her long deep brown hair, which hung well past her shoulders. She also had a bow and a quiver of arrows strapped to her back.

After looking the pair over, Mike let go of his grip on his ebony sword, which was lying under the sheets and relaxed his head back onto his very comfy pillow. "You can pay for the door my old friend."

"Why are you still in bed?" The man in the suit of armor spoke as he walked a little closer to Mike. "We have a wedding to get you to."

"Awe, Eric leave him be. Can't you tell he's heartbroken," the lady said, walking past Eric to sit on the bed beside Mike.

"Did Candice send the two of you here to make sure I finished the job?" Mike asked, turning to face the girl sitting next to him.

"No. She got word of the old man's death a day or two after you killed him." Eric said after taking off his helmet revealing his wavy jet black hair and his deep blue colored eyes. "She however sent me and Shelby here to see why it was taking you so long in returning home."

"All to make sure I was safe and sound I bet." Mike said with a laugh knowing that Candice would never fear for his safety, after all, he was one of the best assassin's she had ever trained.

"Maybe, you above all others should know that she never lets on what her true feelings are when it comes to anything relating to us and the order," Shelby said. "Now, get dressed. We have a long walk ahead of us."

"We will meet you downstairs," Eric said, walking back out of the now broken doorway. "And don't forget to pay for the broken door on your way out."

"What is it?" Mike couldn't help but ask, when he noticed Shelby making no signs of following her big companion.

"She is sad, you know," Shelby said, turning to look Mike in the eyes, and she couldn't help but notice his pain and hurt as well. "She is sad that it is her wedding day, and the one standing next to her isn't you."

"If it was me, the both of us would be stripped of our ranks and everything that comes with it," Mike said, lifting himself up on his elbows, so he could look at his friend. "We would become hunted and more than likely killed."

"Your fighting skills wouldn't leave you nor would the power that Candice has to grant," Shelby said, finally standing up off of the bed. "Maybe the two of you could finally grow old together."

"I truly wish it was that simple," Mike answered.

"I wish it was as well," Shelby replied, turning to face the broken door.

"You and Eric will be able to live forever and with each other," Mike continued as he slowly sat up on the edge of the bed and let his legs hang over the end, his feet planted fully on the ground. "He loves you as much as you love him, and for that the two of you should be happy with each other and worry about me less."

"You are like a brother to us and I fear we will not be able to be happy as long as you are heartbroken, my friend," Shelby told him, taking two more steps towards the door. "Candice loves you."

Mike watched as Shelby walked out of the broken doorway and stared off into the empty hallway for a few moments before getting the rest of the way out of bed and walking towards his dark blue armor. It only took him a matter of minutes to get it fully on and all of his weapons ready to go.

He found himself now standing in front of a mirror, and he couldn't help but admire how he looked in his leather armor, as he reached up and ran his fingers through his short, dark brown hair. He always kept it cut short so it would be out of his sight. He never could figure out why some guys let their hair grow long, so they could wear it in a ponytail.

His skin was always tanned, which made his hazel colored eyes stand out even more, and as he stood there starring at himself, he couldn't help but remember the days when it was Candice standing in front of him starring back, and he had to force himself to look away and leave the room.

The rest of the inn was small and very uninteresting and Mike tossed a handful of gold coins on the desk at the front door to cover the broken door and room. He headed off into the sun light with his two good friends, and his heart sank with every step he took, knowing damn well that they would only lead him closer and closer to Candice's wedding.

"Is something wrong, my love?"

Candice had heard those words spoken to her many times over the last month and here she was again forced to smile and lie to her soon to be husband. "I am fine, Kevin, I promise."

"You just don't seem to be yourself today," Kevin said, walking over to his soon to be wife. "Are you getting nervous about our wedding?"

Candice couldn't help but turn to face Kevin, who was in so many ways a great and good-looking man. He stood easily over six-feet tall, and currently he was wearing a finely cut, white and grey, cotton striped, three-button suit and tie with matching pants and white runners, something that always made her smile. He also had a perfect smile and was wearing a white hat which was currently covering his short red hair.

Even now as her eyes drifted towards the long sword hanging from the left side of his belt, she fought hard to hold back a small laugh knowing that he wasn't trained to fight with it. Kevin was a grand bishop and was raised to be noble and kind, not a skilled swordsman. It was that thought that made her think of another man but that was a long time ago and in what seemed like a different life. "I promise I am fine, and I am looking forward to our wedding."

"I am happy to hear that, my love," Kevin said, after giving his future wife a kiss on the cheek. "Think of how embarrassing it would be if you backed out three days before our wedding."

"I have no plans on backing out now, I promise you that much," Candice continued, trying her hardest to smile a real smile. "I have just been stressed out with all the assignments as of late, and a group of the assassins have let to return home."

"And you are worried about them?" Kevin asked, sitting on the edge of their giant-sized bed.

"Of course I am worried about them," Candice answered, looking towards the glass doors leading towards her balcony. "Not for their safety, that would be foolish, but they should have returned by now, and it is odd for them to be late."

"I am sure they are on their way," Kevin said, watching his soon to be wife closely, trying to get a read on her true emotions. "Assassins have always been an unpredictable sort."

"Yes, I'm sure you are right," Candice replied, turning to face Kevin once again. "People will start saying the same about you if you do not hurry to your final tux fitting, you are already late."

"Yes I almost forgot about that," Kevin agreed, walking right up to Candice and gently giving her a kiss. "I will see you this evening at the dinner party. I love you."

"I love you too," Candice said, turning to watch Kevin leave their bedroom, closing the door behind him.

Candice found herself once again standing in front of the full length mirror that hung in front of her shower, and she couldn't help but look at herself standing there in her red and black leather amour and once again a real smile found its way to her lips.

She knew that in three days she would be forced to put on her wedding dress, and for the first time in a very, very long time she was nervous about that. She hadn't worn a dress in what seemed liked ages, and she knew it would be nice for a change to be rid of the leather armor and be a true lady for a day. Maybe she would even leave her duel war axes behind.

Her hands found their way towards the ebony handles of the axes that were strapped to both sides of her belt, and she couldn't help but run her naked fingers over the cold steel of the blades. Even though it had been a few hundred years since they had tasted the flesh of another person, she knew they were just as sharp as ever.

Her pale, grey-colored eyes found their way back to the front of her half done up leather jacket, and she reached up to do the zipper back up but part of her didn't want to, part of her knew that the fact that she wasn't wearing a bra, and the zipper was that low made her feel sexy. By showing of the V-shape of her chest, she was reminding everyone that she could be both a beautiful lady and the leader of the Order of Assassin's.

The sparkle of the ebony dagger shaped pendent hanging around her neck caused a ton of mixed feeling to rush through her all at once. She had gotten it as a gift from a man who loved her more than anything else in the world, a man who was not the guy she was planning on marrying in three days, a man she had taken in and trained to be the greatest killer in all of the world.

Mike was only eight years old when Candice found him floating on a single piece of wood in the middle of the ocean when she was traveling from the merchant islands to the east, back towards the Temple of Legends.

She had saved the boy and brought him back with her and learned on the journey home that he had been floating on that single piece of wood for almost five days. It was then that she realized he would be the perfect assassin, strong and tough with no family to miss him.

Over the next twenty years she mentored and taught Mike everything she knew about fighting to staying alive to hiding, and with the help of the other priestess, they molded him into a finely tuned killer. On the day he turned twenty-eight, she had granted him his immortality and let him loose on the world.

By doing so, Candice realized every time he had returned from a mission that not only was he getting better and better at killing, but she was also falling in love with him. She knew that by the way Mike would return her smile that he too was in love with her.

A tear slowly rolled down her cheek as she thought back to the days of them meeting in secret, and all of the time she spent cuddled up in his arms during the cold winter nights, all the way up until he turned his back on their love, telling her that she could never be with him and that she deserved a life with a man she could love in the open, a man she could marry and have babies with.

This time her fingers found their way to the coolness of the ebony pendent and she lost herself in the mirror once again. That was until she suddenly realized that she was no longer alone.

"You were so easy to sneak up on," Mike said, as he watched Candice turn suddenly to face him, both her hands on the handles of her axes and her dark brown hair moving smoothly as she turned.

"How did you get in here?" Candice asked, trying to keep the smile from showing on her lips.

"You trained me to be one of the best assassins in the world, and then you are surprised at my skills of sneaking into your room," Mike said, while walking out of the small bathroom and back into the main bedroom.

"I didn't think you would come," Candice said as her eyes darted towards the main door, hoping Kevin didn't return, finding Mike in their private bedroom.

"I am simply returning from my mission," Mike explained, pulling the golden cane from the back of his belt and tossing it onto Candice's bed. "The child killer is no more."

"So I've heard," Candice said, biting her lower lip, fighting all of her urges to say more.

Mike knew that she wanted to say more to him, but he also knew that he couldn't afford to hear her words. Not so close to her wedding day, not with all of his feelings threatening to drive him mad as he looked upon Candice and how beautiful she was now standing in the same room as him, something he had avoided doing for some time now.

"Are you planning on staying?" Candice asked, seeing Mike looking towards the open doors leading to the balcony, clearly the way he had let himself in.

"Well that might not go so well if your future husband were to return and find me here," Mike said with a slight laugh as he turned back to face Candice. "What if he tried to attack me?"

It was Candice's turn to laugh a little at that. She knew that if Kevin were to return and find Mike here, he would most likely try to attack him and force Mike into defending himself, which would likely lead to Kevin dying or Candice stepping in on behalf of her soon to be husband. But even she didn't know if she could take Mike anymore in a fight.

"And what about my wedding, will you be coming to it?" Candice dared to ask.

"Wouldn't it look bad if your top assassin didn't show up to your wedding?" Mike asked, looking again at the doors leading to the balcony. "What choice do I have?"

"You have always been one to make your own choices whether I have agreed to them or not." Candice said, walking right up behind Mike, her chest almost against his back. "I will not blame you if you did not come."

"You would not blame me but it would look bad for the both of us," Mike said, while trying his hardest not to turn and face Candice. "If I was not there it would show that I felt guilty or even betrayed by you marrying him, and that would spread rumors, something neither of us can afford at this time."

"So you will pretend to be happy that I am getting married?" Candice asked, while trying to fight back the tears threatening to overtake her eyes.

"You will marry Kevin, and maybe one day you will learn to love him. The two of you will live a happy life together, and you will have babies. One day you will retire and grow old and die with him." Mike said, and he couldn't help but feel a pain in his chest at his own words.

Before Candice could even say a word, Mike turned around so fast it caused her to step backwards out of shock and even more so when his lips met hers. Before she knew what was happening, she was kissing him back. She had always loved him, but she always knew for the safety of them both he was right about her marrying Kevin and not him.

The sound of the doorknob turning on the main door caused her to turn away from Mike's embrace, knowing that Kevin would be more than likely walking in on them, and in fact it was Kevin who came bursting into the room, a tux in one hand and a dozen roses in the other. It was his smile that really caught her off guard, and she turned to face the doors leading onto her balcony to find them empty.

"The flowers are for you," Kevin said, and Candice still found herself staring out the doors. "And were you just talking to someone?"

"Of course not, my love, I was simply going over my vows for our wedding," Candice said, turning to face Kevin and hoping the tears weren't still showing in her eyes.

And once again Candice was caught off guard by a kiss and this time it was by her future husband, and she found herself kissing him back as well, but her heart didn't seem to feel the same now as it did a minute ago, while she was kissing Mike.

Mike couldn't help but walk a little faster as he neared the edge of the city. He wanted to put as much distance between himself and the temple, a place he had just not only kissed his forbidden love but the same place he had to hear another man kissing that same woman, something that made him nearly storm back into the room and kill the man.

But he knew that wouldn't solve anything and it would only lead to him having to flee and go into exile, this way would be much better he figured, this way he would still get to see Candice from time to time, even if he never got to hold her or kiss her ever again.

He felt his heart slowly begin to calm as he looked upon his small little cottage nested in between a few large pine trees that were mostly overgrown and hid most of the outline of his place in their large branches, but he wouldn't have had it any other way. He loved living outside of town and everyone who knew he lived there, mostly wished to avoid him anyway.

Now his cottage looked even more amazing because the large trees were covered in snow and ice and so was the ground around his house. A snow-covered ground that he knew would never be stained red with blood. He found his nerves begin to relax even more, as he approached his house.

He reached for the doorknob and turned it with ease, knowing it wouldn't be locked, it was never locked. No one would be dumb enough to enter his house and try to steal anything from him. Well almost no one he realized as he opened the door and walked inside, he couldn't help but notice a small chest sitting on his small table in the kitchen, something he knew he didn't leave there when he left.

Even though it was something new, Mike knew what it was and who had left it there for him. He couldn't help but remember the days when he would return from a mission, and Candice would be there waiting for him with his payment. But he knew those days were gone, and all he would ever find upon returning home now was a chest filled with gold.

He picked up the chest, and without even opening it to check out how much was inside of it, he walked into the small living room area and knelt down right in the center of it. He reached down and pulled on the small latch carved into the floor, revealing a trapdoor, leading into a massive space, which was his basement.

He flipped the chest over and watched all of the gold coins fall out of it, and into the giant pile of gold already filling the hole under his house, and he couldn't help but wonder what he was going to do when the hole was fully filled up with gold. It was then that he realized he might need to by a new cottage, a big one with a bigger basement.

That brought a slight smile to his face, as he looked down at all the gold he had. Everything he had earned for the most part over the last hundred years was stored in the space under his cottage.

Mike tossed the small chest into the fireplace along with some kindling, and in a few minutes had a fire going. He could already feel the warmth of it, as he walked from the living room to the small room in the back of the cottage, the room he used as an armory.

Again he turned the doorknob knowing once again that everything would be the same as it was when he left, and he found his way to one of the few bare manikins and began stripping his dark blue leather armor off and placed it on the manikin. It wasn't until he was down to just his shorts that he ran his fingers along the small hole in the chest piece of his armor where the crossbow bolt had sliced right through it. He felt a slight bit of guilt wash over him because he knew he should be dead, and if that was the case, four people would be alive at that moment.

He then attached his belt, which held his two ebony daggers on it and the harness with his two ebony swords before leaving the room and heading to the ladder that led to the loft and his bedroom, a room he realized felt so bare now that he was in it alone, knowing that Candice would never be there waiting for him to come home ever again.

He fell into his bed without a second thought, even though he knew he needed to shower and get ready for the grand wedding dinner, which was to be held in a few hours, but he couldn't bring himself to get up, couldn't bring himself to care. He knew he would be at the wedding and he would have a fake smile on the whole time, but this was just a dinner party and he knew that he would not be missed.

After a few minutes of laying on his oversized bed, Mike found that he couldn't find a comfortable position, and the softness of the black silk sheets on his naked skin was starting to bug him, not to mention the fact that the sheets were a gift from Candice and he knew that they too would soon find their way into the fireplace below.

Even as he lay in bed by himself, he was having a hard time thinking about anything other than Candice. She had been a big part of his life for a very long time, and he didn't want to believe that he was truly losing her, but he knew that with her getting married a lot of things would change between them.

Mike couldn't help but look around his small loft and the small amount of things that he owned or even had in it. The room itself was only about fifteen-feet by fifteen-feet with four solid walls and the small opening leading in and out of the room. The wall to his left housed a window that looked out towards a very small frozen pond but most of the time it was covered by the tree branches.

He had one dresser in the room that sat against the wall across from the foot of the bed, since the day the cottage was made, everything in the room had been there since that day. Once the walls to the loft were built, there would be no way to get it out or new stuff in, but that didn't really matter to Mike anyway.

He kept one manikin to the right of the bed, which housed his very finest of armor and weapons. He also had a few hidden traps, just in case someone tried to tamper with it. That suit of armor was almost the same as the rest of the armor he wore, but it was crafted with a light weight metal that flexed like leather. It was hundred times tougher though, and it was more a pitch black color with a little blue mixed into it.

Again the suit of armor came with two swords in a harness on the back and two daggers in a fancy belt harnesses, but unlike all other weapons he was used to wielding, these four were by far the finest, perfectly balanced and sharp enough that they could cut through a fine suit of armor like it was no more than melted butter. These weapons he had stolen from the grand armor in the temple itself, weapons Candice didn't even know he now possessed. The weapons themselves were crafted out of some rare metal that the world ran out of a long time ago, which allowed them to slightly glow a faint dark blue color. It was another reason why he felt like he needed to steal them.

The swords and daggers were crafted as soon as the priestess started granting assassins the gift of immortality as a means to keep them from running wild. Always the head of the order of assassins would keep the weapons close at hand and train with them because only their blades were able to kill an immortal.

Candice thought the daggers and swords were not suited for her when she took over as the leader of the order of assassins, and she had them locked away for safe keeping and crafted her duel ebony axes to take their place.

That thought now made Mike finally smile as he thought about her face if she ever discovered them to be missing. He knew though that if anyone ever figured out what had gone on between Candice and him, they would try to steal the weapons from the armory themselves, and that was something he couldn't risk, so now he left them mostly in the open in his bed chambers.

With those weapons in hand, Mike knew he would be unstoppable. He was already the best at what he did, be it in hand to hand combat or any type of swordsmanship, and most of the other assassins looked up to him with both respect and fear in their eyes. However, using the weapons for power was something he was never interested in. He stole them for the protection of others if it came to it.

"Hey are you ready to go?"

Mike knew someone had entered his house, but he wasn't in the mood to get out of bed and he didn't feel threatened at all knowing that there was only one way to get to him, and he had the high ground, so to speak. Plus, he recognized the voice right away and knew if she would never come to harm him. He also figured if Shelby was here, Eric would not be far behind.

"Am I ready to go where?" Mike asked, even though he already knew the answer.

"See I told you he wouldn't be coming," Eric said.

"He will be coming whether he wants to or not," Shelby said with a slight laugh

"And you are thinking you can make me?" Mike asked while trying his best not to laugh as well.

"Nope, I don't think I can make you but either you come down here dressed and ready to go, or I am climbing up this little hole to get you."

"Fine, I will be down in a minute, but I hope you are not expecting me to wear anything fancy," Mike said, sitting up in his bed, while cracking his neck.

"No, why would I expect you to wear anything fancy," he heard Shelby say as he walked over to his dresser. "It is only a dinner party for the woman you are madly in love with and her future husband who isn't you."

"Shelby, leave him be. I'm sure he's already feeling bad enough on his own."

Mike stopped listening as he started digging through his dresser, looking for something that would be fancy enough for this dinner but not enough for the two people who would be there celebrating their future wedding.

"Hurry up already or we are going to be late, and you know how much I love a good party."

"I think what she means is how much she loves to get drunk at a good party, and then I am forced to carry her home afterwards."

Mike fought hard once again to control a laugh, which almost escaped him as he heard Shelby's hand slap hard against the back of Eric's head. He didn't know where he would be if he ever lost the two of them. They were his rock that kept him grounded, the closest thing an assassin could have to a family, he always figured.

"I will be down in a second, don't you worry," Mike said while pulling out a few pieces of clothing. "And I'm sure there will be plenty of wine left by the time we get there."

This time he couldn't help but laugh when he heard yet another slap hit the back of his best friend's head.

Chapter 3

"I still can't believe you are not wearing a dress tonight."

"I told you before, the only time you are going to be seeing me in a dress is on our wedding day," Candice said while taking one final look at herself in the mirror. Gone was the tight red and black leather outfit, and in its place was a pair of silk pants, running shoes, and a silk see-through shirt with a blue tank top underneath.

She couldn't help but smile as she turned around to see Kevin standing tall in front of her wearing let another one of his pin striped suits, this time black and with green strips, matching shiny dress shoes and white crane to top it all off. This time she though she noticed he wasn't wearing a hat and had his red hair styled so it was spiked at the front.

"None the less, you still look beautiful my love."

"Thank you," Candice said, trying to keep herself from blushing. "Shall we go now?"

Before she even knew it, she found herself walking side by side with Kevin, their arms linked together as they entered the grand dining area. She had walked into this room thousands of times before but never had she expected it to look the way it did now, so much so that the sight alone almost left her breathless.

The room was massive in size and was the second biggest area in the temple and at this moment almost ever squire inches of the room was covered in hundreds of thousands of blue roses. They seemed to be everywhere from the centerpieces on the tables to hanging from the lights in the ceiling. She could hear the sound of soft music playing but couldn't see a band anywhere in the room. On top of that, everyone was dressed up in fine suits and fancy dresses, and for the first time in her very long life, she suddenly felt like every eye was turned her way, and she couldn't help but feel underdressed.

"Do you love it?" Kevin asked, his voice bringing her back to the real world all around here.

"It is so beautiful and amazing," Candice found herself saying as her eyes darted around the room. "How did you know I loved blue roses?"

"We are to be married and you are wondering if I knew what your favorite type of flower was?" Kevin asked, and she couldn't help but hear a little bit of hurt in his voice.

"It is just that I have never really spoken of flowers with you, let alone talked about which ones are my favorite," Candice said, trying her best not to hurt the feelings of her future husband.

"Okay, well maybe I got a very helpful tip from one of your close friends," Kevin said, and this time she heard something else in his voice.

"And which one of my friends was this kind?" Candice asked, already knowing the answer even though it confused her very much.

"Your favorite assassin was nice enough to inform me of the love you had for blue roses," Kevin said. "But, yet us get to the party and greet our many guests."

Candice knew there was some type of pain in his voice as he talked about Mike, but she also knew he would never openly call her out on it either. Whatever happened between her and Mike was for private between the two of them, and she knew that Kevin would respect that even if he didn't like it.

She found herself once again walking side by side with him as he led her through the many small gathering areas where the guests seem to be split into different groups. From the priests to the priestess, the assassins, and of course all the ladies and noblemen from all over the world, they had come to pay their respects to the soon to be bride and groom.

After a quick scan of the crowd, she noticed right away that Mike was not anywhere in it, and a part of her suddenly felt sad but at the same time she didn't blame him for not showing up. After all, she had loved him once as he had loved her, and she knew this would not be an easy few days for him. Hell, she was half expecting him to show up on her wedding day to kill Kevin and run away with her.

A few of the faces she recognized but a lot of them she knew Kevin must have invited for the fact that they were high ranking in the world, and he wanted to prove that he had made his way to the top. She didn't want to believe it fully and she knew Kevin loved her, but he always seemed to be equally in love with power.

So she found her way into one of the small groups of assassins and quickly felt at ease among the people she had grown to not only train and respect but trusted above all others, she never kept guards around her because she knew as long as she was inside the temple, she would have friendly eyes upon her and watching over her.

Her group of assassin's were just over 150 and they all had quickly turned into the family she had lost when she was so young and brought to the Temple of Legends all them years ago. Like almost everyone who came here to train or teach, she was an orphan and she figured that was why everyone here shared a closeness that few others knew. It was a closeness brought on by losing everyone you loved in this world.

The time started to pass by like a blur and before she knew it, she was already sitting at the head table with Kevin sitting beside her, waiting for dinner to be served. It was then that she noticed three late comers entering the grand room through the far door, most likely trying to sneak in unnoticed, but she knew right away who they were. Eric was dressed in a fine forest green suit and tie and his left arm was linked with Shelby's who was wearing a matching strapless dress with a very revealing cut down the front of it.

As her eyes landed on the third of the group she could have sworn her heart would stop, then and there as her eyes met his. Like always, Mike wasn't dressed up in any type of eveningwear. Instead, he was wearing a dark blue hoodie with a zipper up the middle, and dark blue jeans and black and white sneakers. She also couldn't help but notice he was the only one in the room with a sword hanging from his hip.

"You shouldn't stare so hard at your guests," Kevin said, forcing her to tear her eyes off of Mike and back towards him. "They might find it rude."

Mike knew right away that they wouldn't be able to enter the grand dining area this late and with Shelby wearing a dress which was showing off more skin than it covered, however he only felt a few eyes turn in their direction as they walked through the far door. Only a few but it seemed to be the few who really mattered.

He quickly scanned around the room looking for a table that had three open seats and his eyes betrayed him faster than he had hoped and he found himself looking towards Candice, who was staring back at him, and he wished that she would snap out of it quickly and go back to her other guests.

He found his right hand on the hilt of his ebony sword as his eyes found their way towards Kevin as he spoke something to Candice, which caused her to look towards her future husband and away from him. With a final silent breath, he found his seat beside Eric, and another assassin he recognized but couldn't remember her name for some reason.

"I told you bringing a sword here tonight wouldn't go unnoticed," Eric said, and Mike could feel his friend give him a slight slap on his back.

"I am sure it was the sight of my sword and not me that caught everyone's attention," Mike said while leaning a little closer to his friend to insure others wouldn't hear their conversation.

"What else could it have been?"

"Maybe it was his fancy hoodie and jeans that caught their attention and made them all feel under dressed."

Mike couldn't help but smile, knowing that he could always count on Eric and Shelby to help him get through anything, even if it came with slight jokes and he knew he would do the same for the two of them. He often wondered when they would come to terms with their love and retire from being assassins and finally get married, after all they have been together for close to hundred and sixty years.

It was always the sight of the two of them that both brought a hope and sadness to him because not only did it show that living forever could be amazing if you were with the one person you loved, but at the same time it was that same thought that made him sad as his eyes locked on Candice once again, knowing he would live forever without having her by his side.

He felt himself biting down hard on his lower lip as he watched Kevin wrap his arm around Candice's shoulder, and a part of him wanted to walk right up to the man and slap the smug smile right off of his face, but how could he do that without calling himself a hypocrite. This wedding was his idea after all. He was the one who pushed her away and right into Kevin's waiting arms, so how could he now feel any sort of jealousy.

"Your meal is served, sir."

"Thank you very much," Mike said as he handed four gold coins to the waiter as he placed a rather large serving of duck in front of him.

"I am not allowed to except tips this evening sir."

"Don't think of it as a tip then," Mike said with a slight laugh. "Consider it payment for the fine job you are doing this evening."

"Very well sir, and thank you very much."

Mike smiled again knowing that by tipping the man when he wasn't supposed to would get back to Kevin, and in a small way it would be like a slap to his face. Kevin looked down at servers and maids like they were no more than peasants, and at the same time, Mike knew there would be nothing Kevin could do about it because Candice would never let the man lash out at any of the servers in her temple.

"Why are you always trying to stir the pot?"

"How boring would our lives be if I didn't stir the pot from time to time?" Mike offered, knowing Eric must have been able to read his thoughts behind his reasons for tipping the man.

"I hope to be standing next to you on the day Kevin grows some balls and calls you out," Shelby said, and Mike found himself smiling again at that.

"You never know, he might be able to take you in a fight if it comes down to blows."

"That would be a very interesting fight indeed," Mike said, thinking about the fight in his mind, knowing that if Kevin ever did make a move against him, it would be a short fight indeed.

Dinner went by in a blur as Mike tried his best to focus on anything other than Candice, and for the most part it was working, but every once in a while someone would come up to him and tell him how great it was that she finally found true love. If only they knew the truth about it.

Soon his plate was being taking away and again he paid the waiter another four gold coins and again he felt slightly better about himself, only a little bit but that was a start.

It wasn't until the music started and people began walking to the dance floor that he realized it was time to go. He didn't want to be around to witness the soon to be bride and groom slowly dancing together, their body's right up against each other's.

"Do you care for a dance?"

Mike turned around in the direction of the voice that had just spoken to him and was rather surprised to find a fellow female assassin looking back at him. The same one that was sitting next to him at the dinner table.

It was then that he fully noticed her as she was standing tall in front of him, almost as tall as his own six foot frame but she was slender and attractive and in a stunning orange dress that hung down to just past her knees, but showed off her figure perfectly. She had the most amazing blue eyes as well, which went well with her dirty blonde short hair, which hung down to her shoulders.

"I don't know if it would be a good idea for you to dance with me," Mike said, quickly scanning the room, one of his many bad habits.

"Are you scared that I might out shine you on the dance floor?" She asked with a slight shy smile on her face, something that was very rare among assassins he realized.

"Of course not. Normally I would be more than willing to accept your invite to dance," Mike said, looking again towards the main table, just in time to witness Kevin and Candice sharing a kiss. "But what the hell why not, let's dance."

Mike took her out to the dance floor, took her hand in his, and he couldn't help but notice the warmth in her bare skin against his. How long had it been since he felt someone else skin besides Candice's. How long had it been since he allowed himself to feel anything?

"I hate to sound rude or anything but what is your name?" Mike asked, feeling dumb that he recognized her but couldn't remember her name.

"My name is Alexia and don't worry about it, I am nowhere near the legend that is yourself," she said, looking towards Mike. "We aren't all as stunningly awesome as you are."

Mike could tell right away that she was teasing him, but a part of him knew it to be true. Everyone knew his name only because of the actions he had accomplished over his lifetime, and what a grand life time it would seem if you were someone looking in from the outside.

They reached the dance floor just as the music slowed down and he couldn't help but notice Alexia's shyness come back out again as she tried her best to get close to him for the slow dance. It had been years since he had danced with anyone other than Candice, and that was never in public so he reached forward and wrapped his arms around Alexia's hips and pulled her close to him.

"It is simple really."

"What is?"

"All a lady has to do is get one slow dance with you, and the entire room seems to notice."

"Don't worry, I am sure they are all looking at you in that dress and not at me in any way shape or form."

"Yeah I am sure that is it."

Mike couldn't help but smile because for the first time in a long time he wasn't thinking about anything other than that very moment, and it felt very strange doing something just for him. He knew that not everyone was watching them, but he was pretty sure that the important people were watching very closely.

It was when Alexia finally loosened up by resting her head on his shoulder that he caught a brief smell of her hair as it brushed past the side of his head, and he couldn't help but wonder if it was the smell of oranges or if he was losing it. He could feel the softness of her dress against his palms and her body against his, but he knew he would only allow himself this one dance with her before leaving. He couldn't let Alexia fall into Candice's bad books over a dance or two with him.

Just as quickly as the slow song started it had ended, and he knew it was time to go. Too many people were watching them now, and that was something he wasn't used to. He much preferred to go very much unnoticed.

"Thank you for the dance, my lady," Mike said, as he gave a slight bow.

"The honor was all mine, kind sir," Alexia said with her cute little shy smile showing once again.

"I am sure we will see each other again soon."

"Most likely at the wedding and maybe we can have another dance?"

"Yes maybe we can."

"I look forward to it then, master assassin."

Mike couldn't help but smile at that as he looked once again into her blue eyes to realize she was teasing, something he wasn't used to. Most people would be too afraid of him to risk teasing him. "As do I."

"Have a good night, sir."

"And you as well, my lady."

With that, Mike turned and found the nearest exit, which would lead him out into the fast falling snow, something he was happy for because he knew he would soon get lost in it and block out all of the staring eyes, which seemed to still be glued to his back.

He couldn't help but wonder what kind of attention he drew towards himself tonight, but he didn't really care. For the first time in a long time, his heart didn't seem like it was quite as black. All he had to do now was get through the wedding, and then the week that followed.

Chapter 4

Mike found himself pacing the small, lower-level of his cottage dressed in a nice black and dark blue suit with a tie knowing that he wouldn't be able to show up to wedding wearing whatever he wanted. Such disrespect wouldn't go unnoticed, and he didn't want to stand out in a crowd twice in one week.

He could see the snow falling outside of his window and he wondered how the courtyard would be set up to get everyone shelter from the snow and cold. It was then that he also wondered why anyone would get married this close to the end of the year, the coldest and snowiest time.

He never really minded the snow and the cold but he knew that this day was going to bother him and even as he paced back and forth he kept reaching for the hilts of the two daggers he had hidden away under his jacket. He knew that no weapons allowed meant no weapons allowed, but he also figured two daggers wouldn't really hurt anyone.

He was so lost in his pacing back and forth, and his thoughts so locked on making it through the day that he didn't even realize it, when someone knocked on his front door. It wasn't until the second or the third knock that he found himself walking towards it.

He was even more surprised when he opened the door and a lightly snow covered Candice stormed past him to stand in front of his fireplace. He didn't quite know what to make of it, her being at his house on the day of her wedding, so he just stood there with the door open and the cold winter wind blowing on his face.

"Are you going to close the door or make me freeze to death?" Candice asked, finally turning to face Mike.

Mike didn't answer right away, instead he just kept staring at her standing in front of his fireplace wearing a pair of faded jeans, a sweater, and a fur coat and leather boots. He couldn't help but wonder how odd the choice of clothing since it was her wedding day and all.

"Why are you here?" Mike asked, closing the door and then leaning up against it.

"We need to talk."

"About you being here and not at the temple getting ready for your wedding?"

"You know why I'm here Mike."

"I know why you think you are here, but like I said before, there is no way you and I can work out without us losing everything we love or worse."

"You fear death than?" Candice asked, while trying to read the emotions on Mike's face.

"You and I both know it is not my death that worries me."

"This is true, after all, who would be able to defeat the great and powerful master assassin."

"Why are you really here, Candice?" Mike asked while watching the logs burn in the fireplace. "The real reason this time."

"I am here because I am in love with you and not Kevin." Candice managed to get all of that out before her voice began to crack.

"And you are hoping that we can figure out a way to be together so you don't have to marry him?"

"Yes."

"Give me your two axes and then we can be together forever."

"But why do you need my axes for us to be together?"

"Because if we were to get married, it would be like us going against every rule and law there is," Mike said, finally walking a few step closer to Candice. "You are the leader of the Temple of Legends and I am no more than a pawn you control. If we were to get married, you would be breaking you oath as leader, and would be overthrown or sentenced to death. Do you honestly think I would just sit by and let that happen?"

"So you would need the axes to kill the assassins who came after us," Candice said, knowing it to be the reason before she even spoke the words.

"Kevin will make a great husband and one day an even better father. In time you will learn to be happy with him, maybe even love him." Mike didn't realize how much the words truly affected him emotionally until he finished saying them.

"What about you, Mike?" Candice asked, closing the gap between her and Mike, leaving only a few inches between them. "Don't you deserve to be happy?"

"This is the life I chose to live, nothing more and nothing less. I love what I do and who I am," Mike said, lying about all of it. "But I will always love you as you love me, but like I said before, there isn't any way we can be together."

Mike was caught fully off guard as Candice leaned towards him and pressed her soft lips against his while reaching her arms behind his back to pull him even closer to her. He couldn't help but kiss her back because this was something he wanted to happen ever since he broke it off with her ten years ago. This was something he needed.

It wasn't until his right hand was running up the softness of the back of neck that he truly realized what they were doing and forced himself to pull away from her. He forced himself to take a few steps back and look into her beautiful tear filled eyes.

"If I can't have you at all then I needed one last kiss to remember you by," Candice said as she wiped the tears from her cheeks.

"I will always be here you know. It is not like I'm dying or moving away."

"I know you will always be in my life," Candice said, running her finger through her hair to straighten it back out. "And I want you to know that I will always love you."

"I will always love you as well," Mike said with a smile on his face. "Now let's get you going so you aren't late to your own wedding."

"I guess I should go now or I will never want to leave," Candice said with a smile on her face. "Lose the daggers before you show up to my wedding."

"I will, but only if you promise to say the right name during the ceremony."

"We have a deal then."

With one last kiss she was gone and Mike found himself staring off into the falling snow long after her figured disappeared. He hated himself so much for letting her leave, but he knew he was making the right choice. He knew he would learn to accept it one day.

Candice had a thousand different feelings running through both her heart and mind as she walked back to the temple, and none of them seemed to be about the fast falling snow all around her. She knew she was right for going to see Mike one last time before she got married, but she wasn't sure if she made the right choice by leaving and not staying with him.

She loved him more than anything else in the world, but she also knew he was right, they couldn't get married without starting a civil war amongst the order, and she couldn't bear to think about something bad happening to the Temple of Legends or even the assassins because she couldn't force herself to move away from something she couldn't have.

She also feared that if someone did discover her love for Mike that a contract would be taken out on him behind her back, not that she worried about his safety or anything, but she did fear that something bad could happen. Even though he was immortal that didn't mean they couldn't trap him and imprison him forever. She made a side note to make sure the two swords and two daggers were still safely locked away after the wedding.

The thought of the wedding made her think about all the other feelings she had going on that weren't about Mike, even though she knew she had to see him one last time, she now felt guilty about betraying Kevin by kissing him. She felt like she was both wrong and right but didn't know which one to lean more towards.

She knew she could never tell Kevin about the kiss the two of them shared just now or even about the one the other day. She wasn't scared about breaking his heart, but more so about him going after Mike in a fit of jealousy. Mike at that point would be forced to kill him because of it, which would make Mike an outlaw and would force Candice to put a hit on his life and that would mean using the very weapons she carried on her all the time.

She couldn't help but laugh at that thought anyway because she knew if it came down to that very situation, she wouldn't even be a match against him anymore. She didn't think anyone alive would be able to defeat him in a fight.

She couldn't help but notice the snow even more now as she got closer and closer to the temple and couldn't wait to see how the courtyard was going to look, even if she was marrying the wrong man, it was still her wedding day, and any woman would want her wedding day to be perfect.

She tried her best to put Mike out of her mind and move on with the day and with one final look backwards towards his small cottage, which was both too far away and the snow was coming down way too hard to see, it she entered the main door to the temple and headed off to find her wedding dress.

Chapter 5

"Sir I have to pat you down to check for weapons before I can let you in."

"I don't understand why you have to check me for weapons when you let everyone else in front of me enter without even checking them," Mike pointed out while lifting both of his arms upwards.

"I am sorry sir, but my orders were to only check you for weapons and not the others."

"Of course they were," Mike said, as the doorman started patting him down. "But I promise you I have no weapons on me."

"She told me you would say that and I should check you none the less."

"Candice knows you so well, my old friend."

"Shut it Eric or I will make him check you next," Mike said, just as the doorman finished his search.

"You may enter, sir."

"Thank you for your fine search," Mike said, while handing the doorman a handful of gold coins.

Mike entered the walkway leading towards the courtyard before the doorman could even complain about not being allowed to accept tips and when he was about half way down, he turned back to find Eric rushing to catch up, wearing a fancy cotton three-piece suit.

"Where is Shelby?" Mike asked, finding it odd that she wasn't with Eric.

"She is Candice's maid of honor."

"I didn't know that."

"Yeah I don't think Candice has any real friends outside of us and you."

"She will have Kevin now."

"Do you honestly not have a single weapon on you?" Eric asked.

"It feels very odd indeed," Mike said with a nod. "It almost feels like I am naked."

Mike came to a sudden stop as yet another doorman blocked their path at the final door leading into the courtyard. This one was a little bit older than the last but still wore a black and white servant suit and white gloves; gloves that were currently holding a clipboard, which his eyes were locked on. "Your names gentlemen so I can make sure you are on the list?"

"Are you kidding me?" Mike asked, forcing the doorman to look up from his clipboard.

He couldn't help but smile as he watched the doorman's face turn a very pale white color as he realized who it was he was talking to. After all, everyone knew of Mike's fighting skills and of his killing skills.

"I am so sorry," The doorman said, pushing the door open and stepping to the side. "You may both enter."

"Oh I love how well you are able to scare the servants."

"Do you honestly think I like scaring people?"

"Maybe if you lost a fight once in a while, people wouldn't fear you as much."

Eric's words were lost to him as he walked out into the fully snow covered courtyard. Well, almost fully covered. As he looked around, he could see that all of the chairs were lined up in groups of four and each group had a covered roof over top of it keeping the chairs clear of the fast falling snow.

His eyes followed the covers up to the massive beams that stretched from the temple itself outwards towards the courtyard's main wall. He counted 40 such covers hanging down and each beam seemed no more than a foot wide and three thick but were easily 70 feet off of the ground.

Right down the middle of the clusters of chairs and covers was a single walkway of dyed pink snow leading from one of the temples many doors towards a dome shaped small building where two people currently stood: a high priestess and Kevin.

Mike suddenly wished he had brought one of his daggers because he knew that he could have thrown it from where he stood, nearly thirty feet away, and still gotten a perfect hit on the man. Kevin was wearing a pure white tux with matching white dress-shoes and a hat, along with a very bright red tie. Even the man's buttons were of the same bright red color.

"You still look better, my friend."

Mike smiled again as he turned to face Eric, who was also looking off in Kevin's direction. "Thank you, my friend, but I was honestly just thinking about how well his tux would look with one of my daggers through his heart."

41

"Well, I guess it would match his tie and buttons then"

"Where do you want to sit?" Mike asked, looking around at the small clusters of chairs, which were slowly beginning to fill up.

"Towards the back, I think is best," Eric said while pointing towards the back group of chairs. "I don't want to see the look on his smug face when he kisses her."

Mike agreed with that as well, and the two of them headed off towards the back set of chairs. He found it very difficult to find a comfortable way to sit in such a cup shaped, pink and white chair, so he finally gave up and dragged a second chair over, leaning back in his, and resting his snow covered shoes on the other one.

"Is this seat taken?"

"It is all yours, Alexia," Eric said before Mike could even get a word out.

He couldn't help but notice her once again as she sat almost perfectly in the cup shaped chair. She was wearing a lot more clothes this time and had her hair tied back in a ponytail, but her bright blues eyes still stood out nonetheless. So much so that he had a hard time focusing on the rest of her, which was covered in a tight fur coat and jeans with a pair of leather boots, which came up to almost her knees. "Perfect day for a wedding, I think."

"I would have always preferred a summer time wedding myself," Mike said with a laugh.

"Don't be a party-pooper, Mike. A wedding in the snow can be amazing," Eric said, and Mike couldn't help but hear the sarcasm in his voice.

"You boys just don't understand the beauty of a wedding like us girls."

"Well I understand how cold this wedding is going to be."

The ceiling above them started to glow a faint pink color almost as if on cue and Mike could suddenly feel waves of heat pulsing down upon them. "The smug bastard has thought of everything."

"Don't be jealous. Like I said before, you are still by far the best dressed out of you and him."

"I will have to agree with Eric on that one as well."

It was then that Mike noticed that Alexia had been watching him almost as closely as he was watching her. It seemed odd at first, but he didn't think a whole lot about it.

"So are you here alone Alexia, or is your date off wandering around with these fine ladies and noblemen."

"Sadly, I am here alone today, like most days now that I think about it." Alexia said with a faint laugh. "Not all of us assassins have our soul mates like you and Shelby."

"See Mike, I told you that you weren't the only lonely one in this grand world of ours."

"Now I am really missing my daggers, my friend."

"Why is that?"

"Because I would so use them right now to keep you quite."

"Do you think you are good enough with them to defeat me though?" That made all three of them laugh and that is when Mike noticed the soft sounds of music begin to play.

"Looks like it is starting"

Candice started pacing back and forth inside the small dressing room, trying her best to look away from the many mirrors all around her. Trying, but mostly failing.

Even she was surprised by how amazing she looked wearing her smooth white wedding dress. It was strapless but hung to her body perfectly showing off her slender frame. She was also wearing a feather crown on top of her head, which had larger white feathers in the back, which hung down and covered most of her brown hair. The only thing she hated about her outfit was the clear pink glass colored heels she had on her feet. She longed for her running shoes already.

"Quit your fussing missy, you look amazing in that dress."

"Thank you Shelby, but I feel so awkward wearing it," Candice said, looking once more towards her friend, who was wearing an amazing pink dress that hung all the way down to her feet. "You make wearing a dress look so easy."

"I have been wearing them for a very long time," Shelby said, trying her best not to laugh.

"Do you think I am making a mistake?" Candice asked, now that she finally had Shelby alone.

"I think either way you are making a mistake, but I truly believe this way you will come to regret far less in your long lifetime."

Candice couldn't help but wonder what Shelby was going on about because all she truly knew at that moment was how bad she was feeling and she knew she shouldn't feel this sick to her stomach if she was meant to be getting married today. She figured this day would come and no matter what she did or thought about she wouldn't be happy, but she knew she had to marry Kevin, if not for herself but for Mike's sake. Maybe once she was married, he might go in search of his own life.

"Do you think he will ever forgive me for doing this?" Candice asked as she walked over to the open window and silently closed it. She couldn't afford for anyone to overhear her.

"I think that Mike will learn to move on as soon as you learn to move on. You have to keep in mind it was his idea to break off your relationship and push you into marrying anyone who wasn't him."

"Well then I guess we shouldn't make this day any longer than it needs to be," Candice said while turning back towards the mirror one final time.

"Just lock eyes on Kevin as soon as you reach the courtyard, and don't even try to find Mike in the crowd. Act as if he isn't even there."

"That sounds easy enough."

Candice knew if she delayed this day any longer, she wouldn't be able to go through with the wedding, so she forced her feet to walk towards the exit, the whole time her mind kept telling her to turn and run.

She couldn't help but think about Mike as she walked into the small hallway that would lead her to the main entrance of the courtyard. A courtyard where she knew he would be, watching her every move, and a part of her knew that if she looked into his hazel eyes one last time, she would break down and cry.

She knew what Shelby said about just focusing on Kevin would be the only true thing that would get her to follow through with this wedding. She loved Mike with all of her heart but she couldn't risk making him suffer or losing him altogether, so she figured by breaking his heart today he would begin to heal tomorrow.

She felt Shelby's right arm link around her left and she knew they were getting close. She could hear the soft music playing and she could have sworn her heart was going to burst right out of her chest. She had never felt it beat as fast as it was at that very moment. As the double doors in front of her swung open and the cool breeze from the outside hit her face, she couldn't help but relax slightly.

For the first time in a very long time she felt a sense of joy in her heart as she stepped out onto the pink snow walkway, and she found her eyes drifting around at all of the pink and the fancy set up with the chairs and heaters, paying close attention not to look at the people just her surroundings. Then she saw Kevin looking tall and proud and waiting for her at the end of the walkway.

She could have sworn she felt moisture begin to form in her eyes as she thought about how great of a job Kevin did in setting up the courtyard and all of the hours he must have spent getting ready for this day. Maybe she could fall in love with the handsome man waiting for her at the end of the walkway, joy written all over his face.

Every step she took she found herself wanting to look around and try and catch a glimpse of Mike. She couldn't help but wonder how he felt as he got searched for weapons. She couldn't help but think about their kiss earlier that day, seeing him all done up in his dark blue suit.

Again she had to force herself to focus on Kevin as Shelby kissed her on the cheek and whispered good luck into her ear.

She felt like she was in a dreamlike state as she took her place standing next to Kevin, her right hand finding his left, even after the priestess started talking, she found herself not even hearing a word, focusing only on Kevin.

They went through their vows quicker then she thought they would, and again she was glad she did that right because she felt like she was slowly beginning to lose herself in the grand day that was to be her wedding.

"You may kiss the bride."

Candice heard the words just as Kevin's lips found hers and again she didn't fight back, she just kissed him back like she meant it, like a wife should kiss her husband for the first time. She could feel her heartbreak at that thought and could feel the tears begin to roll down her cheeks. It was real now in her mind and on paper, she was married to Kevin, which meant she might risk losing Mike forever.

She felt Kevin take her right hand again as they turned to face the crowd for the first time since the ceremony had started, and she was about to find him in the crowd, she needed to see what emotions were on his face, she needed to know if he still loved her.

All of those thoughts quickly came to a crashing stop as she felt a sharp pain just under her neck and when she looked down to see what had caused it, she heard screams break out from all around her. She realized quickly that the metal arrow sticking into her chest just above her heart was the reason for the panic.

She felt herself fall into Kevin's arms as he lowered her to the ground and she looked up one last time to see Mike pulling himself up the beam holding the heaters above the chairs, and then he was chasing another man on the very small and very high up cross beam. She lost focus of it all as white spots took over her sight and shortly after that, everything went black.

Chapter 6

Mike wasted no time at all pulling himself onto the top of the cover above the chair he was sitting in, wasted no time getting up to the crossbeam, and with a quick look back towards Candice to see her laying very still in Kevin's arms, he started running as fast as he could towards the fleeing man who had taken the shot.

Every step he took was like three compare to the fleeing man and he figured he would catch him before he made his escape, and he found himself slowing slightly as the man turned to face him. Well it wasn't a man but a boy, he couldn't have been any more than fifteen years old.

Again he found his footing and full speed hoping to catch this boy before he reached the wall of on the far side of the beam and most likely his freedom. It was then that he noticed a second person climb up onto the beam just to the right of him and slightly in front of the fleeing boy.

He recognized Alexia even before she jumped from the beam next to his onto the one he was standing on, a few feet in front of the boy which forced him to come to a standstill, arrow set on the bow string, which was currently aimed right at her.

"What was the point of attacking her?" Mike asked as he came to a stop about four feet from the boy's back.

"What do you mean?"

"She is like the rest of us, and your arrow stood no chance of killing her," Mike said, reaching towards his belt, his very empty belt he quickly realized.

"It wasn't supposed to kill her," The boy said, still holding his bow aimed at Alexia.

"Then you must know that if you shoot that arrow at her now, it will not kill her either," Mike said, taking another step towards the boy.

"It might not kill her, but it will hit her with enough force to make her fall from this beam and that is a long way down, even for an immortal."

"So if you didn't mean to kill Candice, why come here in the first place?" Mike asked as he looked towards the crowd gathering around seventy feet or so under him.

"I was sent here to deliver a message to her, nothing more and nothing less."

"And what was the message, boy?" Mike asked, walking a few steps forward.

"The fact that you guys can live forever means we can destroy your lives for a very long time," The boy said, not even realizing Mike was getting closer to him. "Take today for an example. Even though it was her grand wedding day, I was able to strike her down for no other reason than the fact that I could."

Mike was about to say something when the boy turned so quickly towards him with such balance he got off a perfect shot, well it would have been perfect if Mike wasn't quicker at slightly turning and raising his hand to stop the arrow.

The metal arrows tip found his raised right hand and sliced right through his palm and would have went completely through it if he didn't grab the rest of the shaft with his left hand stopping the arrows flight.

He couldn't help but winced as he pulled the arrow through the rest of his hand and the blood began to really flow when the metal feathers at the end of the shaft cut the hole even bigger in his hand.

It wasn't till he had the arrow fully out and in his right hand did he realize that the boy was moving towards him, with another arrow set and ready, Alexia right on his heal.

Mike couldn't do anything but watch as the boy once again turned the other way and let the arrow fly, this time striking Alexia right in the left knee causing her to stumble. The boy followed his arrow attack with a sideways swing with his bow catching Alexia on the side of her face causing her to topple over sideways and right off the beam, luckily landing one of the covers over the chairs and not the solid ground ten feet below it.

Mike turned back, just in time to see the boy drop the bow from his hands and grab the hilt of his short sword, and again Mike cursed himself out for not bringing any weapons. He looked towards the metal arrow in his left hand and figured it would have to do.

"If you try to attack me, boy, I will be forced to kill you," Mike said, flipping the arrow over in his left hand.

"I am dead either way, so may as well go out fighting a legend," The boy said. "You are him, aren't you?"

"I am who?" Mike asked.

"The master assassin everyone is afraid of."

"I am Mike and I am an assassin but I try to stay away from whatever titles people seem to want to give me," Mike said, watching the boy walking closer and closer to him.

Mike couldn't help but feel sorry for this stupid boy who wished to fight him for no other reason than to die, even that thought caused guilt to creep back into his heart at the very moment, here he was once again about to take the life of another innocent person, and a boy at that.

"Who sent you here?" Mike asked as he readied himself for the boy's first attack.

"You will find out soon enough, I would think."

And then it was on, the boy came at him with skill and speed, which would have topped must humans but not Mike. He was far beyond the skills of a simple mortal, but yet he still found himself on the defensive, trying his best to walk backwards, defect the blows of the boy's sword with the arrow, and all the while also trying not to kill him at the same time.

After a few minutes of watching the boy fight with ease and skill, Mike reached out with his wounded right hand and grabbed the boy's sword arm and pulled the boy towards him, at the same time, he launched his right knee up towards the boys chest and it impacted with such force he could hear all the air leave the boys lungs.

Mike found himself taking a step back once again as the boy remained leaning over on his knees struggling to find air, trying his best to regain himself.

"I have no plans on killing you, boy, so you may as well throw down your sword and surrender," Mike warned, watching the boy very carefully.

"Very well then," The boy said as the hilt of his sword fell from his grip and landed with a clang on the ground below.

"I can't however guarantee you that her husband won't kill you," Mike said, reaching his wounded right hand towards the boy to help him up.

"You should have killed me, you know."

"Why is that?"

"Because I am thinking that this is going to hurt you, whether you are immortal or not."

Before Mike realized what was happening the boy's right hand came forward towards his out stretched hand, with a dagger and he wasted no time in stabbing it right through Mike's already wounded hand.

The pain and the force of the stabbed caused Mike to lose his balance slightly but it was still enough for the boy to lunch himself forward with a tackle, causing Mike to stumble backwards as he lost his footing and he landed on his back.

The boy wasn't so lucky though, and after the two of them landed on the beam Mike could feel him slipping off of it beside him. He rolled himself over and with his right hand, grabbed the beam and with his left hand he grabbed the boys left shoulder under his arm.

They both rolled off the beam at the same time and Mike could feel his arms explode with pain as he fought to not only keep his grip on the beam above him but also onto the boys arm. He could feel his right hand slipping from both the weight and the blood on the beam but he was determined to save this boy for some reason.

"Just yet me fall, I am dead anyway."

"Shut up, you little shit, and pull yourself upwards," Mike said, looking down towards the hanging boy.

He then had no choice to let his right hand go as he reached down to stop the boy's second dagger attack, this time aimed at his chest. He grabbed the boy's arm and stopped it just as the tip of the dagger entered his flesh, and then they were both falling.

Just as quickly as it started, it ended with the boy hitting the ground just underneath him and the force of the fall plus the placement of the dagger, caused it to slam right into Mike's chest, all the way to the hilt and even more so as it broke the bones of his ribs.

He heard the boy's body crunch under him as his own weight crushed the smaller boys frame. It was the sound of his head smacking solid ground, which caused him to hear and see nothing as unconsciousness pulled him in.

Alexia didn't know how to feel as she sat on the edge of her bed, looking down at the bandage still wrapped tightly around her knee. It had been five days since the wedding and her nasty fall from the beam, but she knew it was nothing compared to Mike's fall.

Even as she turned to face him lying on her bed she was amazed that he was still alive and breathing. She couldn't help but notice the dark bruises lining the left side of her face and most of the side of his head and even worse than that was the nasty wound he took to the chest from the dagger when he hit the ground. The daggers blade cut through his skin easily enough, slipping between two ribs but the force of the fall slammed the dagger's hilt in as well breaking the two ribs and causing a lot of damage.

It had been five days since the wedding and still she was both surprised and saddened by the fact that he hadn't woken up once. The priest who treated his wounds said it could take some time for his injuries to heal and the blow to his head could take even longer to heal after he woke up.

All things aside, she knew if they were both mortals they would have both been killed that day, but even an immortal could only take so much. Even though she knew he was healing every day, she figured it could still be a while before he came to.

A slight knock at her front door caught her attention, and she had to force herself to look away from Mike's wounded body and back to her own wounded knee. The arrow had done very little damage, but it still needed to heal and only time would get her back to normal.

She mostly limped her way to her front door and opened it without even thinking, already knowing who she was going to find on the other side. It was the same person who stopped by once a day at this very time for the last five days.

"How is he doing today?" Candice asked as she walked into the small entryway of Alexia small condo.

"Still in his own dream world but his wounds seem to be looking better every day," Alexia said, closing the door behind Candice.

"And how are you doing?" Candice asked while looking at Alexia bandaged knee.

"Every day I can put a little bit more weight on it, and before you know it, I will be back to running and dancing."

"Thank you again for watching over him here."

Alexia thought back to when she first came to after everything that happened, and she found herself lying in a very small cot in the hospital wing of the Temple of Legends, a hospital that seemed to be swarming with every single person at the temple. It didn't take her long to realize that all of their attentions were turned towards Mike, who was lying in the cot next to her. Shelby and Eric wanted him to recover at their place, but since Candice was sending every assassin out in search of clues as to who sent the boy in the first place, well every assassin but her she realized. So it was an easy decision for her to volunteer to watch him at her place.

"It is no trouble at all. I am just happy to be of some use," Alexia said, limping her way to her plush leather couch and mostly falling backwards into it. "You can go see him you know."

Alexia watched as Candice turned to face her bedroom door, but like every day so far, she just starred at it and didn't make a move towards it. It was like something was holding her in place, keeping her from seeing Mike, like she half expected to walk into the room and find him dead.

"I am fine and I am happy to hear he is getting better every day."

"You loved him didn't you?" Alexia asked as she watched the tears form in Candice's eyes.

"Is it that easy to tell?"

"It took me the first two day to figure it out, but I realized why you never go in to see him."

"Why is that?"

"Simple really. You feel guilty that he is lying in there badly hurt because he risked everything to catch the boy who attacked you, and you feel that if you never got married, he wouldn't be where he is now," Alexia said as she watched Candice sit on one of her two recliners.

Alexia noticed that she looked different today though. She wore her normal red and black leather outfit and had both of her axes on her hips. Her dark brown hair was pulled back into a tight ponytail. The fact that her front zipper wasn't fully done up, allowed her to see the bandages she had on her chest from the metal arrow. "Now it is my turn to ask you if you are fine."

"I just have a lot on my mind, that's all."

"Being a married woman and the head of the Temple of Legends can be a handful I bet," Alexia said, reaching her left hand down to rub her knee, which was slowing begin to throb again.

"Yes it can be and it is also stressful just sitting around waiting to hear back about whoever was stupid enough to attack me on my wedding day and why they did it."

"Tell me about it. I feel pretty useless as it is, sitting around here with a gimped knee and no way to really help out."

"You are helping out by keeping Mike safe and making sure someone is here when he comes to."

"It should be you who is by his side when he finally wakes up."

"I am a married woman now, and we both know how that would look if I sat around here day and night watching over him while my husband was at home alone."

"Which brings me back to my question about you being in love with him," Alexia continued, watching to see how Candice would react.

"I loved him once, yes, but it was a long time ago; and let's face it, we could have never worked out anyway, and I trust you will keep this information to yourself."

"I promise I won't tell a soul. I will send word if he comes around later today or tonight."

"Thank you again for everything, Alexia."

Alexia watched as Candice got back out of the recliner and headed towards her front door, only stopping once to turn and face the bedroom door before heading out into the hallway closing the door behind her. "What have I gotten myself into?" she thought out loud, now that she was finally alone.

Chapter 7

Mike couldn't help but reach for the left side of his face as he tried to force his eyes to open. Every part of him was screaming out in pain, but he couldn't figure out why he was struggling so hard to wake himself up. Even the touch of his fingers on the side of his face hurt, and he knew something was wrong right away.

Even after he managed to get his eyes to open, he struggled to see through the blurriness to figure out where he was. He could tell right away he wasn't in the hospital or even his own cottage by the belonging that were all around him, which mostly consisted of a few stuffed bears and bookshelves jammed pack with books. He also noticed a manikin in the far left corner of the room, which currently had a suit of dark brown leather armor hanging from it, plus a sword and dagger.

He tried to lift himself upwards a little more to take in the rest of the room, when he was hit by a sudden rush of light, and he felt a strong urge to throw up. He leaned over the side of the bed, not wanting to ruin whoever's sheets it was he was using, and found a trash can instead.

It all came rushing back to him as he began to throwing up into the trashcan, the arrow striking Candice, his rushing after the boy on the beam, watching Alexia fall off the beam shortly before he too fell to the ground below. Now he understood why his head and face hurt so much.

"Oh my god, are you okay, Mike?"

When he felt that he could handle it safely, he looked away from the trashcan and towards the slender female crouching beside him as he hung over the side of the bed, he recognized her right away, even though she was wearing simple pajamas, which consisted of a pair of flannel pants and a tank top. Her blonde hair was a mess.

He suddenly felt embarrassed leaning over the side of the bed and throwing up in the trashcan just beside him with Alexia this close to him, and he quickly found himself trying to lie back down in bed. With Alexia's

54

help he found it a lot easier this time around, and with a few more pillows behind him, he was in a more upright position.

"Where am I?" Mike asked, once again looking around the small room, a room he knew he had never seen before.

"You are at my place, silly," Alexia told him.

"What happened after I fell from the beam?"

"Would you like to hear the long story or the short one?"

"The pounding in my head is telling me to listen to the short one," Mike said, struggling to not laugh, knowing that even doing that would hurt right now.

He did his best to listen to Alexia as she retold the story and events that led up to him laying here in her bed. He was even more shocked when she told him that he was out for almost ten full days, something that was never heard of before when it came to an assassin.

He didn't like the part of the young boy's death, but he realized enough on his own that there was no way he could have kept him alive during the fall. His right hand found the spot on his chest, which was still covered in bandages, he then let out a slight sigh knowing that he should have died along with that boy ten days ago.

"And she comes to see you every day but never really sees you."

"What do you mean?" Mike asked, looking up from his chest towards Alexia.

"Every day Candice comes at about the same time to check in on you, but never once has she found her way into my room to see you."

"Has she already been here today?"

"Yes about two hours ago or so."

Mike let out another sigh knowing that he wasn't feeling up to seeing Candice now, not while he felt and looked so weak. He didn't want anyone to be able to feed off of his weakness. "Thank you for everything you have done for me, Alexia."

"It was nothing, really, don't worry about it. It isn't like I was able to go anywhere myself, so I figured us gimps should look out for each other."

"Do we know who ordered the attack?"

"Sadly we haven't been able to figure it out yet but Candice has every assassin out looking for any leads."

Mike wanted to keep going but he felt what little energy he had slowing begin to leave him and all he wanted to do was fall back to sleep. He knew he had just slept for ten days straight, but he figured his body would need more rest to heal. He tried his best to readjust himself in the very comfortable bed without causing any type of shooting pain. "How many rooms does your place have?"

"My place has just this one bedroom, a living room, kitchen, and bathroom."

"Where have you been sleeping then?" Mike asked, suddenly feeling guilty that he had been stealing her bed this whole time.

"On the couch in the living room. It is a big sized couch and I am not that big so I have made do with it, but it seems like I can't get comfortable anywhere with my knee always throbbing and what not."

"Thank you for helping me out that day," Mike said as he watched Alexia limp from the bed to dresser across from it.

"I wasn't very much help if you remember it correctly. I mostly got in the way and got shot by an arrow."

Mike could hear the sadness in her voice, and he knew she must have felt guilty somewhat about letting him down even though there was nothing she could have done to have changed the outcome, well aside from jumping under his falling body.

"How is your knee?"

"A lot better than it was ten days ago. But it still hurts most of the time."

"Yeah it will be like that for a while I am betting, but the more you use it, the faster it will heal."

"And how is your hand?"

"It seems to still be attached to the rest of my arm, so that is good," Mike answered while lifting his right hand up, which was still mostly covered by bandages. "Is it bad?"

"Well at first it looked pretty messed up with two different holes through your palm, but it began to heal right away and now you just have some pretty nifty scares but the priest said it would take time for the nerves in your hand to fully heal."

"So you have been looking after me and changing my bandages this whole time?" Mike asked, feeling slightly embarrassed once again.

"Yeah, but it is no big deal, really. I figured I had to change mine everyday so why not change yours as well."

"At least it will be a wedding we will always remember," Mike said, which made them both laugh a little.

"And if we ever start to forget it, we will always have our scares to remind us of it."

"So what are your plans for the night?"

"Nothing really. Maybe I will have a small dinner, and I have to run to the store to stock up on food and what not, well more like limp to the store."

Mike couldn't help but notice the small smile on Alexia perfectly shaped face as she reached up and brushed her bangs out of her eyes. Even in the dim light of the bedroom her amazing light blue eyes seemed to gleam nonetheless.

He had never really paid any attention to any other women he had ever come into contact with, most of his life, he was always in love with Candice and only ever noticed her. Alexia was different in so many ways. From her skin tone to her dirty blonde hair, her blue eyes were the brightest he had ever seen on anyone, and even as she stood across from him in her PJ's, he couldn't help but notice her tall but slender frame, how her tank top was both tight enough to show the outlines of her small breasts, yet loose enough to leave a little to the imagination.

It was then that he noticed that she was watching him as closely as he was watching her, and he felt his cheeks turn red. He was glad he was covered in bruises to hide his embarrassment, but the whole time he found his eyes locked onto her own blue eyes something about them caught his attention and he couldn't look away.

He reached up to run his finger though his short, dark, brown hair when he realized he was trying to use his right hand, which was fully wrapped up. Once again the two of them shared a laugh and then he tried to use his left hand to undo the bandage on his right but found it far too weak to be of any use.

"Allow me to help you."

Mike watched her as she walked back towards the bed and sat down as close to his right side as she could, facing towards him. He watched as she crossed her legs, pulling his right hand into her lap. He could feel her cold fingers against his exposed arm but he didn't notice the coldness over her soft touch. He watched as she slowly began to unwrap his bandage with both skill and ease, and he figured she most have been doing this a few times a day while he was out.

"Are you sure you can handle the sight of you disfigured hand?" Alexia asked, once she had the bandage fully off and closed both of her own hands around his.

Mike could tell she was joking by the smile she had on her face, and he was about to tell her that he was ready to see it when he realized that her hands on his was a feeling he hadn't felt in a very long time. Something he didn't know if he was ready to feel again in his life at that moment, or if he would ever be able to feel anything like that ever again.

"I am sure it looks fine, after all I was in your fine care as you nursed me back to health," Mike said as he watched Alexia's cheeks brighten a slight shade of red for a change.

He could feel her squeeze his hand one last time before letting it go and he watched her carefully for a few more seconds as she readjusted herself on the bed by leaning backwards and resting her elbows on the mattress and again he found his eyes drifting over her body one more time before stopping on her eyes and the smile she had on her face.

He turned his attention back to his right hand knowing that a lot of his skilled relied on his ability to use his hands in perfect unison with each other, and at first he clenched his finger inward and made a fist and smiled again knowing at least he would still be able to hold a dagger or a sword with a good grip.

The scars didn't look as bad as he thought they would, but he knew if he wasn't immortal his hand would be totally useless to him now. The damage it took from both the arrow and the dagger would have been enough to get his hand amputated, let alone the fall would have killed him before it ever came to that anyways.

"You will be good to go in a few days, I bet."

"I hope so as well because if I lie around here for too long I will start to get fat," Mike said while patting his stomach, which was still muscled in a fine six pack.

"If you're hungry I can make you something to eat?"

"I don't think I can handle food right now, but thank you for the offer. I am not even sure if I have to energy to do anything more than what I am doing."

"Maybe you should get some more rest and allow your body to heal a while longer."

"I would normally disagree with you because clearly I have been asleep already for ten days straight, but my eyes won't fall for that bluff," Mike said as he slowly inched his way downwards till the back of his head found the pillow.

"I will only be gone for a little while, but I will check on you as soon as I get back from the store."

"Thank you again for everything you have done for me, I will forever be in your debt," Mike said as he watched Alexia get off the bed and walk towards the dresser once again.

"Don't you worry about it, just get better soon, and we will call it even."

He couldn't help but watch as she dug through the dresser with ease till she finished finding a handful of clothes and with one final smile she headed out of the bedroom and out of his sight, a part of him wanted to get up and follow her but the other part of him screamed out that it needed to sleep and he slowly realized his eyes were closing.

Chapter 8

The next morning came or at least Mike hoped it was the next morning, and he didn't sleep through a week or more again. He already felt a little bit stronger, even as he sat fully up right in the bed, he didn't feel sick at all and his eyes only slightly blurred.

He pulled the cover off of him and shifted his legs so he was in a sitting position on the side of the bed, and he worked on wiggling his toes to try and bring some life back into their numbness. He knew it would be funny if he tried to stand now and by funny he meant landing face first onto the ground.

He even started to rub one foot at a time with both of his hands for no other reason than to test out the strength he had in his hands and before he realized it, he started to feel his own grip on his feet. Every part of his body that he moved or even slightly shifted hurt, and he figured that it would be that way until he was able to stretch out some of his muscles.

He finally just gave in and began to stand, keeping his left hand on the bed for support, and before he knew he was standing fully upright, with a few quick cracks to his back and neck, he found himself slowly walking around the small room.

First he made his way towards the manikin in the corner of the room and he ran his fingers along the smooth leather armor until his hand stopped on the hilt of the dagger hanging from the belt. His fingers found their way around the hilt of the dagger and he could feel his grip tighten around it, but he quickly released his hand and pulled it away, this was after all someone else's dagger.

Next he searched the top of the dresser to find only a few photos of Alexia from when she was a little girl to more recent ones of her. He smiled as he picked up the one of her on the day she was granted immortality. For each person that day felt different, but the look in her eyes in that photo told him that she was more than happy to be a part of the Temple of

Legends.

The only other thing on the dresser was a white and gold locket on a silver chain, and he ran his fingers over that as well but also quickly removed his touch from it. He was a person who was big on privacy and he felt others should be granted theirs as well.

Just outside of the bedroom he saw a small hallway leading into the kitchen and a door leading into the bathroom, so he headed down the one leading to kitchen and was surprised at how much orange there was everywhere, from the walls to all of the kitchen appliances to even the cabinets.

The rest of the condo was pretty small and he found his way into the living room after only taking a few steps out of the kitchen. He walked over to the wall across from him, which had the only window looking outside, in the room and pulled the orange curtains open slightly. It was then that he realized they were on the fifth or sixth floor of the building.

A slight movement to his right caught his attention, and he found himself looking from the window to the couch set against the right wall, and the slender figure sleeping away on it. Alexia was wrapped up so tightly in her thick cotton quilt that he figured even if she tried to get up in a hurry, she would find herself very much trapped in her own blanket.

He wondered to himself if he could ever get a good enough of a sleep that he could find himself that trapped in his blanket and not even realize it, something he knew couldn't happen because he was never one to let his guard down.

He noticed a full-length mirror hanging on the wall beside the door leading out of the condo and walked towards it, determined to see how much damage he really did do to himself. The bruises on his face weren't as bad as they felt to the touch, mostly just large blue puffy marks.

Next he pulled off the bandage from his chest and took in the new scar on the right side of his ribs, almost in a perfect circle shape of the dagger's hilt that smashed through his ribs. The area all around it looked even more bruised than his face, but he didn't feel a whole lot of pain while he poked at with his finger.

Every other part of his body seemed to be slightly red with some bruises thrown in here and there but he knew the worst of it was his chest and hand. It was also then that he realized he was standing in the middle of Alexia's living room in only his shorts and he hoped he had more clothes around somewhere.

"Good morning, and I am happy to see you up and about."

Mike turned to face Alexia who was still wrapped away in her blankets but now fully awake and watching him as he looked himself over in the mirror. "Not as bad as I thought it would be," he said, turning back to the mirror again.

"Nope, you still look like you, which is always a good thing."

Mike laughed as he thought about that and figured it was a good thing as he turned back around to face her lying on the couch now struggling to unwrap the blankets from around her, something that made him laugh a little more. "So, do you always sleep that exposed to an attack?"

"Who would dare attack me while the most dangerous assassin was in the room right next to me?"

"You are a very funny girl," Mike said, smiling again. "I wouldn't by any chance have a change of clothes here, would I?"

"Well, after you woke up yesterday I figured you would need some clothes, and since everyone is so afraid to go into your place, I decided to buy you a few things while I was at the store yesterday," Alexia said, pointing to the large paper bag on the kitchen counter.

"Thank you. It might be a bit awkward with me hanging around here half naked all the time," Mike said, walking back into the kitchen.

"Speaking of half nakedness, do you mind not looking this way until I find my shirt? I seem to have misplaced it amongst my blankets.

Mike just smiled again as he began pulling out the different pieces of clothing in the paper bag while fighting every urge he had to turn around and sneak a peek at Alexia. The first thing he found was a pair of jeans and quickly removed his shorts and replaced them with perfectly fitted pair of jeans. Then he found a tight, long sleeved dark blue shirt and pulled it over his head, struggling through the pain in his shoulder and chest as he did so. The next made him smile again as he pulled out a white and orange zippered hoodie, and he quickly put it on. Again he was amazed at how good she was at picking out his size.

He sensed Alexia approach from behind, more then he heard her silent footfalls, and he could tell right away that she was favoring one leg more than the other. He couldn't help but wonder how long it would take for her to get back to hundred percent again.

"Would you like me too make you some breakfast, or would you rather go out to eat?"

"I think staying in is best for now," Mike said, turning around to face Alexia who had indeed found her shirt, a very bright orange long sleeved shirt. "I'm still slightly embarrassed about being seen in public."

"This is true. I would hate for someone to tease you and hurt your feelings," Alexia said as she opened the fridge door. "Especially since you do not have any weapons too stab them with."

Mike knew again she was teasing him, and he was slowly getting used to it, normally most people feared him too much to even talk to him. "Guess I will have to make a trip to my place sooner or later to get some of my gear," He said as he watched her crack four eggs open into a frying pan. "I have a question for you though?"

"Ask away, kind sir."

"What is with all of the orange you having going on here?"

He watched as she dropped the last egg but was able to catch it before it smashed onto the counter top, and he suddenly felt bad for asking the question. He knew he touched a nerve he had no right to touch. "I'm sorry for asking. I didn't mean anything by it."

"It is fine, and I should have expected it from someone with such a keen sense of their surrounding such as you," Alexia said. "All I can remember about my mother is an image I have in my head. Whether it is real or made up it is all I've got. It is of an image of me and her standing by a river somewhere, and she is wearing the brightest orange dress I have ever seen. So, I guess the color has kind of stuck with me my whole life. It makes me feel like a part of her, like she is still with me even after all these years.

Mike could feel the emotions behind her voice and could relate to it like almost all assassins could. Almost all of their stories started with losing everything and everyone they loved, they all had their own memories of the past, of a life that was left behind a long time ago.

He placed his right hand on her shoulder, and in a single touch he was able to show her that he not only understood her pain, her lose, everything there was to understand about her, he knew he would come to learn. They were so alike in so many ways, but just by looking at her now, he understood that she was different than him as well. She hadn't lost all of her innocents yet. She hadn't been through as much death and blood as he had.

"Do you remember anything about your parents?"

Her question caught him of guard, even though he should have known it was coming. After all, he started the conversion about her past, so he couldn't expect her not to ask about his. "I lost them when I was eight-years-old. We were off sailing on our boat when a freak storm came out of nowhere, and our ship was no match for it. My father got caught by the main mast and was dragged under right away, but my mom was able to get me safely on a piece of floating wood, and she covered my body till the storm gave out. It wasn't until the next morning that I realized she had a piece of plastic embedded in one of her lungs, and she died while I was asleep. I floated on the wood for what seemed like years until Candice found me and brought me to the temple."

"I am sorry for your lose and that you had to witness your parents death." Alexia said, reaching her one free hand up to her shoulder and placing it on top of his hand.

"It was a very long time ago," Mike said while looking at how smoothly she was able to flip the eggs with only one hand, how her hands worked just the way she had trained them to something he understood better than anyone else.

"A lot of sharing so far, and we haven't even had breakfast yet."

"And after breakfast, I am so calling dibs on the shower first."

"What? How is that fair? This is my house, mister, and my rules."

Again Mike couldn't help but smile as he ran his finger down her back as he removed his hand from her shoulder. He watched as she tried her best not to arch into his touch, and as she tried her best not to notice. "Okay, you can shower first, but then we have to take a walk to my place."

"Good I can finally see how my other half lives."

"Trust me, it isn't anything to get excited about."

"No you trust me, it is the simple things in life that count."

"This is going to be a very interesting friendship we have here, isn't it."

"I am thinking so, but you have something else to worry about first."

"What is that?" Mike asked as she flipped two eggs up into the air and caught them on a plate with her other hand.

"Your friend will be here within the hour and I am sure she will be excited to see you up and about."

The mention of Candice made something inside of him stir, but he knew it was nothing more than him being nervous about seeing her again after everything that happened at her wedding. He knew he made the right choice by getting her to marry someone other than him, he just hoped that she had come to terms with it.

"That should be fun," Mike said as he took the plate from Alexia and as she handed it to him, their hands briefly touching.

The two of them ate in silence and before he knew it, she was entering the bathroom and he heard the sound of the water turn on. He found himself pacing back and forth in the small living room, part of him wanting to stay where he was while the other part of him wanted to walk into the bathroom, strip naked and join her in the shower. That part of him was very much winning at that moment and every lap he took, he found himself getting closer and closer to the hallway leading to the bathroom.

That was until a soft knock from the front door quickly snapped him out of it and he found himself walking past the kitchen counter again, this time grabbing a small butcher's knife as he passed. It wasn't much he knew, but in his hands it would be deadly, or at least he hoped it would be.

He hesitated a little bit longer at the front door, until a second soft knock followed the first. He found his left hand going for the doorknob before he knew it, he knew who was behind the door and he figured she was the reason Alexia wanted to shower first.

He was no sooner engulfed be a giant hug before the door was even fully open. Candice threw her arms around his neck with enough force that it made him stumble backwards and he almost lost his footing. Everything was still sore, and he suddenly realized how much it still hurt when she wrapped her arms around him.

He watched as she quickly pulled herself away from him and straightened her clothes. She did her best to hide the moisture, which was forming at the bottom of her eyes as he heard a second set of footsteps leading towards the door. He gripped the knife even tighter even though he already knew who it was.

"So the hero finally rises after his grand fall," Kevin said, while walking into the small living room, wearing another of his smug suits and hat, this time is was an off shade of grey.

"When did you wake up?"

Mike looked her over closely before answering her. She looked like she always did, wearing her black and red leather armor and her duel axes always at her side. He noticed right away though that she wasn't wearing her ebony dagger pendant around her neck. "Early last night I guess, but I just got out of bed this morning," He said, looking away from her back towards Kevin.

"Well it is good to see you up and well, none the less," Kevin said as he walked past Mike with a slight slap to his back before sitting on one of the recliners.

"I agree with Kevin, it is very good to see you up and about."

Mike knew she could read the anger on his face at that very moment, and could sense the rage building inside of him. Even as he watched her reach out and remove the knife from his hand, he knew that she knew he wanted to stab the smug bastard.

"Where is Alexia?"

"She is in the shower."

"When she is done, I need to talk to the two of you about something important."

"Can it not wait Candice?" Mike asked, looking back into her pale colored eyes. "I have been asleep for like eleven days, and I could go for a shower myself."

"Like the lady said, it is important, and we don't have time to dick around."

Mike found himself facing Kevin once again. Before he even realized, he had turned towards the man. He smiled as he watched Kevin reach for the hilt of his sword. He knew that he could kill him before he even got a chance to stand up from the recliner.

"It can wait until the two of you are ready. Swing by my office when you have time."

Mike watched as Kevin got up and took the very roundabout route around him and back towards Candice and then his smug smile returned. "Enjoy the shower, my little buddy," Kevin said as he walked out the front door.

"If it wasn't important, I wouldn't be asking you to come to me so soon."

"Next time leave the dog at home."

"He is my husband, and you will treat him as such."

"I will treat him like the scum he is."

"A scum you forced me into marrying because you didn't want to marry me yourself."

"I will be in your office as soon as I can."

"Bring Alexia. It involves the two of you."

With that, he watched Candice walk out the front door as well, and he found himself slamming the door behind her, regretting it as soon as it happened.

"That doesn't sound too good, eh?"

Mike turned to see Alexia standing in the middle of the kitchen wearing only a towel, she hadn't even dried herself off fully, and he could see the little beads of water roll down her shoulder from her hair. "You heard all of that?"

"I would make a pretty bad assassin if I didn't realize people were in my house, let alone know what they were saying."

"I am sorry about slamming your door," Mike said, once again trying his best not to stare at the half naked girl in front of him.

"I am sorry that you had broken your own heart and put yourself through all of this for the future happiness of someone you love."

"It also brought me a freedom I didn't think I would ever find," Mike said, surprised at how well Alexia knew the situation between Candice and him.

"We have all fallen in love at one point and time in life. If it is meant to be then go with it, and if not, live and learn, my friend, live and learn."

"Have you ever been in love?" Mike asked.

"Maybe I have, maybe I haven't. That is a story for a different time though. You need to shower and I need to get dressed."

"Another time it is, then," Mike said as he walked past Alexia and couldn't help but notice her once again wrapped only in a towel. "First the shower, then my place, and then off to work."

"It's a date."

Once again he couldn't help but smile as she teased him, something he knew he would have to get use too sooner or later if he planned on being around her all the time, which he fully planned on doing.

Chapter 9

"Holy crap your place is nice."

"It gets the job done," Mike said as he walked towards the ladder leading to his bedroom.

"I love it, it is so rustic, way out here in the woods with a real fireplace. The next time one of us falls seventy feet and needs to recover, we are doing it here for sure."

"Deal," Mike said as he started up the ladder. "Give me a few minutes to get changed and then you can follow me up if you'd like."

"Better yet, can I check out your weapons room?"

Mike watched as she walked towards the room on the left, which served as his armory and couldn't help but smile. She was wearing her tight brown leather assassin's outfit with both a sword and dagger hanging from her belt. Her blonde hair still hanging freely down and he once again noticed the front of her outfit. The zipper was low enough to show off the top half of her breasts. It was then that he cursed girls for having boobs as built in distraction factor that guys couldn't use. "Yes you can," He said as he finished his trip up the ladder, thankful she agreed not to join him.

He knew he didn't really need anything from his bedroom but he had to reassure himself that both the suit of armor and the weapons he stole, still remained where he had left them. He couldn't risk them falling out of his hands now.

He let out a sigh of relief as he finished climbing into his room and saw that everything was right where he left them, nothing seemed missing and he couldn't help but run his fingers over the leather armor, feeling its softness against his fingertips.

He couldn't wait for the day when he would finally get to wear it, the day he finally had a reason to free himself from all of the crap, which was slowly eating away at him from the inside out. He could hear Alexia in the room under him and he figured the quicker he rejoined her, the safer his secret would be.

The climb back down took even less time than it did going up, and he found himself nearly walking right into Alexia as he entered the door leading into his armory. He watched as she slowly walked around each set of armor he had, as she carefully looked at and touched every weapon that she could.

"How many people have even seen all of this stuff?"

"Honestly, just you and me," Mike said as he took his two favorite ebony daggers off of one of the manikins and hooked them to his belt.

"I thought you were going to change?" Alexia asked, after she turned to face him for the first time since he entered the room.

"I liked this outfit, so I changed my mind," Mike said, looking around at the rest of his gear.

"You are a very odd man."

"Thank you."

"You have a lot of stuff in here, you know."

"Yeah, I have been collecting it for years now."

"Does one man really need like 50 daggers?"

"You never know when you are going to need more than 45 daggers at any given time."

"True, I guess. All I have is like two or three weapons in total."

"What happens if you lose one?"

"Then I am short a weapon till I can afford to buy a new one."

"Tell you what, then," Mike said, as he looked everything over once again. "Help yourself to anything you want in this room. Well anything but the suits of armor and ebony weapons."

"You would really let me choose anything I want from here?"

"Yes and then we will have to go."

He watched as she made her way around the room once more before she came to a complete stop right in front of the small weapons rack hanging on the left wall. He knew that something had caught her eye and he guessed what it was before she even reached out and touched it.

He watched as her fingers ran along the length of the fine and sharpened blade of a very old and very rare short sword. It was about a two and half feet long and was made out of a rare green ore. The hilt was made out of the same ore but melted down and shaped into the head of tiger. He received the sword as a payment for one of the very first mission he had completed.

"You can take it if you want," Mike said as he watched Alexia right hand close over the hilt of the sword.

"It is so beautiful, and I have never seen a green sword before."

"Yes, I believe it is one of a kind."

"And you are sure I can have it?"

"Yes, I am very sure."

Mike watched as she removed the sword from the rack and practiced a few quick swings testing out the blade and how well it was balanced. He was kind of surprised at how well she handled a sword. He knew every assassin was trained with almost every type of weapon, but she seemed more comfortable with the sword then most did.

He smiled as she replaced her own old sword with the new green one and he couldn't help but notice the faint smile on her face. "Are you ready to go?" he asked, leaning against the doorframe.

"Only if you promise we can come back here one day, so I can continue to look at all you stuff."

"It is a deal."

"Lead the way then."

Mike smiled again as he walked from the armory back into the main quarters of his cottage. He once again sensed Alexia following him more than he heard her, and he also noticed that she wasn't limping as badly when he turned around to look at her one last time before they walked out into the snow.

"You could have been a lot nicer to him, you know," Candice said as she watched Kevin from her desk as he starred aimlessly out the window.

"I have no clue what you are talking about."

"He risked a lot for us, and you could have at least shown some respect."

"All he managed to do for us was land on and kill the only person who could have given us any real answers about who ordered the attack on your life."

"It doesn't matter anyway. I have everyone out looking for answers, and I am sure we will have them in no time," Candice said, finally looking away from her husband and back towards the stack of papers in front of her.

"I truly believe you put too much trust and faith in one man."

"He is more than just a man and you know that," Candice said, trying not to let the anger in her voice show. "He one of the best assassins ever."

"And that should give him power to do as he pleases?"

"As long as he isn't breaking any of the rules or bringing harm to anyone who didn't deserve it, then I don't give a damn what Mike does?"

"I think you will not stand up to him because you are far too afraid of him."

"Anyone who wasn't afraid of him would be a fool, a very dead fool and very quickly if they didn't show any fear at all when it comes to him and who he is."

"You think none will rise up and match him?"

Candice again looked up from her papers and back towards her husband. A part of her wanted to get up from her chair and slap him so hard it would knock his hat right off his head, but she knew she couldn't afford to strike him here and now, not this soon after the wedding.

She also knew that just because the two of them were now married, it didn't put him in a position of power, nor did it give him the right to attack and or act like he was better than anyone who served under her. She was the leader of the Temple of Legends and not him, and she hoped he realized that before she had to remind him of it.

It had been eleven days now since their wedding, and even though she found herself getting frustrated with Kevin more often than not, she also saw a side to him that she was slowly beginning to like, maybe even more then like, but she knew she needed to get past Mike fully before she could come to terms with that.

"What are you thinking about?"

This time he caught her fully off guard by asking her a simple question, well to him it would seem like a simple question, but in order for her to answer it she would need days and days to explain it all. "Just trying to find some kind of order in all of this chaos," She said, figuring that was as good enough of an answer as any.

"Are you thinking about him?"

"What do you mean?" Candice asked, even though she didn't feel up to going down this path.

"I am talking about the feelings you have for your master assassin friend."

"I have no feelings for him, he is simply a good friend who I have known for a very long time."

"What did you want to do tonight?"

"I was hoping to get an early night's sleep if you are interested in joining me," Candice said, glad that Kevin decided to change the subject before they got into yet another fight over Mike.

"Don't you think if I join you, it will lead to a late night instead of the early night you are planning on?"

"Yes, I am sure it will lead to a late night, but I would love it none the less," Candice told him as she watched Kevin slightly blush. Even now that they were married, they had yet to find time to sleep together with all the crazy events happening around them. Plus, with her chest almost fully healed, she felt a lot better as well.

"Then it is a date, my love."

"Who doesn't love a good date night?" Mike said as he walked through the open door leading into Candice office with Alexia right behind him.

"A simple knock would have sufficed." Kevin angrily stated.

"Tell you what. When it says your name on the door and not hers, I will try knocking."

Mike watched as Kevin's cheeks slowly began to change a few different shades of red before he was able to get himself back under control, even though he wished deep down inside that Kevin would try to attack him, just so he could embarrass the man even more.

It was however, the redness in Candice's cheeks that quickly made him realize that he may have crossed a line, not that he cared or anything. It was just always good to know where that line was after all. "So you needed to see me?" he asked, while taking a seat in the chair to left of the desk.

"I have recently received a contract of the upmost importance and you were requested by name to be the one to carry it out," Candice said, as she pulled out a few pieces of paper from in front of her.

"Why does everyone always request me?" Mike asked, even though he already knew the answer.

"The client is offering a small fortune to you as payment."

"I already have a very large amount of money, why would I need more."

"Fifty thousand gold coins is something you should learn to take seriously."

Mike couldn't help but hear Alexia let out a small gasp from the seat next to him, and before he knew, it he was smiling as he turned to face her. The look she wore was even more priceless then the gasp she just let out. "What is the job?"

"I will need the two of you to set out for the Merchant Islands as soon as you are both healthy enough to travel. Once there, you will need to track down a small band of thieves who stole something of great importance to our client and he wishes to get it back." Candice said reading over the paper in front of her. "He says the band is led by a rather large woman and that she will try to protect this item with her life. He says that he is only interested in the safe return of the item, but if you need to kill the band to get to it, then so be it."

"I am confused about one thing though?" Mike asked, turning back to face Candice who was finally looking his way as well.

"And that would be what?" Kevin asked from the other side of the room, forcing the two of them to turn and face him."

"The grown-ups are talking right now if you don't mind," Mike said, turning back towards Candice.

"The client is a rich and powerful prince who wishes to remain nameless for now and also a good friend of mine."

"I get it now," Mike said, trying not to laugh out loud. "You get this great contract shortly after the two of you get married from one of his good friends and we should just jump at."

"You know damn well we take all offers seriously," Candice said, this time trying to keep her anger in check while talking to Mike.

"Well you can tell your prince friend that I have enough gold to buy him and everything he loves, and that I am not interested in this deal." Mike said, standing up from the chair he was sitting in and began turning towards the door.

"I told him that you have already agreed to his terms, and that you would leave as soon as you were well."

"Well isn't that convenient," Mike replied, sitting back down in the chair.

"I will charter you a boat as soon as you are ready to leave."

"No need to do that, you and I both know I own my own boat, and have a great captain to sail it for me."

"You have an answer for everything don't you?" Candice replied, trying her best not to look Mike in the eyes.

"I will not accept his money though," Mike said, and again he heard Alexia gasp beside him. "However the full payment can go to Alexia for helping out with this mission, and for the cost she put out watching over me while I was injured."

"Fine. So when do you think you will be in good enough shape to travel?" Candice asked, looking from Mike to Alexia and then back again.

"We will leave tonight."

"We will?"

"Yes we will," Mike said, answering Alexia's questions. "It is a three-week journey from port to port, and that will give me all the rest and time I need to heal."

"Sounds good to me. I will arrange for the money to be sent along with you for expenses and room and board from the treasury," Candice said, pulling out a blank bank form from her desk.

"I don't need any money and the two of us will be fine," Mike said, once again standing from his chair.

"My good friend is expecting you to complete this job as quickly as possible."

"You can tell your good friend that I will now be moving a lot slower since you decided to open your mouth once again when the grownups were talking," Mike said, looking back towards Kevin who face was once again a very deep shade of red, and his right hand was on the hilt of his sword.

"You should really learn some respect you know." Kevin said, trying his best to keep his rage in check, after all he stood a small chance of winning this fight.

"If you wish to teach me some, feel free to try?" Mike said, turning his body to face Kevin as well. "I am a very quick learner."

"You are both acting little children," Alexia said, catching them both by surprise. "If we are to leave tonight, I will need to pack some supplies and what not, so be a good gentleman and walk me back to my place."

Mike felt her hand on his shoulder, and he quickly shifted his gaze from Kevin back to Alexia. He no longer felt the urge to see how far the blade of his dagger would go into Kevin's soft chest, and he lost even more of his anger when she smiled at him.

"Once you have the item, you will need to deliver it in person to the address written inside this sealed envelope," Candice continued, handing a single grey envelope to Alexia. "After you exchanged the item he said you will be paid in full."

"Is there anything else we will need to know?" Alexia asked, a she tried her best to keep her eyes on Candice and not on Mike next to her.

Mike suddenly stopped listening to the two ladies talking as he noticed something on Candice's face. After all of the years he had known her, he came to learn that she was the greatest at hiding her emotions from everyone but him, and now he could see something in her eyes, something he had never seen before, something he knew was good but would come at a great price.

He suddenly realized that she was finally taking his advice and moving on. She was going to try her best to love the man standing across from him, and she would give herself to him mind, body, and soul and she would one day have his babies and fall in love with him.

She was slowly beginning to do everything that he wanted her to do, and he suddenly realized that he might have made a mistake by letting her go. His heart felt broken, but he knew deep down inside this was the right place for them both to be at this time.

"I am sorry for being a real asshole just now," Mike said, reaching his right hand out towards Kevin, who after a few minutes of hesitating finally returned with a hand of his own.

Mike figured that Kevin would be stuck in his life for a very long time now but in terms of years he realized that Kevin would be nothing but a sour patch in his life span, but he figured he would play nice for Candice's sake more than his own. "I will send word to you once we reach the port on the merchant islands," Mike said, turning back towards the door, and Alexia who stood there smiling back at him.

"Thank you very much and have a safe journey," Candice said as she watched the two of them leave side by side. She didn't quite understand Mike's sudden change of heart towards Kevin, but she knew it most likely had to do with her.

"Well that went well, I think." Kevin laughed, as he turned to face Candice

"You should be glad he didn't kill you."

"You wouldn't have allowed him to kill me."

"You talk as if you think I would have been able to stop him."

"Clearly he realized his mistake by challenging me, and that is why he apologized to me."

Candice knew it had nothing to do with her husband, but she needed to pick her battles now and she knew that she would need to start taking Kevin's side more often than Mike's if she planned on making their marriage work. So instead, she just smiled at him. "Just don't forget our date tonight," she said as she focused her attention back on the stack of papers in front of her.

Chapter 10

Mike closed his eyes and he couldn't help but feel the wind blowing in from the ocean as he sat on the end of one of the small piers, the water almost right below his feet, the waves slowly washed past him. He always hated the ocean because it took his family from him but in that same moment it also brought him to where he was today.

He had walked Alexia back to her place while giving her directions on where she was to meet him on the docks. He then returned to his own house, only this time he did change his clothes, into the stolen leather suit of armor and the four weapons that came with it, weapons he could use to kill an immortal if he needed too. He didn't know if he could trust Alexia with this knowledge, but at the same time something didn't feel right about the mission, something felt out of place. He wanted to make sure he covered his tracks the best he could, and this time leaving the armor and weapons at home seemed wrong.

At first, he couldn't believe how stiff the armor felt, but after wearing it for a short while, it seemed to form better to his body, to flex better to his every movement. The leather was a lot thicker than his normal outfits and crafted with metal throughout it to harden it against all attacks. Even the glowing blue dagger he held in his right hand felt almost weightless, but he could tell the blade was sharp just by looking at it and with a quick jab downwards he stabbed it into the wooden pier he was sitting on.

It was then that he wondered if he was right to steal items as beautiful as these, but a part of him knew that their power was locked away for a reason. He also felt wrong keeping them locked away as well, they needed to be free, like he needed to be free.

"It is going to be a cold trip to the Merchant Islands this time of the year."

Mike stood up and turned to face Alexia who was also almost at the end of the pier. On his way up, he grabbed the hilt of the dagger he had stabbed into the wood, and put it back into its custom harness, a harness, which also blocked out the glowing light of the blade. "My ship has built in heaters so I think we will be fine," he said as he took Alexia's two bags from her.

"And here I was thinking we would have to cuddle together to stay warm below deck."

"You packed a lot of stuff, I see."

"We will be gone for almost two months if not longer, and a girl needs her things, you know."

"We are also traveling to an island where there is a shop every two steps," Mike said, teasing her for a change.

"So are we swimming to your boat or just waiting here till we freeze to death."

"The captain is just fueling it up and then he will be here, I think." Mike sent word as soon as he returned home to his captain to ready the crew and ship but he knew his captain often worked at his own pace.

"So that was an interesting encounter back there, eh?"

"Does this whole thing seem weird too you?" Mike asked, turning to face her.

"Everything seems to be weird when it comes to you."

Mike could tell she was joking around by the smile on her face, even in the fading light of the sun and he couldn't help but reach out and brush the snowflakes from her hair with his finger. "Thanks, I think."

The sound of a horn sounding behind him forced them to turn around just in time to see a ship fast approaching the pier and it wasn't a sail boat but instead it was a 40-foot-long custom built steam boat, lighter on the water and could maintain a faster speed without the help of the wind. It was a three level boat with the first level being mostly the engine room and the crew chambers. The second was the deck and the top was the captain's post, and the two main bedchambers. The whole ship was painted in a fine metallic deep blue color, which almost blended in with the ocean itself.

"This is your ship?"

"Yes, this is my ship," Mike said, catching the main tie ropes as they were tossed down towards him.

"How much money do you make? I feel like I am getting ripped off on my contracts now."

"How old are you?"

"I turn 51 this year."

"And how old were you when you became immortal?"

"I was 25 years old then."

"I have been doing this for 74 more years then you. It is like a lifetime of earning money. Give it time and you too will be able to buy a lot of crap you don't need."

"You really are an old man aren't you?" Alexia said as she took his out reached hand and entered through the doorway.

The inside of the boat was almost as amazing as the outside as they rounded their way through the lower level of the ship to the stairway leading to the upper level. The floors were all done in a fine oak hardwood, and the walls were of simple designs painted a plain white color. The main floor was pretty much the same until they came to stop in the middle of a hallway with a door on each side of them. Mike knocked on the red door to his left as he placed Alexia's bags in front of the blue door.

A man in his late forties answered the red door and even though he stood straight and proud, you could see the age behind his eyes. This man was the captain of the Sea Sparrow II and also one of Mike's oldest mortal friends. He hired captain Jason Lightcid back when the man was no more than a boy, 16 or 17 years old, and he has been the captain of his ship ever since.

"It is good to see you alive and well my old friend," Mike said, giving the man a slap on the shoulder.

"Yes it is, and yes you are right I am feeling very old indeed."

"This is my friend Alexia," Mike said, taking a step to the side so Jason could see her better.

"She is another assassin, I see."

"How can you tell that about me just by looking at me?"

"It is simple, girl. All of you seem to have a sadness in your eyes that not even a hundred life times could fix. Good people you are, but living forever is something I couldn't do."

"You wouldn't want to sail the seas forever?" Mike asked, already knowing the man's answer because he had always answered the question the same way every time.

"I would love to sail the sea forever but I couldn't sit around and watch everyone I know and love grow old and die. That is why the few of you immortals should take great joy in each other because you will never have to feel that pain of losing everyone you love as long as you have each other.

My name is Captain Jason Lightcid, and it is an honor to meet you Alexia."

"The pleasure is mine," Alexia said, with a slight bow.

"So where are we off to this time, boy?"

"I am almost 80 years older than you, and yet you still call me boy."

"You are only as old as you look, and I have known you almost my whole life. You have never changed while I have grown old and grey."

"You are young at heart, old man, and we set sail for the Merchant Islands," Mike answered.

"A fair course indeed, and fair whether we shall find."

With one more bow to them both, Jason walked off towards the Captain's deck to start them off on their three week-long journey across the ocean. Something Mike was both looking forward to and worried about. Once again something didn't seem right about all of this.

He opened the blue door and walked into his main chambers on the ship, with Alexia right behind him. The room was almost as big as his entire cottage was, and was decorated with the finest art and furnishings money could buy. This was the one place where he liked to show off a part of his wealth, not to brag about having it, but because he felt truly happy on the open seas, so he figured he would style his chambers as nicely as he wanted too.

"I am really starting to not like you."

Again Mike found himself smiling as she teased him, everything around him he had earned over the course of his life. Some of it bad, and some of it good, but by being who he was it meant people would pay him more than they would anyone else. "This will be our living area from the next three weeks," he said, placing her bags beside the bed, the very large bed.

"This is room is like the size of four of my places put together."

"You can have the bed, and I will sleep on the couch over there. The bathroom is to the far right and the kitchen to the left. There is a spare room in the back where I have a few sets of armor as well and some weapons if you need anything, and feel free to help yourself to anything else you find on the ship," Mike offered, walking towards the double-sized couch, which was just as big as most people's beds.

He didn't know what it was but he always felt more at home on his ship then he ever did back living in his cottage. Maybe it was the sense of freedom, or maybe it was the fact that he could be alone for once. He always figured that the ocean didn't care who or what he was and he never felt judged by anyone when he sailed the open waters.

The first few times he traveled out on the ocean he was scared for his life. He kept having flash back of the day his parents were killed in the storm. It was part of his training to conquer his fear of the water; an assassin couldn't fear anything. Candice had brought him out on the water, weeks at time, until he finally found himself being able to move around the ship feely, even fight on it with skill. She broke his fear of the water by the time he was ten, and now he loved it more than anything else, well he loved sailing on it, but he still didn't freely swim in it.

"It is a very nice ship you have here," Alexia stated, making him focus on her once again.

"Thank you, it means a lot to me."

"I can sleep on the couch you know, if you want your bed."

"You can have the bed and I will sleep on the couch. After all, I have slept in your bed as of late, forcing you to be on the couch, so it is only fair."

He watched her as she fell onto her back onto his bed, the soft feather filled comforter fitting around her body perfectly. He smiled as she closed her eyes, clearly taking it all in. "And if you feel up to it, we can train on the main deck whenever you want, to try and get your knee used to combat again."

"I will only train with you if you keep those weapons far away from me."

"So you recognized them after all, then."

"I have never seen them personally but I have heard legends of the weapons with the glowing blades, legends I don't want to personally test."

"Legends are no more than a story told by the old," Mike said, lying on the couch-bed.

"Legend had it those were locked away in the royal armory, an armory, which was said to be foolproof."

"Once again you shouldn't believe all of the legends you hear."

"So you did steal them?"

"Yes, but only to keep them falling into the wrong hands," Mike explained as he starred at the clear ceiling, and the stars slowly beginning to come out.

"You thought that once she got married to Kevin he would find a way to get into the armory himself and steal the weapons."

Mike didn't answer her question but then again he didn't even think he had a real answer to give her. He stole the weapons for the safety of every other assassin, but he couldn't figure out from whom or why. Maybe he really stole them for no other reason than the fact that he could.

"I won't tell anyone if that is what worries you."

"I trust you or else I wouldn't have let you see them so clearly. That isn't what is worrying me."

"What is it then?"

"Fifty thousand gold coins is a lot of money to offer for any contract, even the ones requested of me. It just seems off, seems like we aren't being told everything, not that Candice lied to us, but maybe she doesn't even know all of the facts." Mike said, pulling out the glowing dagger once again, losing himself in its soft blue light.

"Yeah I got the feeling that Kevin wasn't telling us something that he knew, like he was holding back information."

"Guess we will have to wait until we have this item that was stolen in our hands."

"You don't like this part of the job, do you?"

"What part?"

"The part of having to kill people who may not deserve to die but end up dead because they were in the wrong place at the wrong time or because they tried protecting something that you needed."

Mike knew she couldn't have been more right about him. He knew that they would track down this band of thieves and get the item back, but what he couldn't tell was whether or not the thieves would part with it freely or if he would be forced to kill them and take it. He only liked killing people if they truly deserved to die, and after all, for all he knew these thieves might not have even stolen it in the first place. Maybe he was being sent there to steal it from them.

"So how do you plan of finding these thieves?"

"I'm planning on offering people money for information," Mike said, knowing that money would always make people talk because it always came down to either money or his dagger that would always get him what he wanted.

"I guess this is why you are the best of us."

"I am sure you are just as good as I am. Like I said, just give it time and who knows what you will become."

"Guess we will find out in the morning, which of us is the best after I kick your ass during out training."

They both shared a laugh from their separate beds and he couldn't help but wonder what she would be like to fight, what her style and combat training was, and how good she really was with a sword. He flexed his right hand around the hilt of the glowing dagger, and he held it there tightly, hoping that his hand would feel fully healed soon and then he wondered if it ever would be same as it was. He had never suffered such damage to any area of his body before like he did that day. Even the dagger to his chest didn't bother him as much as his hand. "You never know, you might be better than me in a fight."

"Only if you let me win or if I attacked you in the shower when you weren't expecting it, but then again I bet even in the shower you don't even let your guard down."

"Try it out one day and find out for yourself," Mike suggested and again they both shared a laugh.

"Well, now that we are on the subject of showers, I think I am going to have a quick one and change into something a little bit more comfortable."

"My house is your house, and like I said earlier, help yourself to anything you want. The towels are by the door and the shower is big enough for like five people to enjoy." Mike turned his head slightly and watched as Alexia quickly unpacked a change of clothes and headed off towards the shower. He continued to watch as she walked past him, and again he couldn't help but notice her body wrapped in her tight brown leather armor.

"If you are going to stare at me, you may as well join me then."

"I wasn't staring at you," Mike said as he felt his face turning red with embarrassment.

"That is what I figured," Alexia said with one more of her soft laughs before entering the bathroom, leaving the door open just a crack.

He figured it might have been her way of inviting him to join, or maybe she just didn't want the door closed. Either way, he stayed laying on his soft couch-bed staring now back up towards the stars, wondering what kind of trouble he had gotten himself into with this girl, or maybe it wasn't trouble at all. Maybe this is what he needed to finally become free again.

Chapter 11

Mike could feel the ice frozen on top of the deck of the ship. He could feel his leather clad foot sliding lightly on the surface, like every day for the last two weeks he woke up early and found his way to the deck, to the waiting eyes of the entire crew.

He looked at them all, gathered around the railings and windows that over looked the open part of the deck. He wondered again if they all gathered together to watch him or Alexia, who was standing ten feet in front of him.

He knew if he was part of the crew, he would be here for her too, looking at her in her tight, brown leather assassins outfit. He watched her now as she pulled the green sword he had given to her out of its harness, and watched as she took a few steps closer towards him.

He didn't even bother reaching for his own weapons because he knew what her first attack would be. He knew that she would come in fast and hope to make him lose his footing on the icy deck. She had tried this everyday so far, but it always failed.

Mike noticed Jason standing at the window of the Captain's quarters looking down towards them. It was the first time in the two weeks of their sparring that he noticed his old friend. He often told Jason of the many stories of his journeys and missions, but he knew Jason always doubted them at one point or another. Guess he figured today would be a good day to come and find out the truth.

Mike knew Alexia was coming towards him, but he matched his old friend's stare for a moment longer, just one moment before turning back to Alexia who was almost right in front of him now. He smiled as he began to step slightly to the right and she matched his course with a simple adjustment to her run. At the last second before she ran right into him, he faked to the right once more and turned on the ball of his foot quickly to left, only to find a green blade of a sword waiting for him there.

He dropped to his knees and slid right under the blade reaching for the hilts of his daggers at the same time as he reached the side railing of the ship. Still on his knees, his dug the back of his feet into the railing and pushed himself forward with all of his strength. He went from a dead stop to lunging back towards Alexia in a blink of an eye.

She crashed into him with her sword still ready meeting his forward attack with his daggers, and so their dance began again, sword on dagger and dagger on dagger. He was surprised at how good she was at duel-wielding weapons the first time they sparred together, but as the days went by, she kept correcting her mistakes and getting better and faster with both weapons.

He could tell she still favored her sore knee and he tried his best to center his attack so she would be forced to put the weight on her good knee and not her bad, but like all acts of combats, sometimes things happen that you didn't expect to happen.

She came on again with a downward slash with her sword as she jabbed forwards with the dagger and he met both attacks with his daggers. He even managed to block her swiping low kick with a quickly jump and a flip backwards.

He landed on his feet with ease, and only slightly slid backwards on the icy deck, only to find Alexia already in front of him, sliding on her knees with both of her weapons pointing his way. This time he jumped forwards in a semi flip, and just as Alexia went under him, he lashed out his daggers and again blocked her attacks, until she spun at the last second and grabbed onto his foot. He felt her pull backwards while he was still in the air, without his feet being able to get under him, he face-planted hard into the wooden deck.

He got his hands under him and pushed upward and with another quick spin he was back on his knees and facing a now smiling Alexia but it wasn't until he stood up that he realized something was wrong. His eyes began to blur and he was seeing white spots where there shouldn't have been any. Before he could stop the fight, he was able to see slightly through the blur, and he caught sight of the yet again fast approaching Alexia. This time he was only able to half block her dagger attack with his own and when he reached down to block her sword slash, he over reached and took the blade of her sword to his right wrist. He felt his fingers go numb and heard his dagger fall to the ground.

With speed he could no longer keep up with through his blurry eyes, Alexia grabbed his now weaponless hand and pulled him closer to her. He went to dodge low, but clearly she was expecting that and he was met with her knee hitting him in the side of the head. Again more white spots showed up in his eyes.

Even though he was clearly wounded, the two of them were still moving fast enough that he figured most of the crew weren't fully keeping up with the attacks or their movements. He managed to push himself away from her, and he reached his right hand to the hilt of the sword on his back, the whole time trying to blink the whiteness from his sight.

He pulled his sword free with lightning speed just in time to match her sword strike. The steel on steel launched a spray of sparks into the sky all around them. This time he caught her by surprise with his strength of the sword blow. This was the first time he had used one of his swords while sparring with her.

She hesitated for just a second to long as he forced her backwards on the icy deck with his sword attack, just long enough for him to catch her left hand with his as he let his other dagger slide to the floor as well. It was his time to pull her close but just as he did he felt her knee give out on her.

She stumbled into him and with their hands all tied up, she crashed into him and he slightly lost his footing on the ice and found himself falling backwards before he could stop it. He managed to push both of their swords free of their falling bodies, but that only made the impact with the deck even more painful. He heard his head smack the deck more than he felt it. He did how ever feel her weight as it slammed into his chest, which knocked the wind out of him.

He found himself trying to blink away the blurriness again while he fought to get air back into his lungs. He could feel Alexia push herself slowly off of his chest, which only made it harder for him to get the air he wanted. Within seconds, she was off of his chest and laying on her back beside him.

"That was interesting," Mike said, between each difficult breath he took.

"I so would have beaten you too if it wasn't for my stupid knee."

"You can always try again tomorrow."

"By the way what happened to you?"

"What do you mean?"

"After I made you face plant onto the deck, you seemed out of it afterwards."

"I think my head isn't a hundred percent healed yet," Mike answered as he turned to face Alexia who was now on her side facing him. "After it bounced off both the deck and your knee, I couldn't get the blurriness and the white spots to go away."

"Maybe we should take a break for a few days then, just to make sure you are going to be fine. We are, after all, on a very important mission."

"Maybe you're right. It would suck to have a run-in with a band of thieves and have my head go all wonky on me."

"It might be a bit of distraction."

"You seem to be a bit of a distraction."

"What do you mean?"

Mike couldn't help but laugh as he looked around at crew who still stayed around to watch the two of them laying on the icy deck, most of them men. "You seem to be distracting them from their jobs," He said, motioning towards a few of the crewmembers close by.

"They could be staring at you in that sexy black outfit of your as well you know."

"They could be true, but I am almost positive they are here for you."

Mike sat up slowly, this time hoping to limit the amount of blurriness that came to his eyes and he was somewhat happy when nothing at all happened. He made a mental note not to hit his head again anytime soon. He watched as Alexia started to rub her left knee with both of her hands and he turned himself to face her.

With his legs crossed and sitting right beside Alexia, he lifted her left leg up and placed it straight across his lap. With his right hand still slightly numb, he used his left to hit the deck and crack of a few chunks of ice. He grabbed a chuck of ice in each hand and placed one on top of her knee and the other right under it.

"Thank you."

"Maybe we should take it easy for a little while for your sake as much as mine," Mike said, trying his best not to stare at her as she propped herself up on her elbows to look at him.

"Only if you promise me a rematch as soon as we get home."

"It's a deal."

He could feel her eyes on him as he ran the ice up on down her sore leg. He knew it couldn't be doing much because of the thickness of her leather pants but it was the thought that counted. After all, he was the one who had reinjured her knee, and there was no way of knowing if she would be hundred percent by the time they reached the Merchant Islands.

That didn't really bother him though because if she wasn't then they could take it easy for a little while longer before going after the band of thieves, which would make Kevin angry but would make him happy because he was starting to like hanging out with Alexia more and more as the days went by. He also couldn't wait to see her expression when she found out that he also secretly owned a small bungalow on one of the smaller beaches there.

"I think your ice has melted all over my leg."

Mike found his eyes drift back from whatever spaced out area they were in back towards her leg, which was indeed slightly covered in water. He laughed at the sight and he noticed her smile back at him. It was odd, really, how he could be around her. He didn't have to hide his laughter or anything else they shared when they were in the open like this, something he could never do with Candice.

"I would offer to pay you for your thoughts, but sadly I don't have any money to offer."

"Tell you what. You can ask me any one question right now, and I will be hundred percent honest with you," Mike said, finally looking back into her blue eyes-- eyes that seemed to light up a little too much at his statement. "You can have one question a day but only one, so make it count."

"And you promise not to get mad at me no matter what I ask."

"I promise."

"How long were you and Candice in a relationship?"

"Just over thirty-five years," Mike answered. Without even thinking about it, he figured his secrets would be safe with Alexia.

"That is a long time, and I honestly didn't have a clue until she started coming to see you every day while you were at my place."

"Thirty years compared to the rest of the time I have been alive, really isn't that long if you think about it," Mike said, as he tried to figure out if he should remove his hands from her leg.

"How long has it been since you two called it off?"

"Just over ten years ago, shortly before she met Kevin for the first time."

"Okay, now it is your turn."

"It is my turn to do what?"

"Ask me anything you want to know about me, and I will give you an honest answer."

Mike knew this could be his perfect chance to learn anything he wanted about his new traveling companion, but he couldn't settle on just one question to ask. Even as he sat there watching her stare off into the distance of the ocean and the open water, he tried his best to keep his eyes from drifting lower to the rest of her body but like always he failed. "Do you really like being an assassin?" he asked and smiled at her once again as she turned back to face him.

"Honestly, I am not sure anymore. I travel away from the temple more now just for fun and to see the world, then I do it for contracts. It is part of the reason why I don't have as much money as I would like to have, but I have seen so many places and met so many different people it somehow seems worth it to me, but I always find my way back home."

"If it helps any, I think that your fighting skills are perfect and it seems like your outlook on life is far greater than most assassins."

"Not nearly as perfect as yours though."

"Trust me on this. You don't want to be like me when you get to live as long as I have."

"I would ask you why, but I will save that for my question tomorrow."

"No matter what happens during this mission, never forget who you are, and never try to become like me," Mike said, finally giving her back her leg.

"I make no promises, but I will try my best to be as good as a person as you are, even if you try your best to hide that person all the time."

"I can live with that, I guess," Mike said, offering his hand to her to help her up and off the deck.

As soon as they were both on their feet again, he noticed that Alexia was struggling to walk with her once again sore leg and he gently but quickly picked her up with ease. It happened so quickly that he felt her wrap her arm around his shoulder tightly as if she feared he would drop her.

"Next time, a simple warning would be nice."

"Where is the fun in that though?"

"Good point, but let's speed this up a little. I need a shower, and you may need to help wash my back while I try to keep myself standing upright."

Mike felt his cheeks turn red once again as he tried to figure out whether or not she was joking around with him or if she was serious. Either way, he found his legs moving a little faster as they got closer to their room.

Later that night, Alexia found herself sitting on the very front of the ship, her legs hanging over the edge, while she rested her head on her arms as she stared off into the distance. She had hardly ever been on the open water like this before, and she found herself lost in the sights and sounds of water all around her. Even the taste of the splashing seawater wasn't that bad.

She left the room shortly after Mike had fallen asleep. She couldn't help but smile again as she thought about him trying his best to stay awake and talk to her. She knew the hit he took to his head must have affected him a lot more than he was letting on, so she decided to let him sleep.

She passed very few members of the crew while she walked to the front of the ship and guessed they must have all been asleep as well. The ones she did pass met her with smiles and nods but hardly any of them spoke a word to her.

So, she was a little surprised when she heard footsteps walking up behind her, but she didn't even look away from the ocean in front of her. She figured if someone on the ship really wanted to attack her she could deal with them without even trying.

"If you don't mind me saying, if you are going to jump, you should jump from the back of the boat and not the front. You have more of a chance of being run over if you jump from here."

"I was just enjoying the view, that is all," Alexia said, finally turning to face the captain of the ship.

"The moon is full tonight and well worth the viewing in my eyes as well."

"Yes it helps to keep one centered."

"That was quite the show you two put on earlier."

"Yeah it was pretty fun until the end."

"I didn't know the boy could move like that."

"Trust me, he wasn't even trying," Alexia said, a slight smile showing on her lips. "He has been holding back this whole time for my sake."

"And why would he be doing such a thing."

"Because Mike is truly the best of us all, he has skills that cannot be matched."

"So, he was sparing your feelings then."

"No. Every day he has been using more and more of his skills," Alexia said, again turning back to the open sea ahead of her. "I think he has been training me this whole time."

"Yeah that seems like something the boy would do."

"Yeah, he is a good man, even if he doesn't show it to the world."

"That is because that leader of yours got deep into his head and his heart. I have watched his downward spiral over the last few years. He lost the love of life and the adventure he used to have when we first met."

"So you knew about the two them as well?" Alexia asked, surprised that Mike would allow anyone to find out the truth about him and Candice.

"That is the thing about a hidden and forbidden love. It always stays forbidden, but never hidden. Sooner or later the world will share your secrets whether you want her to or not."

"Did you ever meet Candice?"

"A few times, yes, but never on this boat if that is what you are wondering. The boy has never brought anyone abroad before. You would be the first."

"What did you think of her?"

"I think that in the two weeks you have been sailing with us, you have been able to fix what it took her thirty plus years to break."

"What are you talking about?" Alexia asked, trying to figure out if this conversation was a good one or a bad one.

"I have not seen the boy smile in years now, haven't even seen him laugh like he used to when we were young men together. I feared he lost that part of himself, but I am glad to see it is still inside of him."

"You think I am good for him?"

"I think that is something the two of you will have to figure out on your own."

"I am starting to see that this is going to be a very interesting mission after all."

"You are very young at heart and for that you are lucky. I wish you the best of luck, Lady Alexia but for now I must leave you and retire myself;

even an old man needs his rest."

"Have a good night and thank you for your kind words," Alexia told him as she watched the captain walk back down the deck and through one of the many doorways.

She didn't know what to think about at that moment, so she just went back to staring off into the distance. She didn't come along on this mission because she hoped to find love, but more so because she didn't want Mike to go alone. Even if she didn't have a choice, she knew there must be a reason why she was here.

She stared at the moon for a very long time, and soon the sun started to rise up out of the ocean itself, or at least that is how it looked from where she was sitting. She knew she would have to return to her bed soon but she didn't have the heart too look away from the beautiful sunrise.

Chapter 12

Mike watched the waves slam into the side of ship with very little interest. The first few times he had been at sea, the waves brought fear into his heart but not now. Nothing seemed to bring fear to his heart anymore.

But it wasn't the waves that brought him to the side of the ship that early morning though. Instead it was the sight of a second ship coming towards them. It was still too far away for him to make out the flag, but he could still see it was black, the mark of a pirate ship.

The part that really worried him was the fact that his own boat stood out on the open seas and almost everyone would avoid it even pirates but it would seem this set of pirates did not care who he was or maybe they were so new to the lifestyle that they didn't even know who they were approaching.

"Should I raise the alarm?" Jason said, looking off towards the pirate ship off in the distances.

"I will deal with this myself, just keep everyone safe and out of harm's way."

"You will deal with a ship full of pirates on your own?"

"It wouldn't be the first time," Mike said, turning to face his old friend. "I assure you I will be perfectly fine, and at the end of the day you will still be the captain of my ship."

"When will you figure it out, boy, that you aren't on your own in this life?"

"I will learn that as I look into the eyes of the person who is beside me, as I take my final breath."

"I will go now and make sure everyone has a safe place away from the fight."

Mike watched Jason run off, down the deck and into the doorway. His eyes turned back towards the ship, which was fast approaching his. A ship which was slightly longer than his with three massive sails. He thought about turning around and getting Jason to go at full speed to outrun the ship, but then he realized that wouldn't be as much fun.

He could see the boarding plank on the side of the pirate's ship as it grew closer and closer and the fact that there was only one, only assured him that these pirates were not professionals. He couldn't help but laugh at his dumb luck for running into these fools on the open seas, but after today they would think twice about attacking another ship.

He could now even make out the shapes of the many men standing on the side of the ship waiting for the boarding plank to be put in place. He watched as their captain steered the ship alongside his, as it inched closer and closer.

He watched the four men on the ship throw their grappling hooks onto the side of his ship, watched as the boarding plank smashed through one of his side railings, something that made him a lot angrier than it should have. He even watched as the first man began walking towards him on the plank, a giant of a man standing almost eight feet tall, covered from head to toe in fur clothes with a great axe strapped to his back.

And again Mike found himself smiling.

Alexia found herself running as fast as she could down the narrow hallways leading to the main deck. She could feel her knee burning and knew it wouldn't hold out for long, but she had to make it to him, she had to help him.

She ran passed many members of the crew doing their best to lock down as much of the ship as they could, so even if Mike lost the fight, the pirates would be hard pressed to even get inside the ship. She almost ran right into one of the female crewmembers as she reached the last door that would lead her to his side. She tried opening it, only to find it sealed shut.

"You need to open this door for me now?" Alexia said, turning to face the female Member of the crew standing by her

"I cannot, I'm sorry. Only the captain can unlock the doors when we are in a full lock down."

"Where is the captain now?"

"Last I saw him, he was on his way to his quarters to watch the outcome of the fight."

She found herself moving back the way she came before the woman even finished talking, and again she could feel her knee wanting to give out but she just pressed on harder, even though she knew she would pay for it later on that day.

She rushed right past the blue door, which would lead her back into her room, straight down the hallway, and right into the half open door leading into the captain's quarters. She found herself running right past Jason and right up to the main window overlooking the deck.

She got there just in time to see the last of the pirates walk off the boarding plank onto the ship and slowly began to form a circle around Mike. She only counted about twenty of them as she watched the big man in the center approach Mike.

"Why have you come to my ship?" Mike asked, watching the big man get closer to him.

"We have come for whatever treasures such a nice ship as yours will have, plus the women who are unfortunate enough to be found aboard you ship."

"Have you not heard of the name of my ship or of me?"

"You are nothing more than a man standing in the way of our loot."

"Well, in that case, I am from the Temple of Legends on an important mission, and I do not wish to be delayed any longer."

"So we should just believe you are one of the legendary immortal assassins?"

"Believe me or not, but I am a master assassin and my name is Mike," Mike said as he watched some of the pirates in the group let out gasps of fear, and others even took a few steps back. "So I will let you have this one chance to turn around and leave my ship."

"And what if we decided to stay?"

"Then I will be forced to kill you all."

A few more of the pirates took another step or two back he noticed but the big man in front of him was either really dumb or just stupid because he reached over his left shoulder and pulled his great axe free.

Alexia could see Mike talking, but she couldn't hear anything that he was saying. She could guess it must have been something good because a few of the pirates started walking backwards. She figured maybe they would make it through the day without any blood being spilt; that was until she saw the big man pull his great axe free.

"You have to open the doors and let me help him," Alexia said, turning to face Jason.

"It isn't safe to open the doors now, and the safest place for you is here with us."

Alexia turned back to the window just as the big man lunged forward at Mike. His great axe swung behind his head as he readied a mighty forward chop, and just as the blade of the axe was inches from Mike's head, she watched him move with such great speed to the side, the axe blade slammed hard into the wooden deck becoming very much embedded in it.

Again she watched him move with some much speed as one of his blue daggers found its way into his right hand. Shortly after that, it found its way into the back of the man's neck. She could see a look of fear wash over the big man's face, as he realized that the end of his life was at hand. She could see the color wash away from his face, as the blood began to spill down his neck. Even though the window blocked all sound, she could have sworn she heard the sound of Mike pulling the dagger free of the man's neck and the sound of the man's dead body landing on the wooden deck.

It was then that she watched all chaos break out on the deck, as bodies crashed together some trying to get back to their own ship. Almost all of them rushed towards Mike, who now had both blue glowing daggers in each hand. Even from the distance, she both feared and loved the beauty of the weapons.

Mike pulled his dagger free from the back of the big man's neck and watched as he fell to the ground dead. He watched as some of the pirates began to flee, but more turned to face him, all of them with weapons in hand and all ready to avenge their fallen leader.

The soft blue glow of his twin daggers somehow made him feel at ease, as if nothing else in the world mattered at that very moment. He looked around at the remaining pirates, all of whom were about to attack him and all of whom would be dead very soon.

He would have felt guilty for taking the lives of these men but he figured they were far from innocent. Most of them were most likely murderers of women if not worse, and that was a good enough reason for them to die this day, but he figured he wouldn't take any joy in the killing.

He looked up towards the captain's quarter's main window, and his eyes found Alexia right away. He knew she must had have been mad when she realized all of the doors to him were sealed, but all he saw on her face now was panic. It was like she was truly worried for him.

It was as if she could read his thoughts as she stared at him now. She smiled back at him and he couldn't help but smile as well. He didn't know what it was about this girl, but he knew she was different. He knew that if she could, she would get to him now even if it meant dying. He figured if it were possible for them to die, he wouldn't mind dying by her side.

He rushed forward with a speed that couldn't be matched by a mortal man and lunged both his daggers into the shoulders of the closest pirate. The impact was so intense that both Mike and the pirate went airborne for a few seconds. As the pirate flew backwards, he used his feet and pushed off the dead man's chest lunging towards the next two pirates who were unfortunate to be in his way. Each of his glowing daggers found their necks as he forced them to the ground with his attack.

Alexia watched the set of pirates' land on the ground, each one of them with a dagger sticking out from their throats. She watched as he killed three pirates within seconds and without even trying. She knew then that he was indeed holding back when they trained together.

She now watched as three more of pirates tried to organize some plan of attack. They started to circle Mike, like a shark around its prey, but she couldn't help but smile once again when she thought about how this prey was a far bigger shark than the little ones about to attack him.

The first came forward with a lazy thrust of his sword, but she could tell it was more of a distraction than a real attack, as the pirate behind Mike lunged forward at the same time. His battle-axe aimed low. She watched as Mike reached out and grabbed the guy in front of him. He pulled him forward with so much strength that it sent the man stumbling just in time for Mike to jump on his back and out of the way of the low swinging axe, which now laid very much embedded in the pirate's head.

Again she was forced to wonder if there was a limit to his fighting skills and speed, and again she found herself staring at him and him alone.

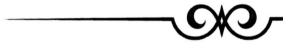

Mike turned back around after he heard the crunch of the pirate's skull, knowing that another attack would be coming his way shortly. He finished his spin with his daggers ready to attack, and just as a metal hammer swung inches from his face, with his left dagger he stabbed upwards slicing through the man's forearm and with his right he aimed low sinking his dagger right into the man's lower chest, hitting him in the lung.

Another sword came down towards his right side as he struggled to pull his hand free of the dying pirate's body, and he found himself exposed for the first time during the fight; however, luck was with him as the blade simply bounced off his tough leather armor.

As the sword fell short of its mark, Mike left his daggers in the man who was now lying very dead on the ground and reached behind him grabbing the hilts of both the swords he kept on his back. As he pulled them free of their harnesses with such amazing speed it was like one great blue blur as the blades came to life with their blue light.

The pirate who had just failed with his poor attempt of a sword attack, backed away suddenly as he came at the man with both swords spinning at his side. His right wrist brought the sword downwards with both strength and speed as the one in his left hand shot off to the side to parry another attack from a second pirate trying to join in this fight.

He watched as the second pirate started to smile thinking they had finally organized enough of an attack to overwhelm the assassin, but again Mike fought the two of them with ease. His left hand keeping one at bay with blinding defensive strokes of the blue sword, and he went on the full offensive with his right hand.

He knew it would only be a matter of time before one or the other screwed up and he would get his shot to kill them both, but he was enjoying this moment, the freedom that came with fighting. Not so much the killing, but during the fight he always managed to fully clear his head and think about nothing else.

When he was in this state of mind, he noticed every little detail about the fight and the people he was up against. The one he was attacking was slowly beginning to sweat and slow on his defensive maneuvers, while the one he was parrying kept attacking too quickly, making it easy to block his attacks. It was however the third pirate who was standing on the plank, aiming an arrow at him that made him wonders what to do next.

He waited until he heard the twang of the arrow leaving the bowstring to suddenly step forward, causing the guy who was attacking him from behind to also come forward and take his place on the deck. This was followed by the arrow, which was aimed at him in the first place. Now, with only one attacker left besides the man who was quickly trying to find a second arrow, Mike focused on just attacking the man now, and both of his blades started to go into a blue glowing dance, which had the pirate back stepping for his life. His life was ended as the tip of each of his glowing blades shot through different areas of his chest.

He turned just in time to deflect a second arrow with his left sword and off he went again, this time towards the rest of the pirates, who were trying to escape back to their own ship. He came face to face with two bigger pirates about halfway across the plank, and again went into a series of blue glowing skilled moves, which left one pirate dropping to his knees holding his neck and the other falling backwards into the freezing water below.

He wanted to keep pushing forward, but the plank began to move under his feet as the pirate ship began to pull away from his own ship. He turned at the last second and jumped just in time. The plank fell out from under his feet and into the water below. He tossed his two swords midair towards the deck of his ship, and grabbed the edge of the broken rail on his descent downward, causing his body to slam hard into the side of the ship.

He began pulling himself upwards when a series of arrows started impaling the side of the ship all around him, and he tried his best to make himself as small as possible. He knew they could only keep up the barrage for a short time because the ship would soon be too far away for them to aim at him. Arrows started coming less and less and he slowly began pulling himself back up towards the deck of the ship when he suddenly felt a hot screaming pain in his lower back. He knew an arrow had found its mark but he had to focus on pulling himself up.

It wasn't until a small slender tanned hand came into view of his eyes that he realized that Alexia was at the side of the railing reaching down to help him up. He felt her grab him under his right shoulder and begin to pull upwards as he used both his hands to lift himself up.

As soon as he got over the side of the broken railing and back onto the deck, he noticed an arrowhead poking out of the front of his armor, or at least he thought it was through his armor. It turned out, while he was hanging over the side of the ship, it pulled his leather body armor away from his leather pants creating a perfect opening of non-protected flesh, which now had a wooden arrow sticking right through it.

"That doesn't look like it feels too good."

"It looks a lot better than it feels if that helps any," Mike admitted as he reached down towards the arrowhead with both hands and broke it off at the shaft, causing his body to ripple with pain.

Mike was about to reach behind him to pull the rest of the shaft out of his body, when Alexia almost knocked him off his feet as she wrapped her right arm around his neck and her left around his lower back, pulling him close to her.

He looked down into her bright blue eyes, trying to figure out was she was up to, when she quickly moved her face towards his, her soft lips touching his gently at first, but soon she was pulling him closer as the kiss got more intense. He felt her left hand grab the shaft of the arrow and began pulling it out quickly. She was quick at doing so, but the pain still overwhelmed him and he almost lost his footing, but she still held him tight, kissing him the whole time.

It wasn't until he heard the shaft of the arrow hit the ground that he slowly began to relax again. He could feel the blood pouring out of the wound as it ran down both his front and his back, but he couldn't bring himself to think about it now, not while his lips where on hers.

Finally, he had to pull himself away from her long enough to move his hand down towards his wound to see how bad it looked. It wasn't too bad and he knew he would heal, but it would be yet another scar on his body, but at least he would be able to live and tell the story about how he got the scar.

"I guess I now know a very good way to distract you."

"Yes, you seemed to have figured out a very good way of being a much needed distraction in my life," Mike said, looking back into her blue eyes again, noticing her beautiful smile on face.

"Do you want to try it again now?"

Mike was about to say he very much would love to try it again, when he heard the footsteps of the rest of the crew finally making their way towards the deck. He turned just in time to see Jason pull his two blue glowing daggers from the dead pirate's body, and began to walk towards him and Alexia.

"Well, looks like I won't doubt any of your stories ever again now that I have witnessed you in action first hand."

Mike watched as his old friend held out the hilts to his daggers, so he could take them back. Little did Jason know that those very daggers could be used to kill him, not that Mike believed the captain would ever try such a thing or that he would even get close to him if he did try. He just found it very ironic. "Thank you for keeping everyone locked up and safe," He said, while reaching out to retrieve his two daggers.

"It was all in a day's work, but now we will deal with the dead bodies and the blood, and Alexia you should help him back to the room and treat his wound before he bleeds on my ship anymore."

"It is my ship, my old friend, and if I want to bleed on it, I will," Mike said, which forced everyone around him to share a heart filled laugh. "But a hot shower would certainly make this day feel a lot better."

"I check my calculations while you were in the middle of the fight, and I figure we are about three days away from the Merchant Islands. I think it would be best if you two get some rest, and I will send word when the port is in sight."

"Thank you again my friend," Mike continued with a final look towards Jason and his crew. He turned off towards the stairway, which would lead him to his room and his very warm shower.

Chapter 13

They arrived at the docks three days later just as Jason had said they would, and the crew quickly made their way into the busy afternoon market. Mike had little trouble leaving the ship and walking onto the busy boardwalk, but he turned around to find Alexia still standing on the side of the ship staring off into the crowd and the city in front of her.

"Are you coming or do you wish to stay on the ship all day?"

"I'm coming, it's just that I have never seen anything quite like this before in all of my travels."

"The Merchant Islands are some of the biggest trading cities in the whole world, and people come from all over the world just to sell their junk here," Mike said while reaching his hand out towards Alexia. "And I don't really blame them with six different islands filled with shops of every type and some of the most private beaches in the entire world. This place is a safe haven for the scum who wish to sell their stolen wares, and I believe it will be where we find our thieves."

Mike watched as she slowly began walking down the ramp towards him, felt her fingers interlock with his, something he didn't know if he should be getting used to or not but over the last three days the two have them had grown a little closer as they got to know each other better.

He started walking back onto the boardwalk, half pulling her along behind him, mostly because she seemed to get distracted by every single sight there was to see. From all the boats filling the bay around them to the people dressed up in all sorts of colors and designs.

He wondered how anyone could go their whole lifetime and never find their way here, out of all the places in the world. This place was one of a kind, a place where anybody from any walk of life could find a good meal with good company, to a fine place to live. The prices were always fair, and the people would never stop amazing you.

"It isn't what I was expecting, that is for sure."

"It is a world all to its own here," Mike said as they walked through the busy crowd, leading to the west side of the boardwalk.

"Don't you ever feel fully exposed here among all these people?"

"It took me awhile to get used to it. This place has a very low crime rate, and almost everyone here has a lot of money to spend, so the guards enforce the laws to keep the money flowing."

"And what if they realize who we are?"

"They won't figure that out," Mike assured her, walking down the stairs leading to the beach. "That is why we are wearing our normal people clothes now."

"And here I was thinking you had just grown tired of seeing me in my tight leather outfit."

"I don't think I would ever grow tired of seeing you in any outfit."

Mike could feel her staring at him as they walked along the sandy white beach, and he turned slightly to face her and caught the smallest hint of a smile on her face. She looked beautiful again today like always, her blonde hair hanging free around her face, her blue eyes so busy taking everything in around them. He then wondered if it would be possible for her blue shorts to get any shorter on her long legs, but she seemed to wear them well along with her white and blue tank top, which was almost too tight on her. You could tell just by looking that she wasn't wearing anything underneath it.

That is what he always loved about the Merchant Islands. Even if you came in the middle of the winter season, the weather was always super-hot, but if you came during the summer season it was almost too hot. It also meant the women around here often wore very little clothing.

They walked for a good three hours along the beach and the tree line slowly got closer and closer to the water. Mike watched as Alexia took her shoes off and began walking in the ocean along the beach. The water was crystal clear here, and you could swim out for a very long way and still see the ocean floor.

He watched her as she seemed to finally allow herself some time to truly be herself, walking along the water up to her knees, always staring off in the distance. He couldn't help but laugh as a group of fairly large fish swam right up to her feet and in between her legs, causing her to almost jump right out of the water.

"That wasn't funny, you know."

"The only thing that would have made it better is if you fully fell into the water," Mike spouted as he stopped just outside of the water line to look at her as she stared back at him. A smile spread on both their faces.

It was her turn to hold out her hand to him, but he found himself hesitating this time. He didn't mind sailing on a boat across the vast open ocean, but he still couldn't bring himself to freely walk into it. Something about it still brought a slight fear into his heart.

She came towards him then, as if she could sense his doubts or fears. She pulled herself towards him, their lips touching once again in a kiss, and for the first time in a very long time he found himself enjoying his life. After all, how could he not, standing there on one of the most amazing beaches in the world, kissing one of the most beautiful women in the world?

He knew what she was doing before she even began pulling him a little closer towards the water, but he didn't find the strength in him to be able to break their kiss over a little bit of water on his feet, feet he realized were still covered with his shoes.

He felt her soft hands slide under his blue T-shirt as she began to pull it up and over his head. He could feel the salt-water against the wound he had suffered a few days ago. Even though it was mostly healed, it still stung a little as the salt got into it.

Soon the water was almost up to the top of their chest when she wrapped her legs around his waist and her arms around his neck. His left arm went under her to keep her right where she was as his right hand found its way under the back of her tank top.

He finally broke their kiss long enough to look her in to eyes again, her bright blue eyes were sparkling in the sun light, but he could see something deeper in them, some kind of joy she was just beginning to understand.

"See the water isn't that scary of a thing."

"You sure do have a great way of distracting people don't you."

"I told you I did."

"Are you this good at distracting every guy?" Mike asked as his fingers ran along the naked skin of her back.

"You are you only guy I have ever wanted to distract. However, the real question is how many girls have you brought here before to make out with under the sun?"

"You would be the first," Mike said, and shortly after he said it, he felt her lips on his again. This time only for a second before she rested her head on his shoulder as they both took a moment too take it all in.

"So where are we off too?"

He tried his best not to get chills as she spoke so close to ear. He felt her warm breath against his neck, as he felt her fingers running along his lower back "We are going to my super-secret beach bungalow."

"Of course you have a super-secret bungalow on a beautiful beach such as this."

"It's nothing special, but it is still a two-hour hike away."

"Is that your way of saying we should get out of the water?"

"It is my way of saying that if we hurry we can watch the sunset from my deck."

"Lead on then."

Mike almost regretted saying anything as Alexia slowly unwrapped her legs from his waist and lowered herself back down onto her own feet. He did, however, catch quite a show when he looked down at her white tank top, which was now soaked and mostly see-through. He smiled once more as she gave him a wink while she walked past him and back towards the beach.

He followed her back onto the beach, and as soon as his feet were out of the water, he pulled off his now ruined runners and grabbed his sand covered T-shirt from the ground. He began walking, once again, down the beach. He felt her fingers wrap around his, and he couldn't help but wonder where this was all going.

He had never before been out in public with a girl showing this kind of affection so openly. Normally he and Candice had to hide their every move, and they could never go out into public together. He was starting to like this new connection with Alexia.

They walked side by side for the rest of the trip, and soon the beach disappeared into rough batch of jagged rocks and slippery moss. The two of the crossed it with ease, and soon he could see his secret hideaway in the distance. It really was a small bungalow, which sat twenty-feet into the ocean held above the water by stilts. It was made out of mostly wood with a grass and straw roof and had one main door and a deck door, which hung out over the ocean even more. The floor was made entirely out of glass and give him a perfect view of the sea life below.

"It is so beautiful."

"Wait until you see the inside of it, but we have to hurry though," Mike explained, walking towards the wood walkway leading to the latter that would lead them up to the main floor of the place. "Once the tide comes in, the walk way gets covered in water and I don't feel like swimming."

"Do you ever design anything that is simple?"

"I like to keep life interesting."

The two of them made their way across the wooden walkway towards the latter and already the water was slowly beginning to cover it. Alexia climbed the latter first, and he had a hard time not starring at her in her tight shorts as he followed her up.

"Welcome to my super-secret beach house," Mike said as he pushed open the wooden door leading into the place.

Again he watched as she walked into another of his places, which seemed to leave her speechless. This place was simple in layout. The bed was against the right wall, the bathroom to the left, kitchen by the door leading to the deck right in front of them, and of course all of their gear from the ship.

"How did our stuff get here before us?"

"I had Jason take one of the small life boats filled with our gear here as soon as we left the ship."

"You seem to think of everything, don't you?"

"Well I didn't think about the fact that there is only one place to sleep here," Mike admitted, looking at the double sized bed sitting to his right.

"I'm sure we can handle sharing the same bed. We're both adults, after all."

"Well I am all grown up and wise, but you are still young," Mike said, teasing her again as she found her way to her bags.

"Can I ask you my question of the day now?"

"Yes you may."

"How old were you when you completed your first assassination?"

"I killed my first person on my twentieth birthday."

"You weren't even an immortal then, though."

"Candice said it was a true test of my skills to kill a person on even ground and so I did for eight years before I was granted my immortality," Mike continued as he tried to keep his mind from racing back to that day all those years ago. "I'm not really sure if I felt more alive than or right now being here with you."

He couldn't tell what she was thinking as she remained crouched over her bags, looking back at him. She had a smile on her face, but again he saw something in her eyes that he didn't quite know what it was. Maybe she too was afraid about the feelings they seemed to be sharing, or maybe it was something else.

"We might miss our sunset if we don't go outside now," Mike reminded her as he noticed the sun reflection showing just outside of the door leading to the deck.

He was caught off guard once again as she came towards him, her eyes locked on his as if she was looking for something in his soul while he was trying to find something in hers. She had her arms around his neck again in seconds, using the speed only an assassin was gifted with, and he no longer tried to stop her.

As soon as her lips met his he reached down and grabbed her gently by her hips, lifting her slightly up as she wrapped her legs around his waist once again. He carried her to the door leading out on to the deck without even slightly breaking their embrace, and with a quick kick the door swung open and he walked out onto the wooden deck.

He fell backwards into the lounge chair he kept on the deck, and their lips finally parted as she cuddled into his side and they both relaxed in the chair side by side watching the sun slowly fade into the depth of the ocean.

"I want you to ask me something you want to know about me?"

"What do you fear the most in your life?" Mike asked as his ran his fingertips along her bare skin of her legs.

"That I will live forever and never know what it is like to be free or to love someone. That I will always be alone."

"It is a lonely life we have chosen that is for sure."

"Have you ever regretted it?"

"No I have loved my life for the most part, but lately I fell into a dark place I guess. I am slowly pulling myself out of it, but after Candice and I broke it off I basically took any and all contracts just to get away from her and from myself as well."

"Are you still running from yourself?"

"If I was I wouldn't be here with you."

"And are you truly over Candice now?"

"I have been over her for years now. It just took me a while to truly realize that, and you have helped as well," Mike said as he starred out at the stars slowly beginning to pop out in the sky. He could feel her soft blonde hair against the side of his face. He couldn't help but notice her sweet fruity smell as well.

"How have I helped?"

"In a way you have showed me that what I had with Candice wasn't as intimate as I thought it was. We were together for so long, and yet we could never do what you and I did today on the beach, even if it was just a simple kiss."

"Well my lips are always at your disposal, but if you ever try to use and abuse them, I will so kick your ass."

"Do you really think you can take me?" Mike asked as he felt her roll into him even more, wrapping her left arm over his chest and he her legs over his.

"I think that I cou..."

Mike listened to her words trail off, and he knew right away by her breathing that she had fallen asleep on him midsentence. He decided that he would let her sleep, and he took that time to think about the day's events leading up to this moment.

He thought about her kissing him on the beach so she could distract him enough to get him into the water and past his fear of the ocean. He also knew the kiss was more than that as well. She kissed him for the same reason he kissed her back— because she wanted to kiss him, and he was starting to think that he liked kissing her.

But how long would she really stick by him, he couldn't help but wonder. After all, he was just as reckless with his life as he had been with his fighting. Even with the pirates back on the ship, he rushed into the fight for no other reason than he could, and he ended up with another scar. His heart told him to stop chasing them before he reached the plank, but he kept going.

A small part of him wondered if Candice would try anything stupid against Alexia once she realized that there was something more than friendship between them. He didn't think Candice was a jealous person, but you never know how someone will act when love is involved. He wouldn't allow Candice to send Alexia off on any stupid or dangerous missions alone, but he also knew he couldn't over reach as well, without going against the Temple of Legends laws.

Even as Alexia tried to pull herself closer to him, he knew that the simple laws wouldn't stand in his way of what was right and wrong, and he continual to think about it and about her long after his eyes closed and went into his dreams.

Chapter 14

Mike found himself walking down one of the busiest sidewalks in all of the Merchant Islands, and he couldn't help but feel at ease in the hustle of people all around him. It was midday on a Friday, and everyone was out and about enjoying the nice weather, spending their hard earned pay they had gotten for the week.

This time though he wore his two blue glowing daggers tucked away in the back of his belt, but he still walked along the sidewalk in his normal clothes, a simple black shirt and blue jeans and a new pair of white runners.

He could see Alexia shopping on the far side of the street, wearing a bright orange skirt that hung past her knees and a loose fitting T-shirt, which he swore he recognized as one of his own. Even as he watched her shopping, he nearly walked into a group of men playing a game of dice on the sidewalk and only after their shouts did he realize that he wasn't paying attention to anything besides her.

He had to look away from her and carry on with the job he set out to do this day. He knew she would be okay in this big city on her own, and he felt a little bit better as he began to walk down the street again when he caught sight of a handful of crewmembers from his ship close to her.

He wasn't sure where to begin his search of finding a small band of thieves among the large island of thieves, but he had a lot of gold on him and figured that would be a good way to get people talking. His first stop was a black market weapons shop he visited every time he came to the islands. After all, could one person truly have too many weapons?

He kept walking down the sidewalk, blending in for the most part with the passing crowd and animals, which also seemed to walk freely on the streets. He didn't even seem to notice the many looks he was getting from most of the women he passed because he was once again busy thinking about Alexia. He didn't want to carry on with this mission, he wanted to go back to her and spend the day with only her.

He kept thinking about that even as he walked right down the alleyway on his left, and through the third door on his right, before coming to a stop in front of a metal door, which he knew would be locked. He reached into his pocket and pulled out five gold coins and slid them under the door and then stood back.

It took a few minutes before he heard the many locks and bolts on the other side of the door begin to unlock and even longer for the door to finally swing open. He was greeted by an older short man with a beard that hung down to his belt. He was wearing a black smith's outfit, just like every other time he had met the man. He didn't know his name because of the whole black market thing, but he trusted the man just like the man trusted Mike's gold.

"Long time no see, Assassin."

"Likewise, Smithy." Mike figured calling the man that was better than not calling him anything at all.

"Come in, come in."

He wasted no time standing outside as he walked past the older blacksmith and into his shop, listening to the solid metal door locking behind him. It was a great way to make sure one didn't try to grab something and run out without paying.

"What brings you here to my shop this day, Assassin?"

"I am looking to buy a dagger if you have one that I like, and maybe some information as well," Mike said, grabbing a coin purse from his belt and dropping it on the main counter. It landed with a thud.

"What kind of dagger are you in the market for, and I will see if I can help you out."

"This is going to seem like an odd request compared to what I normally ask for, but do you by any chance have any daggers made out of any type of orange metal or ore?"

"Give me a few minutes to search out what rare daggers I have for you, and in the meantime feel free to ask me anything you wish to know, your gold is always good in my store, Assassin."

"I am being paid a lot of money to be here today, but sadly it isn't for a vacation. Instead, I am in search of a small band of thieves."

"You will have to give me more than that, boy. There be a lot of thieves on this island."

"The information I have says that the band is led by a fat woman but I don't have a name, sadly."

"Well there are only a handful of thieves around these parts led by a woman, let alone a fat woman."

"So have you heard of them?" Mike asked as he walked around the shop looking at all of the fine blades, none of which he knew would compare to his blue glowing weapons.

"Their camp is to the west of here just before the great waterfall."

"Yes I know that area I believe."

"Find the waterfall and then look for a cave just beside it, and you will find the people you are in search of. Normally, I wouldn't say anything to you, but these thieves bought goods off of me without full payment, so I owe them nothing."

Mike watched as the blacksmith made his way back to the counter with something in his hands wrapped in a soft silk cloth. "This is the best I can do for you on your request, Assassin."

"I am sure if it is from your shop it will get the job done," Mike said as he walked back to the counter as the older man began to remove the cloth to relieve a bright yellowish orange blade.

"She is called the Settingsun and I am sure you can see why."

Mike reached out and took the dagger into his right hand, and he was amazed at how lightweight it was and how comfortable it felt. The hilt of the dagger was of a simple smooth design with a many pointed sun on the bottom of it. The blade had a jagged curved shape to it. As he turned the blade in his hand, it looked like it was changing colors as the light hit it.

"It is perfect. How much do you want for the dagger?"

"This blade isn't for you, is it?"

"No, it is for a very good friend of mine."

"Is it for a woman?"

"Yes, it is."

"Then consider it a gift from me to you, Assassin."

"Are you sure?" Mike asked, looking towards the older blacksmith.

"In all the years you have been buying from me, Assassin, you have never once brought anything for anyone other than yourself. So, to finally hear that you are shopping for a woman I find myself happy enough in giving you the weapon."

"Thank you very much, and I promise you the weapon will be put to a good use."

"I am sure it will."

"And thank you for the information."

"I also sell diamond rings if you ever find yourself in the market for one. Or better yet, I have a necklace you might like."

He watched as the man reached into one of the lock boxes behind the counter, and he could hear his hand digging around in the box, clearly looking for something he knew to be in there. A minute or two later, he pulled his hand out holding a simple little wooden box and placed it in front of Mike. "This is the finest piece I have ever crafted."

Mike reached out for the little wooden box, but hesitated at the very last second just as his middle finger slightly brushed against the wooden box, and it wasn't till he got a nod from the blacksmith that he dared to open it.

Inside the box he saw the most beautiful orange sun pendant he had ever seen. It looked like it matched the dagger he had just gotten, and he figured it would shine just as bright in the sun. He knew right away it would be something Alexia would love, just like the dagger if for no other reason than the color. The pendant was attached to a slender white gold chain and he couldn't help but wonder how beautiful it would look hanging from her neck. "Dare I ask what the price of such a fine piece would set me back this day?"

"If you have a second bag of gold coins it is yours, and I will even throw in the custom box as well."

"I will take it then," Mike said, willingly dropping two more bags of coins onto the counter.

"I have always loved the way you count, Assassin."

"I would rather keep you happy as my friend than make you an enemy by being cheap, and gold lost its appeal to me long ago."

"You are always welcome in my store, Assassin, day and night. Maybe one day I will be fortunate enough to meet this lady who has finally caught your attention."

"If we have time before we leave, I will try my best to swing by."

Mike watched the blacksmith unlock and open all of the locks again, and the door began to swing open. With one last quick hug, he found himself back on the streets, happy for a change because not only did he find the thieves he was after, but he walked away with two great gifts for Alexia.

He could feel the wooden box in his right pocket and he couldn't wait to see the look on her face when he gave it to her, but he also started to wonder if it was a good idea to be giving her such gifts so soon into their friendship. After much contemplation, he figured it didn't matter as a smile found its way to his face again as he thought about Alexia.

Alexia found herself sitting down at the oceanfront restaurant long before the time Mike and she had agreed upon. She latterly ran out of things to do and money to spend, which she figured he may or may not find funny since it was his money she had spent.

She looked up at the sun and since it was still pretty high in the sky, she knew she would have a long wait till he got to the restaurant. As she sat there, she couldn't help but enjoy the view from her table while she dug her feet into the soft white sand.

She thought back to the night she had fallen asleep in his arms in his lounge chair, and smiled at the thought. She remembered waking up beside him, their bodies tangled up with one and another. Their faces were so close, she couldn't help but kiss him again.

But even after that kiss, she felt him holding back, like something was stopping him from wanting anything more than just kissing. She could see everything he was trying to hide behind his stunning hazel eyes, but she didn't know when and if he would open up to her. She thought about maybe having to force him into answering by making it one of her questions of the day.

She was so lost up in her own world she lost track of time and everything around her, until she heard someone ask, "Is this seat taken?"

Alexia knew someone was standing beside her but she found herself too trapped in her own thoughts to notice him until he had spoken to her. She looked him over and figured he was a young kid no more then maybe twenty-five, wearing a pair of white shorts and a button-up shirt with all the buttons undone on it. He wasn't in the best of shape, but he wasn't fat either, she noticed. "I am sorry, I was lost in my thoughts, but sadly the seat is taken," she said, trying her best not to hurt his feelings.

"A girl as hot as yourself shouldn't be kept waiting."

"Well, I am the one who showed up early, so it is my own fault, really."

"Well guess there is no harm in my keeping the seat warm while we wait."

"Guess you don't know who my friend is."

Alexia wanted to reach across and slap the boy as he sat in the chair next to her, but she figured he was just trying to act cool to impress her. She had known boys like him all her life, overly cocky and under experienced in life, so she just simply shook her head.

"What is your name, pretty thing?"

"If you don't start talking to me like a grownup, I will be more than willing to rip you tongue out and allow you to eat it," Alexia scolded, once again trying not to get too upset.

"I would have never thought a pretty little thing like you would have such a nasty mouth."

"I really do advise you to leave before my friend gets her."

"Do you not know who I am?"

"This is my first time visiting these parts, so honestly I wouldn't know you apart from the pig I walked beside early today," Alexia continued, and she tried her best to hide her smile as she watched his cheeks turn red with rage.

"I will let that rude comment slide due to the fact that you have an amazing body and all, but I will demand some respect from you if you wish to keep talking to me."

"Trust me, I do not wish to keep talking to you."

She watched him reach forward and pound his fist on to the table, nearly spilling her very fancy and very expensive orange drink. She could handle a lot of things in life and let most of it slide unpunished, but this boy was getting on her nerves and she really wanted to hurt him, even if it was just a little bit of hurt.

She could see the sun begin to sink into the ocean and knew that Mike would be along anytime now, and for his sake more than the boy's, she had to try and get this stupid kid to leave her alone.

Mike watched as Alexia and some strange guy talked from just inside the door of the restaurant, and he couldn't help but smile at the annoyed look she wore all over her face. He laughed to himself as he watched the guys face turn a bright shade of red, and he wondered what it was she had said to make him angry.

It wasn't until the guy slammed his fists into the table in front of her that he found himself reaching for one of the daggers in his belt, but he relaxed as soon as he realized that she could handle herself against the likes of some regular guy.

He leaned against the wall to his left and he watched Alexia turn her sights back to the setting sun as she began talking again to the guy, a guy who was clearly not taking her hints to leave. He figured she must have been trying to get the guy to leave before he arrived, fearing what he might do if he saw the two of them together, but it was odd though because he knew he could trust her and so he didn't feel any jealously at all.

He began walking closer and closer as he realized their conversation was getting more heated, and he had to keep Alexia from doing anything overly bad to this guy because that would only cause them more grief with the city guards.

He knew she could sense him walking up behind her because she quickly tensed up and he figured it was because she had no clue how he would react to her sitting there with another guy. "It is good to see you again," He said as he leaned over her left shoulder giving her a gentle kiss on the cheek."

"Yes, I am glad you are finally here."

"So this is the guy who kept you waiting all this time. I see nothing overly special about him," the young boy blurted.

"This is what I had to deal with while I was waiting for you to get here."

"He seems like good company. Do you care if I join the two of you?" Mike asked, pulling another chair over from a different table and sitting right next to Alexia. His right hand found hers under the table and their fingers locked together.

"I was just telling your lady friend here she is one of the most beautiful things I have ever seen."

"Well, she is beautiful, I give you that, but what I really would like to know is what do you plan on achieving here right now?"

"I just wanted to prove to her that I am the better man is all."

"And what makes you think that you are a better man than me?"

"Well, I am very rich."

"Join the club, kid, but she isn't into me because of my money."

"I come from a royal family."

"All of my family is dead, and yet that doesn't seem to both her at all."

"I could take you in a fight and prove I am the stronger man."

Mike had to stop himself from laughing at that comment, even as Alexia let go of all her senses and burst into a loud but cute laugh. He smiled at her again as he watched herself express her emotions so freely, and he knew he was slowly beginning to like her more and more each day.

"I demand to know why that is funny."

"Trust me, kid. I would be able to kill you a hundred different times before you even got up out of your chair."

"Is that a challenge, then?"

"My god it is like talking to a dead tree," Mike said, leaning back in his chair. "You really aren't catching on, are you, boy?"

"You are the one who should be showing me some respect."

"Look these are your options. First, you can freely get up and leave, so my friend and I can share a meal and catch up with each other about what we did today. Second, you can try to act tough and start a fight and the nice city guards over at the table to the far right will come and arrest you. Or finally, I can jab my dagger here so far into your mouth you will never be able to speak a disrespectful comment to another woman again," Mike said, jabbing the tip of his blue glowing dagger into the table in front of him as he finished talking.

"If I were you kid, I would listen to the man," One of the city guards said from across the way. "Trust me, you don't want to tussle with one of his kind."

"I will leave now, but don't you think I will forget about the two of you."

"You can think about me all you want, boy, just know in your heart you will never have me." Alexia snapped back, while trying his best not to laugh anymore then he already was.

Mike watched again as the boy's face turned bright red at another of Alexia's comments and this time he couldn't help but laugh as the boy stormed away from the table towards the exit of the restaurant. He watched the door for a few more seconds before turning back to Alexia who was looking back at him with a puzzled look on her face. "What?" he asked as he pulled his dagger free of the table.

"You handled that very well."

"What did you think I was going to do?" Mike asked, already knowing the answer, his smile still on his lips.

"I figured you would storm in here with your daggers flying, and this whole restaurant would end up covered in dead bodies and blood, and then we wouldn't get to enjoy our meal together."

"You don't really have that little faith in me, do you?" Mike asked, slightly hurt.

"Of course not, I have full respect for you. I knew you would be able to handle yourself like the gentleman you are. It was more like I was having a hard time holding myself back, and I didn't want to get us in trouble with the law."

"The law wasn't going to be a problem."

"How did you get them to back you up by the way?"

"It was simple. I tossed a small coin bag on their table as I walked past them to join you."

"You really do think about everything, don't you?"

"How was your day today?"

"It was pretty good. I mostly shopped and ran into a few people from the ship and saw Jason as well, who agreed to take my bags back to our place for me but mostly I spent the day missing you."

"I missed you as well," Mike admitted, meaning every word of it because all he could think about all day long was her.

"So what did you get up to today?"

"Went to see an old friend who was able to supply me with some good information about our band of thieves and where we could find them amongst other stuff."

"What kind of other stuff?"

Mike pulled out the dagger he had gotten for her, which was once again wrapped in the silk cloth and placed it on the table in front of her. "I got you a gift," He said as he watched her lean forward and run her fingers along the silk cloth.

"You really shouldn't have, but thank you very mu…"

Mike smiled as she stopped midsentence as she finished removing the orange colored dagger, and as if on cue, she held it in her hand and up towards the slowly setting sun. "It is called the Settingsun and it is all yours."

"It is the most beautiful things I have ever laid my eyes on."

"I had a feeling you would love it as soon as I saw it."

She kissed him then, but it was a short kiss. He still felt the meaning behind it, but clearly he caught her off guard with the gift, but in a good way. Something she wasn't used to, it would seem.

"I got you something as well, but it is back at your place, and I fully planned on surprising you with it when we got home."

"I can't wait to see it," Mike said, looking into her blue eyes again. "I have one more surprise for you still. Did you want it now or when we get home?"

"We should wait until we get home, so we can both surprise each other at the same time."

"Sounds like a plan to me."

They both ordered their food to go and ate it as they walked along the white beach in the moon light, heading back towards his place. They walked in silence enjoying each other's company once again after spending the day apart and every step he made he had to fight the urge to kiss her.

Before he knew it, they were back in the safety of his place and he found himself surprised indeed, at the amount of bags, which were placed neatly against the left wall. He could have sworn there was like a hundred of them. "Busy day of shopping I see," he said while sitting on the edge of the bed.

"Please don't be mad, but I may have gotten a little carried away."

"Did you find a lot of things that you loved?"

"Yes a lot of nice clothes and books and such."

"Then it was money well spent, and no, I am not mad."

He began reaching into his pocket and quickly pulled out the small wooden box as soon as she looked away from him and began digging in her own backpack. He watched her as she was crouched over, clearly trying to find what it was she had bought for him and he couldn't help but stare at her. She truly was beautiful.

"Okay, I found it. Should we open them at the same time?"

"Seems like a good enough of a plan," Mike said, handing her the wooden box and taking the black box from her.

He watched as she opened the lid of the wooden box and he could have sworn her jaw was about to fall right off of her face. He knew right away he had picked the perfect gift for her again. His fingers traced the lining of the black box, which he held in his hand, and he slowly began lifting the lid. Inside of the black box was a perfectly carved sword and dagger made out of wood, which hung from a small sting of tread. "It is amazing," He said as his hands traced the two small wooden carvings, feeling the smoothness of them.

"It would seem we think alike. Can you help me put mine on?"

He smiled as she walked over to him and sat between his legs on the edge of the bed, pushing herself back gently into his chest. He reached into the wooden box and pulled the pendant and chain out and clasp it around her neck, he brushed her blonde hair off to the one side as he did it, leaving most of her left neck exposed.

She turned to face him and before she was able to say a word, he pushed his lips against hers, gently at first, but the kiss quickly turned more intense as she turned slightly to face him better. He felt her lower back with his left hand and he ran his finger up her spine from the bottom to the top as he felt her arch her back as he did it.

Soon she had turned fully around and was now straddling him on the edge of the bed. He kept his left hand on her back to keep her from falling backwards, and the whole time their lips never parted. His right hand found the front of her shirt and slid underneath it. He felt her let out a soft sigh as his finger ran along her perfectly toned stomached.

He knew she was wearing nothing under her shirt once again, but he ran his hand up her side, feeling the slight bumps of her ribs as he did, but again he hesitated just a little. It was like he had no clue where to go from there. She was far from his first lover but something was different about her and he didn't know what it was. All he knew for sure was that it was a good thing and he didn't want to risk ruining it over a night of lust.

"What's wrong?" she asked, pulling away from him slightly to look into his eyes.

"Nothing, silly girl, I was really enjoying that until you pulled away," He said, stealing another quick kiss from her, which made them both smile again.

"You just seem to keep yourself from going too, far that's all."

"I respect you as a woman, and I would hate for us to regret anything in the morning. I just don't want to rush anything with you," He told her, running his right hand along her neck till it came to a stop on the back of her neck. "If that even makes any sense to you."

"It does, and I think you might be right. I think we get caught up in the moment and with each other and we don't even think about it. But I want you to know that I would never regret anything you and I did together."

"Neither would I, and I am fully enjoying getting to know you better."

"Okay so let's just take this day by day and see where it leads."

"I agree," Mike said, lying down fully on his back.

"But I want you to know, Master Assassin, I think of you as more than just a friend."

"And I want you to know, pretty lady, that I also think of you as more than a friend," Mike said as he pulled himself and Alexia up more towards the headboard and the pillows so he was fully on the bed with her still on top of him.

"I could so get used to this, you know."

"Get used to us lying in bed together?" Mike asked as she rolled off of him and wrapped her arms around him, one under his head and the other over his chest, pulling herself as close to him as possible.

"That too, but I meant I could get used to waking up beside you every morning, so don't go messing this up or else I will kick your cute butt."

"I will try my best not to," Mike said, laughing again as he began to run his fingers through her hair, which seemed to put her asleep. He felt her shift a few more time and then she began breathing softly against his neck. He too could get used to waking up beside her every morning.

Chapter 15

Once again Candice found herself going over the stacks of paper on her desk, which seemed to keep getting bigger and bigger every day. She knew that sooner or later she would have to call back all of assassins from their search in finding out who ordered the attack on her and get them out into the world again completing the many missions which now sat in front of her.

She knew that both Shelby and Eric had returned that morning and were most liking resting before they came to give her their full report but she figured that they didn't find anything or else they would have come to her right away. Besides Mike, they were here top assassins and if they came up empty handed, she knew she would never have the answers she searched for.

So she figured it was best to send out word to the others to return home as soon as possible. They all needed to start making money again. Plus, she too was slowly becoming very bored without any of her fellow immortals around, and Kevin seemed to be out most of time, more than he was at home.

So it surprised her even more so when he came bursting into her office wearing a god-awful teal green suit, and she was glad he didn't have a matching hat on or else she might have laughed at him. She knew he was able to dress himself up well, and he was a handsome man, but she couldn't figure out where he got some of his suits from.

"What is taking them so long?" Kevin asked as he paced back and forth in front of Candice's desk.

"Who are we talking about this time?"

"You know who I am talking about."

"I told Shelby and Eric they could get some rest before bringing me their report so calm down and be patient."

"I am talking about your favorite and that girl. They should have found the stolen item by now, and my friend is becoming very annoyed at how long it is taking them."

"Then you can tell your friend to cancel the contract and I will send word for them to come home as soon as possible and forget about the item or you can tell him to sit on his ass a little longer and have some faith," Candice said as she looked away from her husband back to the paper work on her desk.

She could still feel her husband staring at her but she didn't really have the time or the energy to fight with him over something so stupid. The more she thought about it, the more she realized that maybe it wasn't as stupid in his mind as it was in hers. "What is bothering you so much about all of this?"

"My friend is paying a lot of money for speedy results and he hasn't even heard from Mike since he left here over a month ago."

"You and I both know that these things take time and effort, and I am sure once the job is done I will be the first to know. Then, I will let you know." Candice stated, trying her best not to let her rising anger show in her voice.

"Do you not understand the stress I am under right now?"

"Well if you came home once in a while, maybe we could find a way to fix your stress problems," Candice said, smiling at her husband.

"I am trying to be serious, and all you offer me is useless jokes?"

"You think the fact that I am asking you to come home once in a while so we can have sex is a useless joke?" Candice asked. Her eyes narrowed dangerously as she starred at her husband.

It annoyed her even more so that he matched her stare with one of his own, but his was more like a cross between a whiny baby and a lost dog. It made her want to slap him real hard, something she knew she shouldn't feel towards her husband.

She walked over to the side window in the room and cracked it open, getting a quick breeze of the crisp winter air against her face. It calmed her down almost right away and she quickly allowed the rest of her body to relax as well.

She smiled as she looked out towards the snow covered city and all of the very white rooftops and she even tried squinting her eyes as tight as she could, trying to see if she could spot his house way off in the distance.

Kevin was right about Mike being gone for just over a month now, and even though she was a married woman, she couldn't help but miss him. It was like she was missing out on something now that he was gone. She too hoped that he would returned soon.

She felt Kevin put his hands on her shoulders and she relaxed even more at his touch. They barely spent any time together since their wedding, and even less of that was spent touching each other. She figured she would take this rare chance and go with it.

"I am sorry I got mad at you, but like I said, I am under a lot of stress and I was just hoping there was some way you could reach out to him or even send word to him."

"Mike is not the guy you just tell to speed up his workmanship. He is the best at what he does because no one can match his skills. So, I allow him all the freedom he needs."

"Or maybe it is because you used to have sex with him that you allow him such freedom."

Candice turned to face him then, and was met by a massive slap from the back of his right hand. She knew the blow was coming, but did nothing to stop it. She felt his knuckles connect hard with her cheek and she could taste the blood in her mouth as her lip began to bleed.

She laughed at him then, and again she was met with a second slap to the same side of her cheek. This time, she could feel her skin begin to bruise. After the third shot she grabbed his hand and pulled him close to her face. Her blood covered lips met his, and she pulled him close during their very intense kiss. A kiss that lasted for a good five minutes before she finally pulled away from him.

"What was that for?"

"If you ever lay your hands on me like that again, I will have no problem murdering you and throwing your body into the ocean," Candice said as she watched him take a few steps back from her. "I am your wife, and you will treat me with the love and respect I deserve."

"I am sorry I struck you, my love."

"We will pretend it never happened, and maybe tonight you will be home for a change."

"I will try my best to be home tonight."

"And if you ever talk about my sex life with Mike again, we will have some serious problems."

"I am so done with this conversation." Candice watched as Kevin walked for the door once again, and she could tell he was having another little fit but she just watched him walk towards the door anyways, truly not caring if he was mad or not he was the one who crossed the line and not her.

Eric reached for the door knob of Candice's office door located on the upper level of the temple and was surprised to see the door fling inwards and Kevin storming out of it and right into him. Without a word, he just simply walked past him as if it never happened and headed off down the hallway, stomping his feet the whole way.

He walked into the open door and saw Candice starring off out the window, which overlooked the city, something he was used to seeing. He knew she loved the view from so far up, looking down at the city she loved and protected with all of her heart. He also knew it was the view that reminded her of all of the hours she and Mike spent locked away in this very room.

"So your husband seemed to be in a very chipper mood this fine afternoon," Eric stated as he watched Shelby take a seat on the soft couch, which was pushed up against the far wall.

"Yes, I am sorry you had to witness that. We were in the middle of a fight, which didn't seem to end well on either side."

"I'm guessing it was about Mike," Eric said, after he reached back and closed the door giving them some privacy.

"It seems like everything nowadays has to be about Mike."

Eric knew there was something wrong with Candice as she kept looking out the window. He could tell she was hiding something, even as he walked closer to her. He felt her stiffen under his touch as he placed his right hand on her shoulder, something she had never done before with him.

It wasn't until he turned her gently to face him that he noticed the swelling on her cheek and under her eye, the black marks of a big bruise slowly forming, her lower lip, which was still bleeding. It was her tears that caught his attention the most though, he was used to seeing her cry over losing Mike, but never had he seen her cry before because of an injury, not even on her wedding day when she took an arrow right through her chest.

He was about to let go of her shoulder when she suddenly pulled herself into his chest. He could feel her sobbing even more now as he wrapped his arms around her, supporting her weight when it felt like her legs wouldn't anymore.

"I am so going to kill him." Shelby couldn't help but say as she looked at the sadness which seemed to fill her good friend's eyes at that moment.

"Shelby, you can't touch him and you know it," Eric said looking towards Shelby who was now looking like she was about to lose it. "If you harm the husband of the Leader of the Temple of Legends it will make you an outlaw for life."

He watched as Shelby walked over to the two of them and crouched down beside him. She reached out and took Candice into her arms and he freely let her go. He knew Shelby was only doing this because if she wasn't there holding Candice, she would go off and kill Kevin for hurting someone she loved.

"I am so sorry he did this to you."

"He used my having sex with Mike and turned it into a bad thing. Like I only did it to cause him problems even though it happened way before I ever met him."

Eric left the two of them on the floor, found his way over to the Candice's desk, and he freely helped himself to her personal chair as he stared at the door leading to the hallway. A part of him wanted to chase Kevin down and cut his head off, but he knew if he followed through with that, it would make him an outlaw against the temple. He would be hunted and that would mean Shelby would most likely be hunted too, most likely by Mike if he was the one who was ordered to.

He thought that idea over for a second and suddenly realized something different would most likely happen if Mike was sent after him. He knew Mike wouldn't try to hunt him down to kill him but instead he believed that Mike would use all the resources he had to help him and Shelby disappear forever.

Either way, he knew he couldn't do anything that would ever put himself and Shelby against their two best friends. Even through their breakup, they all remained good friends and he wouldn't be the one to risk losing that friendship now. "Where is Mike anyway?" he asked, looking back towards Candice who was now sitting on the floor with her legs crossed.

"I sent him and Alexia on a mission over on the Merchant Islands. A mission I am starting to think was a big mistake."

"How long have they been gone for?"

"Just over a month and a bit now, he said he would send word as soon as he recovered the stolen item."

"Which I am sure he will as soon as he has. Mike is a lot of things, but he is good at his job and even better at keeping his word."

"So what news did the two of you find on your journeys?"

"Sadly, we heard or found nothing about who hired the kid to attack you on your wedding day. It is almost as if no one ever did it at all."

He watched as Shelby spoke to Candice about their findings and he couldn't help but look her over. She was wearing a green pull over sweater and tight jeans, which seemed to draw his eyes to all of the places he knew he shouldn't be looking at now. Shelby and he went way back, and they knew each other almost all of their lives. He loved her like she loved him, and together they made the perfect match. He couldn't even think about living a day without her in his life.

"Eric, are you listening?"

"No, sorry, I was lost in my own thoughts."

"More like fully distracted by starring at my ass, you mean."

"Well that too," Erick said, smiling again at Shelby and how good she looked to him right now.

"If I get the two of you a ship, would you be willing to travel to the Merchant Islands and track Mike and Alexia down for me."

"Take a few days to think about it because Shelby and I should rest for a bit before we head out again, and I can assure you Mike is more than okay."

"So does my face look that bad?"

"You are still the second most beautiful girl I know," Eric said, trying not to laugh, which only made the two girls giggle.

"See, this is how my man treats women. He will make them laugh so hard they pee themselves before he ever laid a hand on them."

"Well, I am quite skilled at making people pee themselves, but it isn't a very funny trait after the fact though." Eric barely got the words out while he fought to hold back his laughter.

"The two of you should get on your way back home again, and take a few days to do nothing but relax and return to me when you are ready to help me get some of these contracts finished."

"If you need us for anything you know where we will be," Eric told her as he quickly looked over a few of the contracts lying on the desk. "And I will also take these six and get them done as quickly as I can."

"Thank you again for everything you guys have done for me throughout the last few crazy years of my life."

"It is nothing, and trust me, you have helped us just as much as we have helped you." Eric said while grabbing another handful of contracts. After all, Shelby would use this time to relax but he would grow bored quickly.

"I will come visit you two as soon as I can, and we will sit down and really catch up on our lives."

"That sounds like a great plan," Eric agreed as he began walking towards the door.

It didn't take the two of them long to get down the hallways leading away from Candice's office and back down into the lower areas of the massive building, and again he found himself fully distracted by Shelby as she walked in front of him the whole way.

Shelby couldn't help but feel comfortable as she lay fully naked in Eric's arms, wrapped up tightly under their many layers of silk and cotton sheets. She loved nothing more than spending the day naked and in bed making love to him, but she could sense now that something was bothering him, like his thoughts weren't fully with her.

She knew that seeing Candice all shaken up like that had affected him somewhat, but she didn't realize it was this much. She too was having hard time thinking about her best and oldest friend besides Eric in such pain and sadness. She knew right away that the bruises on her lip and her face weren't bad enough to make her break down and cry like that, but instead it was all the stress and sadness she had buried away for so long finally coming to the surface. "Do you think we should have gone after him anyway?" she asked as she ran her fingers along the side of his naked body.

"I think we would have done more damage than good if we did go after him."

"I have never seen her like that before."

"I guess it proves that even she is just as fragile as the rest of us."

"First, everything with her and Mike and now her shitty marriage with Kevin. It doesn't seem right if you know what I mean."

"I do, and deep down inside, I want her to be happy and in love. If that means she shouldn't be with Kevin any more, then so be it, but that is something that she needs to figure out on her own and if it ever comes to that point, I will support her no matter what."

"So you don't want to go and kick his ass right now?"

"Oh trust me, I would love to track him down and give him a good beating, but I would much rather see Mike do it when he returns and finds out what happened between them."

"I bet you they come back married," Shelby said as she rested her head on his smooth chest.

"Who will come back married?"

"Mike and Alexia. Try to keep up my silly lover."

"And what makes you think that?"

"I just got that vibe. You know, when I saw the two of them together at the dinner when they shared that dance and again at the wedding."

"I truly hope he can find something to bring him out of his depression, even if he doesn't see the fact that he is depressed. I can see it every time I talk to him or fight beside him."

"It is almost like his heart just isn't into this life anymore, like it is searching for something far better," Shelby said, thinking about Mike as much as Candice. "It is like he has lost his purpose for living."

"That is never a good thing when you are cursed with the gift of immortality."

"Do you really consider it a curse?"

"No, I love the fact that I will get to live forever with you by my side, and that I will get to love you for all of eternity."

"You are always so smooth with your words and that is why I love you so much."

"So I hope he does find love once again, so he can finally free himself of the guilt of losing Candice. I also hope that Candice can find true love again as well, whether it is with Kevin or someone better."

"You don't plan on using this free time to relax do you?" Shelby asked, already knowing the answer.

"I wish I could, but with Mike gone along with every other assassin basically, I need to step it up and help Candice out anyway I can. So if by completing as many contracts as I can alone will lead to one less thing for her to worry about, then so be it."

"Yet another reason why I love you."

"I thought you were only with me for my rugged good looks and my skills of making you laugh so hard that you pee yourself."

"Well, of course all of that, plus so much more," She said, and then her lips found his once again as she pulled herself on top of him, straddling his naked waist.

Chapter 16

Mike loved moving about in the dead of night, it made him feel so much freer as he slowly made his way to the small clearing that laid a few feet in front of him. He crouched low, just inside the tree line and slowly began scanning the clearing, making sure he didn't miss anything at all.

He could see the giant waterfall to his left and he knew that even if he screamed right now as loud as he could, it wouldn't be heard over rushing water of the waterfall. He could see Alexia to his left as well, she was also crouched, just inside the tree line, and as his eyes scanned back to the right, he could see the outline of the small cave entrance, which would lead them to the band of thieves they were after.

The light of a fire burning within the caves entrance told him that clearly people were hiding out inside the cave and he hoped his information was correct. He wanted to find the stupid item he was after so he and Alexia could finally return to their home and carry on with their new life together, something he very much looked forward too.

He saw the one and only guard whom was on the lookout standing next to the river bank clearly washing something, but he couldn't quite make it out in the darkness. The fact that they had only set up one lookout told him that once again, these were not professionals in any way.

He got to his feet and began running as fast as he could towards the man. His feet made no noise at all as they landed on the dried grass of the clearing, but even if they did, he didn't think anyone would hear him over the roar of the waterfall.

He saw Alexia move into the clearing now as well just as they had planned. She made a straight line for the cave entrance, just in case they did miss a hidden guard, which he figured they hadn't but she needed something to do nonetheless.

He reached the guard as quickly as he could with his speed, and jumped at the last second. His knees connected hard with the man's back sending him roughly to the ground face first. Mike watched as the man's face bounced off a rock on the way down, leaving him very unconscious. He grabbed the man's feet and pulled him back a bit to make sure he wouldn't fall into the river and drown before he too ran off to the cave's entrance.

Alexia was already waiting for him when he arrived, and he looked her over quickly, more so for his own benefit than anything else. He was really starting to like having her around all the time in that tight brown leather outfit. He noticed too that on top of the green sword he had given her, she also had the bright orange dagger on her as well.

He struggled to tear his eyes off of her slightly unzipped jacket and back towards the mission at hand. As he turned back to face the cave entrance, he noticed a quick smile pass her lips, clearly she didn't have a problem with him looking.

He started walking into the cave and the first ten feet or so was almost pitch black but he caught the slight flicker of the fires light from time to time. The closer they got to it, the louder the voices seemed to be growing from within the cave. He could count about five different people talking.

He could feel Alexia keeping a safe distance behind him, but he knew she was watching out for him a lot closer then she needed to. It was good for a change to have someone else along to watch his back. He fully planned on limiting the amount of people he had to kill in order to find the item, and he knew with Alexia so close by, he would be able to force himself to hold back a little.

He could now see the fire a lot clearer as they reached one more turn in the cave's tunnel and he figured the thieves' camp was just on the other side of the turn. He could also hear the voices a lot better, even though they were talking too quiet for him to make out the words.

He turned to face Alexia one last time before walking around the final turn in the tunnel and ended up right in the middle of the circle of thieves. That was yet another reason that made him realize they were no more than a band of rookies and nothing more.

He stopped so suddenly in the middle of the room that Alexia almost ran right into him as she entered right behind him. He watched as all five sets of eyes turned towards the two of them. There were four sets of male eyes, and the other set belonged to a very plump oversized woman.

"What are you doing here?"

"We were sent here from the Temple of Legends to retrieve an item you

132

Michael Long

good thieves stole," Mike alerted them as he looked at the oversized woman.

"We have stolen very little, I can assure you of that." It was one of the guys who spoke and as if on cue they all turned to face the far right side of the cave where a very small pile of goods and weapons laid stacked neatly on the floor. All of the guys looked towards the wall, but Mike noticed the woman's eyes turn towards the makeshift door against the same wall, but further away from the pile of goodies. Clearly there was something hidden behind that doorway and he figured it was what they came here for.

"This is what I am willing to do for you good folks," Mike said, pulling the small backpack from his back and tossing it at the feet of the fat woman. "Inside there is close to ten thousand gold coins and it is all yours if you choose to leave right now and give up all the stolen goods in this room to me."

"I am afraid we cannot accept the offer."

"I am only going to offer you this once. Take the money and leave with you lives," Mike said as he watched the four men stand up. The one closest to the bag of money reached out and grabbed one of the handles and soon all four of them left the way he and Alexia came in, but the fat woman still stood her ground.

"I cannot let you have what you seek."

"You are willing to die for this item?"

"I am willing to die to ensure it never gets returned to that sick and twisted Count Drake and his group of noblemen."

"I can assure you that no matter what you attempt to do, I will get the item this day but I am willing to offer you your life in exchange for it though. Just walk away now."

"I am afraid I can't let you take it from me, assassin."

"That is what I hoped you wouldn't say," Mike said as he watched the woman pull a rusty dagger from the folds of her shirt.

"Sometimes a person has to be willing to die to protect the things they love the most in the world and I hope one day you feel this way about something as well, assassin. I hope you love something so much you are willing to die for it."

"We are talking about a simple item and you are willing to protect it with your life. Why is that?"

"You have no clue what it is you are after, do you, assassin?"

"We were paid to come here and find an item and it isn't my place to

133

ask questions about the job but instead to just complete it," Mike said, taking a few steps closer to the woman, hardly afraid of her or the dagger.

"I can save you from killing me if you make me a simple promise, assassin."

"What is the promise?"

"That if you leave here with the item you will protect it with your life no matter what happens."

"That is an easy promise for me to make because once the item is my hands it will be as safe as it has ever been."

"Say the words, assassin. Tell me that you promise to protect the item with your life no matter what."

"I promise you that I will do everything in my power to keep the item safe on its journey with my life if I need to." Mike found this whole thing to be very crazy, but he figured if his promise would spare him from having to kill her, it was a good promise to make.

"And you there girl, do you promise to do your best in making sure he sticks to his promise?"

"Yes, I promise to keep both him and the item as protected as I can while he is holding on to his promise to you this day."

"Very well then, the item you seek is behind that wooden door hidden under a fine fur comforter. You will know it when you see it, and if you still doubt my words, look for a crossed engraved in the item."

"Thank you for making it easy on us."

"Just stick to your promise, and protect the item with your life."

Mike was about to walk towards the wooden door when the woman turned the dagger in her hand and stabbed it towards her own chest. He watched as the blood spilled out of her chest and he was even more shocked when she pulled the dagger free. He could tell right away that she must have nicked a part heart and would die very quickly, but he didn't expect her to stab the dagger a second time into herself, this time to the neck, leaving her very dead.

He then wondered what kind of item they were truly after, and this only helped him wonder even more if they were being set up on this mission. Nothing seemed to fit right since day one, and now this crazy woman and her crazy promises.

Alexia was about to say something, but he silenced her with his up raised hand. He didn't do it to be rude but more for the fact that he needed to find this item and be done with it already. He walked towards the door and gently lifted it to the side revealing a side chamber in the cave, which seemed to serve as a bedroom.

He crouched low to enter the small chamber and quickly realized that it wasn't any taller on the inside, no more than five feet tall at its highest point. He knew Alexia wouldn't enter just encase this was some kind of a trap and she would need to protect him as he tried to get out of the small cavern.

He found his way to the far side of the wall and he could see the fur blankets lying on a very small shaped bed in the faint candle lit room. He reached down and as soon as his hand touched the blanket, he found himself hesitating, something really didn't feel right about this mission now.

He forced himself to slowly pull the blanket down. What he found under it was more surprising than the woman lying dead in the room outside, but at the same time made her crazy promise all the more real. He had just found their lost item he realized, and it was a little girl fast asleep on a little bed. He knew it had to be the little girl because she had a cross-engraved on the back of her neck, which he found with ease as he bushed some of her hair aside.

He found himself outside the small cavern in a matter of seconds and looking at Alexia, who was also staring back at him with a questioning look on her face. "So did you find it?" she asked, coming a few steps closer to him.

"I don't think we were sent here after any kind of item at all."

"What are you going on about?"

"The only thing in that room is a little girl no more than eight years old with a branded mark of a cross on the back of her neck."

Mike watched as Alexia disappeared into the small side chamber clearly wanting to see what it was that he was going on about. He found his way towards one of the logs by the fire, and took a seat on it. His head was filled with a hundred different thought and he couldn't figure out how any of this was possible, why he was sent here for a little girl.

He tried his best to back track everything that had happened since he left the temple but he couldn't find any sign or link, which would have led him to believe he was after a little girl all along. He found the sealed envelope that Candice had given him and told him he could open it as soon as he found the item.

So he decided to break the seal now and pulled free the small white piece of paper from inside. All that was written on it was a name Count Drake and his address. He already knew where it was because he knew of the Drake family and their private island, which just happened to be a week west from where they were now.

He heard Alexia walking towards him, felt her hands on his shoulders as she rested her chin on the top of his head. He felt her wrap her arms around his neck as she pulled herself even closer to him. He calmed again at her touch, but he was still no less confused about the events at hand.

"The girl must be the thing we are searching for."

"If that is the case, none of this makes sense," Mike told her, turning to face the entrance to the small chamber.

"What should we do?"

"I have no clue, but I know we can't leave her here."

"So you want to bring her with us then?"

"It is either that or we leave her here alone, and who knows what that might lead too."

"And you did make a promise after all to watch over her."

Mike found himself walking back towards the little entrance, and soon he was sitting beside the little bed, the girl still fast asleep in front of him. He tried his best to think about what he should do logically, but something about that seemed wrong. Something about handing this little girl over to the Drake family didn't feel normal, but that is what he was being paid to do.

He looked the little girl over once again and agreed with what he said earlier. She looked to be about eight years old and she had jet black hair, which hung down past her shoulders. Besides the branded cross on the back of her neck, she looked like any other eight-year-old girl.

He reached his one arm under her head as he picked her up with the other, and she still didn't wake up as he tried to maneuver the two of them out of the small chamber. Instead, she just snuggled more into his arms. He knew she wouldn't make a very good assassin being such a deep sleeper, but something about her screamed innocent to him.

He cracked his neck as he stood back up to his full height and readjusted the girl so her head was on his right shoulder and he was holding her fully with both of his arms. She wrapped her little legs around him still clueless as to what was happening to her.

"Where are you planning to take her?"

"Back to my place for now, and once she is awake maybe we can learn something about who she is or how she came to be in this cave."

"Are you as confused about all of this as I am?"

"Yes. Like I said from the start, something didn't feel right about this mission and now it seems like I figured out why," Mike said as he followed Alexia out into the clearing with the waterfall.

They walked for most of the night and found their way back to his small place just as the tide was going out and the sun was slowly beginning to rise. He found climbing the ladder a little bit more of a challenge now that he had a fifty-two-pound girl in his arms, but he still quickly made his way into the house and placed her gently on the bed, were she cuddled up with a few of the pillows, the whole time she slept peacefully.

He then found his way to the door leading out to his deck and he cracked it open letting some of the fresh ocean air into the place. A part of him wanted to leave both the girls there and go off to find out the answers he needed to know, but he figured he would learn them as soon as the girl woke up.

He could feel Alexia staring at him, but he just kept his eyes locked on the ocean in front of him. He tried to lose himself in the world all-around him as the sun started to climb higher and higher into the sky. In that world he was still a free man, in that world he knew he could find the happiness he had been searching for. It seemed like this could be the one moment that would really begin to shape the rest of his life.

Again it was Alexia wrapping her arms around him from behind, which reminded him of the world he truly belonged in, in a world he was also so close to finding true happiness in. He could see his own smile in the reflection of the window in front of him. He could see Alexia standing so close to him, her chest right against his back, and even though there were layers of leather between them it still felt like he could feel her nakedness against his.

He turned and kissed her then, let his lips meet hers for just a few seconds, after all they weren't alone and this clearly wasn't the time to be fooling around. It was out of the corner of his eyes that he noticed the little girl begin to stir, as she sat up in the bed and began to stretch and rub the sleep from her eyes.

He watched as she slowly began looking around the small room, which must have looked massive compared to the small hole in the wall she had fallen asleep in. It wasn't until she finished her search that her eyes fell upon the two of them. She didn't seem scared, just very confused.

Alexia started walking towards her a little bit, but the girl began shuffling backwards in the bed until her back came to rest right against the solid wall behind her. Alexia stopped walking towards the girl and turned back to look his way.

"I know you must be scared waking up in a strange place with strange people but I promise you we mean you no harm," Mike said as he walked passed Alexia, his left hand brushing against her lower back. "Do you have a name, girl?"

He watched as the girl opened her mouth and began to say something, but no sound came out. She lifted her right hand, pointed towards her neck, and gave a slight shrug of her little shoulder. Mike took a few steps closer to her, and it was then he could see the strange small scar along her neck.

"You cannot talk, can you?" Mike asked, and he watched her shake her head slowly. "But you can understand what I am saying though?" She nodded. "Do you have a name?"

He watched again as the girl began to talk with no sound coming out, but he just waited until her lips were finished moving and then they both just stared at each other, each shrugging their shoulders. He knew this could be a long day unless they found a way to communicate better.

"Well, my name is Mike and my friend here is Alexia. We are the ones who brought you here. We came upon your little cave and found you fast asleep inside, so we brought you to a much safer place."

The girl began looking around, and with her hands she made a gesture that looked a lot like writing something down. It was at that point when Mike realized that this girl could more than likely read and write. He started searching through all of his dressers knowing he kept paper and a pen somewhere and he quickly found a handful of pens and some very fancy parchment paper. He handed it all over to the girl.

He watched as she climbed out of the bed and walked towards the small table and laid out all of the new supplies before she started writing on the paper in front of her. He joined her at the table as did Alexia and they both sat on opposite sides of the girl. Once she finished writing, she handed the paper over to him.

What happened to Jen? He read the letter out loud.

"You mean the bigger lady at the cave?" He asked and again the girl nodded. "She was the one who told us to take you away from the cave. She said she had to leave and it was no longer safe for you to be with her."

Again the girl began to write and again she passed the paper back to him. *My name is Misty and she was my nurse.* He read the note aloud once again.

"How come you needed a nurse? Are you okay?" Mike looked at Alexia as she spoke and he could sense some kind of pain there. "Where are you parents?"

The girl started writing on the paper again, and the whole time Mike kept watching Alexia, as if he expected her to break down then and there, which it looked like she was about to do. He placed his right hand on her leg and she placed her left hand on his and again their fingers interlocked with each other.

Jen was the one who helped me after my neck got hurt and I lost my voice. She said I was a miracle child, and I disseevered to live a free life away from evil. I am okay now. It only hurts from time to time. As for my parents, well ... I am not sure. I have never met them.

He squeezed Alexia's hand a little tighter as she fought back her tears and he could tell right away that something about this child reminded her about something in her past, something that he figured she would tell him about sooner or later. The little girl too was watching Alexia as she tried her best not to cry, and soon he noticed that the girl was about to tear up as well.

He was about to say something more, when the little girl got up from the other side of the table and came around to stand right next to Alexia. She wrapped her arms around the much taller lady and Alexia returned to gesture as she leaned down and wrapped her arms around the little girl. Both of them had tears in their eyes now.

He couldn't help but laugh at the sight knowing that they were more than likely sharing some kind of intimate secret about their pasts, but he knew they both needed that hug so he let them have it. He leaned backwards and rested his elbows on the floor as he began to stare out the door once again. He could see the waves out in the distance and he knew that they would all be on his ship heading out once again soon enough. He knew he would have to visit Count Drake to get to the bottom of all of this, but he was unsure if he was going to bring the girl along or not.

He was so lost in his thoughts that he didn't even realize that the girl was standing beside him, watching him as he starred out the window. He couldn't help but offer her a smile when he caught sight of her, and he really looked at her face now. It was the first time he noticed her eyes. She had either been too far away for him to notice or was busy looking down at the paper, but the girl had two different colored eyes. The left eye was a pale grey color and her right was a dark green. He had seen people with two different eye colors before but none like this girl's.

"I guess we will need to take you shopping and get you some new clothes to wear," Mike said, looking the girl over who was a hundred percent dirty, and wearing clothes with more holes in them then fabric.

But I don't have any money, how can I buy any new clothes?

He watched as she wrote it and again couldn't help but smile at how innocent the girl must be. "I will buy you the clothes and maybe a few pairs of shoes," He said, answering her question.

"And we need to get you into the shower so you can clean yourself up and wash your hair."

Mike watched how excited the girl got at the idea of a simple shower and soon she was walking towards the bathroom with Alexia, who returned a few minutes later and straddled his waist again as he remained on the floor leaning backwards.

"So I wasn't expecting this outcome."

"I knew I should have gone with my gut at the start of this mission. Something seemed off and I should have looked into it more," Mike said, lost in her blue eyes once again.

"Be glad it was us who found her and not someone who had worse intentions in mind."

"The quicker we get to the bottom of this the better."

"And what do you have in mind?"

"I guess we go and visit this Count Drake and find out why Misty is so important to him, maybe even find out how a little girl came by a serious injury like that to her neck."

"You don't plan on handing the girl over to the man, do you?"

"I am not sure yet what we are going to do about this girl, but if it turns out she is the Count's daughter then who are we to interfere with that. If I get a bad vibe once we are there, then the girl will remain with us until we get back to the temple and sort this all out," Mike said, running his hands up the inside of her legs, all the way up until they came to a stop on her upper thighs."

"But first we are going to take her out and spoil the crap out of her for the day. Well, maybe all day tomorrow, I am so tired now."

"That is what happens when you spend the night awake chasing after thieves," Mike said, teasing her once again.

"Wait till you see what happens when I take a nap and leave you in charge of an eight-year-old girl alone all day."

"It can't be that hard if you think about it. I'm sure she is just a smaller cuter version of you," Mike said, quickly making sure his lips found her as soon as he finished talking, keeping her from whatever witty comeback she would have.

They both lost themselves in that kiss for what seemed like hours. Their hands roaming around freely, but they both knew in the back of their minds that a little girl wasn't that far away, so they both remained in control of themselves.

He loved kissing her and he wished he could do it every free chance he got, but he knew there was a lot of pressing issues at hand but they could wait he figured, he was going to take a few days to enjoy himself before the three of them set out again.

He lifted himself up with Alexis still in his arms and he lead her towards the bed before gently placing her on her back, his lips parted hers even though they both wanted more and he couldn't help but look into her eyes, her very tired eyes he suddenly noticed, and he figured she could more than likely use that nap. "You can sleep if you want. I can handle watching a little girl on my own for a while," he said as he ran his fingers through her blonde hair, her eyes closing almost immediately.

"Maybe I will try and get a few hours of sleep, and then you can have a few hours yourself."

"That sounds like a perfect plan to me." Mike said pulling the silk sheets over top of her. "If we aren't here when you awake we went into town do to some shopping."

"Okay, just don't lose her or leave her behind anywhere."

Mike couldn't help but laugh as he heard the shower turn off, and Alexia breathing change as she slowly fell asleep on the bed. Now the challenging part was about to begin. He had to figure out a way to keep an eight-year-old entertained and happy. Maybe going shopping was a perfect idea after all because what girl didn't love shopping.

Chapter 17

Mike couldn't help but notice how much Misty reminded him of a smaller version of Alexia as they walked down one of the many crowded streets. She seemed to be in awe as they passed by the many people and shops, just like Alexia was the first time they had walked this same road.

The first place they stopped at was a clothing store, and Misty quickly found a few dresses that she liked. After trying them on, he couldn't help but notice how surprised she was when he paid for all five of them. It was like the girl wasn't used to anything good happening to her.

As they walked down the busy street, he was once again wearing his normal clothes and she was now wearing a really bright pink dress and a pair of white sandals. She had a bright pink ribbon which was now holding the ponytail together at the back of her head.

He watched as she stopped suddenly as a fat pig started walking down the same sidewalk in front of them, and he laughed again when she walked right up to it and begin petting it, like the pig was some kind of dog.

"No, we aren't going to buy a pig," Mike said as she looked at him with her very bright eyes, which quickly turned into fake sad eyes after he said he wasn't buying the pig.

They made their way into one of the less busy restaurants and found a nice quite table on the deck overlooking the pier, he took a seat right beside her at the table, and they both starred off at the many boats parked at the many docks.

"That one is mine," Mike said, pointing towards his ship to the left. He noticed the girl stand up on the chair to get a closer look of it, almost falling over the railing at the same time.

The waiter came next and he ordered a pop while she kept pointing at the orange milk shake, and again he couldn't help but notice how much this kid had in common with Alexia.

Can I order anything I want?

"Yes you can have anything you want on the menu," Mike said with a smile as her eyes lit up once again.

He couldn't help but watch this little girl's face as the waiter placed the giant sized milk shake in front of her. He wondered if he would have gotten this excited when he was her age. It was then that he realized that when he was her age he was found and taking in by Candice and the Temple of Legends. He wondered then how much his life might have been different if it was a simple merchant ship that found him instead. Sure if that was the case he would have long along been dead but he still couldn't help but wonder.

They each ordered a burger and fries and he quickly found his eyes looking back towards his ship. Even from where he sat, he could see a few members of the crew walking to and fro, and he couldn't help but wonder if his life had changed the lives of the many crew members he hired to sail his ship. He couldn't help but wonder if his life had an impact on anyone at all in the world.

He tried his best to feel regular as he sat at the table in his blue shirt and jeans but with a quick glance around the room, he figured if it came down to it he could more than likely kill everyone here, and walk away without a single wound. He didn't know if being an assassin was all it was cracked up to be or maybe he was just stuck in a slump. He found himself in a dark place, and he was having a hard time knowing if he could get out of or not.

Tell me a little bit more about yourself? Mike read the small piece of paper as Misty handed it over to him.

"I was just thinking about that very thing, about myself I mean," Mike answered, looking towards Misty who was watching him with young excitement in her eyes. Maybe a tale or two wouldn't hurt the girl. "I live on this island as well as the main island, close to the Temple of Legends. Have you heard of it?"

Jen used to tell me stories about the people who lived in the temple and she used to say that they were killers, ghost, and nothing more than that.

"Not all of them are as bad as your friend made them out to be, but yes, they are all killers, but only do so to protect what good is left in this world. I have often wondered if what little good that they do is often outweighed by the fact that more people fear them, then they respect them, or that money is the main reason why so many of them still work and not for the greater good."

And how long have you been one of them?

"What makes you think I am an assassin?"

Earlier you were wearing both armor and expensive weapons, wasn't that hard to figure it out.

"Then to answer your question, I have been an assassin for 120 years, and immortal for 100 of those years. I was taken in by the temple when I was about your age."

Are you and Alexia married?

"No, we are just really good friends. I have only just recently started to get to know her," Mike answered, looking back out into the horizon.

The two of them eat their food in silence as Misty not only finished her burger, but also two other helping of fries and again he couldn't help but smile. This little girl was more innocent and free then he would ever be, and he didn't know if he was happy about that or jealous. Freedom would come at a great price and he didn't know if he was ready to pay that price yet.

Am I the reason why you are here?

Her question surprised him even though he should have seen it coming. After all, she figured out who he was but then again, maybe she was the real reason why he was there. Maybe something other than a contract brought him to this island. "I am being paid to find you, yes," he said as he quickly stole the last fry off of her plate, causing her to give him a very serious look, a very cute but serious look.

Jen always said I was important, but she wouldn't tell me why. She said it was why we had to stay hidden in the caves. I have been here for months now, and this is the first time I have been within the city.

"Well you are missing out on a lot that this fine island has to offer."

Like that fat pig that we saw earlier which would have made an awesome pet?

"Like the sights and the sounds of people coming and going all around you, the feel of the sand in your toes and the water on legs, the freedom that comes with being young and not owning a pig for a pet."

How would you know if owning a pig is great or not? Have you ever owned a pig?

"No, I guess I haven't owned a pig," Mike admitted, trying his hardest not to laugh. "Tell you what. Name one thing you want to do right now besides buying a pig, and we will go do it."

I would like to find my own suit of armor.

"You thinking you might be in need of a suit of armor any time soon?"

You said I could name anything I wanted and that is what I want, Mister Assassin man, unless you changed your mind about the pig?

"You are a smart little thing, aren't you?" Mike said again, struggling to keep his laughter to himself as he left some gold on the table for their meal. "Well, let's go visit a friend and see if we can get you some gear."

The two of them left the restaurant side by side and headed back into the afternoon rush of people coming and going and soon they found themselves right in to middle of the crowd. He felt Misty's hand grab his own and at first he looked down towards the little girl who had a smile from ear to ear as she looked around. He realized that she was more than likely holding his hand so she wouldn't lose him in the crowd, and so he did the same as he held onto her hand.

He wasn't used to having a kid by his side and he couldn't even remember the last time he even interacted with a child. The thing about being an immortal assassin with immortal assassins as friends is you didn't get a chance to be around kids often, if at all. He grew up knowing Eric and Shelby and over all those years the two of them never even mentioned having a baby, and so it was with most of the people he knew.

Even now, as he walked down the street hand in hand with this little girl, he couldn't help but think of all the responsibilities that came with it. He was in charge of keeping her safe and protected, and he only just met her that morning really. But at the same time, he also found himself coming to enjoy some of the smaller things in life, like how an eight-year-old girl would be perfectly happy with owning a pig as a pet.

He turned and headed down the dark alleyway, and she followed him without a second look, but he did feel her walk a little bit closer to his side and grip his hand a little tighter. He smiled again as he approached the door at the end of one of the allies and slide a few gold coins under it.

He waited a few more minutes and again he heard the familiar sound of the door being unlocked from the inside. Soon he found it swinging opening, and the two of them walked, still hand in hand, until they got inside. Misty ran off to check out all the cool and very expensive stuff her little hands could find.

"You brought a little girl here out of all places?"

"She wanted to come here and who am I to argue with a little girl," Mike said, patting the old blacksmith on the shoulder. "If you wish, you can be the one to break the little girl's heart and ask her to leave."

"Twice in one week, assassin, to what do I owe this honor?"

"The little girl has a request that I am hoping you can fulfill."

Mike watched as Misty walked towards the old blacksmith somewhat cautious but more so curious as she handed him over a small piece of paper before turning back to her search amongst all of the expensive items all around her.

"Is she serious?"

"It would seem so, and I promised her we would do whatever it is she wanted to do. So here we are."

"Only because I know your money is good, I will see what I can do but no promises."

Mike took a seat on a very old but very expensive red and gold chair, which was off to one of the sides of the shop and watched as the old man and the little girl went about their own little searches of the shop. He pulled out the glowing blue dagger he had tucked away in his belt, and began spinning it in the palm of his hand, losing himself in the blue glowing blur it was making.

He quickly lost himself to everything that was going on around him and back to the mission at hand, he knew he would have to go and see this Count Drake to figure out why Misty was so impotent to the man. He didn't want to think about all the many different reason it could be and he knew in his heart that if he even sensed something was wrong, he wouldn't leave Misty there with him.

But that would mean going against the contract and the temple and he had never done that before. Sure he had broken a few of the minor rules and acted for himself a lot of the time, but he always finished the contracts, and never once questioned his own actions. However, but he did fear that this time would be different. He feared this little girl would end up testing his entire life's course.

He knew he was in over his head with the feelings he was having towards Alexia but at least she lived the same life as him and walked that same grey line. Misty was a kid and she was a world apart from him and Alexia. She was the true meaning of innocents in his mind.

But then again, Alexia came into his life for a reason, so maybe this little girl was here for the same reason and he just didn't realize it yet. Whatever the path they would lead him down, he knew they would be traveling within the next day or two, so he figured he should enjoy the time to relax before hitting the open seas again.

He came back to the world at hand when he felt Misty watching him, and when he stopped spinning the dagger in his hand he noticed she was standing in front of him starring at it as well. Clearly he wasn't the only one who could get lost in it glowing blue light.

"I think I found something that might work here."

Mike watched as the blacksmith came out of one of the side rooms pulling a chest behind him, a very old and cracked wooden chest. He pulled it till he was almost in front of the two of them, and Mike took that moment to slip the blue glowing dagger away and lean forward in his chair. "What is it?" he asked as he kicked the side of his chest, which left a solid dirt mark on the side of his new runners.

"It is a chest for the girl, and don't you go around kicking things that don't belong to you, assassin."

Misty turned and looked his way and after a quick nod she walked closer to the chest and began lifting the lid that only made it few inches up before falling back down again. He was about to reach forward to help her left it when the blacksmith beat him to it, pulling the heavy lid up with ease.

Misty lifted herself up so she was mostly leaning over the side of the chest trying to look at what was inside and he found his hand on the back of her leg keeping her from toppling head first into it before he realized what he was even doing.

Before long she started pulling out a few things at a time until she had everything in the chest on the floor in front of her. He knew right away that he was looking at a small suit of blackish metal armor and he couldn't help but wonder where or why the blacksmith had it, but he was glad that he did.

With the help of the blacksmith he watched as Misty slowly got the suit of armor on, and even though it was slightly too big in some areas, it seemed to do the job right. He could see her smiling face in the slits of the helmet and he couldn't help but laugh this time at the sight of her, standing in front of him dressed in a very odd suit of black armor.

"All she needs now is a sword and she will be set."

Before he could even mention what a crazy idea it would be to give a little girl a sword, the blacksmith pulled out a short wooden sword from behind the counter and placed it in the belt harness on the suit of armor.

"How much is this going to cost me?" Mike asked as he pulled out his pouch of gold.

"It belonged to my son but that was a long time ago, and since it fits her so well you can have it for two gold coins and you word it will be treated no different than your own fine pieces of armor."

"You have yourself a deal," Mike said, handing the man the pouch of gold, which had far more than two gold coins in it.

"I really have to find out who the person was who taught you how to count, assassin, and thank them for doing such a fine job."

"Well I guess we should be on our way before a certain someone starts to worry about us," Mike suggested, giving the blacksmith another gentle pat on the back.

"Every time I see you, assassin, you always seem to surprise me and for that you will always be welcomed in my shop."

"I will see you again and who knows what goodies you will find for me to buy next time."

The two of them found themselves back in the crowd heading back towards the beach, once again hand in hand, and he couldn't help but laugh at the looks some of the people gave them as they walked by. None of them bothered him because he would still see Misty smiling wide under the helmet. He had surprised himself at how easy it was to make a little girl happy with only a few small gestures.

Alexia found herself waking up in a very quiet and very empty house. She had to fight the urge to roll over and fall back to sleep because she knew if she did that now, she would be awake all night again and for some reason she looked forward to sharing the bed that night with Mike.

She quickly stretched her back and neck before getting out of bed and out of her leather armor, which she was surprised she was able to sleep in, in the first place. She walked over to the door of the deck and opened it up so she could feel the oceans breeze on her naked body. Even though it was hotter outside of the house then in, she still enjoyed the slight breeze on her skin, so much so it started to give her a chill that ran down her spine leaving goose bumps all over her body.

She found pair of lose fitting sweating pants and a light T-shirt and figured that would be enough for the day, since she had no plans of doing anything at all. She grabbed a bottle of water and found her way out to the deck and sat right on the edge of it. She could feel the warm water against her toes as she watched a sailboat cross the ocean miles away.

No matter how hard she tried not to think about it, she knew that they would be on a boat soon enough heading to a place she didn't want to go. She knew it was part of their mission to return the girl to this Drake guy, but something about it didn't seem right. She also thought this whole mission seemed odd from the start, and now this little girl being the item they were being paid so much money for, just made it even worse for her.

She tried to figure out why a man would pay so much money for a little girl and then she tried to block out all of the horrible thoughts that suddenly came rushing into her head. Some of them she had long ago forgotten, but always stayed just within reach of her mind, never truly letting her forget her past, never allowing her to fully move on, or even trust another guy fully.

It was the image of Mike and her kissing in the ocean when they first got to the island that brought her out of her dark thoughts and back on the road she now walked. She didn't know a lot about him, but from what she did know she knew she could trust him. After all, his life seemed just as messed up as hers and they both had a lifetime to try and fix their mistakes, so why not try to fix them together.

She also knew that she could be getting way too far ahead of herself by thinking that as well, and knew that anything could happen once they completed this mission. He could even go back to the life he had been living, solo and disconnected from everyone, and maybe he loved that life.

She knew she would have to wait and see what the rest of this mission had in store for the two of them, well I guess the three of them now, she figured, now that Misty had come into their lives. Yet another thing she wasn't fully prepared for. She was still in the prime of her life and enjoying it to the fullest, even if she was single and alone, but now she had Mike and a little girl to worry about. She figured she could deal with him easily enough, but she had no clue what she was going to do with a little girl in her life. And what if this mission ended badly, and she stayed in their life for even longer? Was she ready for that?

Again the mission came back to her main thoughts and she knew that if Mike refused to turn Misty over to Count Drake, it would mean that the contract would become void. To break a contract after accepting it and fulfilling it would be a huge break in the Temple of Legends laws, so much so that it could lead to one of them if not both of them being thrown out and stripped of their tittles or even worse to become outlaws and hunted down and killed. All of her life serving as an assassin she had never heard of anyone doing this, and she felt somewhat relieved when she thought about the fact that Mike had stolen some of the more powerful weapons that could kill an immortal. Although she knew he had some of them, she figured that he didn't have all of them. She knew of at least two axes that would work just as well.

She heard the front door open and she couldn't help but smile as she turned to face the pair as they walked through it. Mike was wearing his normal jeans and shirt but he still looked good like always and Misty was wearing a really cute but ridicules suit of black armor, which caused her to laugh out loud when the girl came up to her and wrapped her arms around her in a big hug.

She watched Mike over the top of Misty's armored helmet and smiled again as he went about placing all of the new clothes he bought today into a small suitcase, which she figured he got as well for when the three of them left. That thought made her heart jump in her chest, and it took her a few minutes to clue into the fact that Misty was still standing in front of her, but now with her hand reaching out with a piece of paper in it.

I have a sword just like you now, and Mike got me this cool suit of armor even though all I wanted was a pig. He said a pig isn't what a girl should want as pet, but I really liked this pig.

"It is a very fine blade you have there, and I am sure a pig would have made a perfect pet for an eight-year-old girl," Alexia said, raising her voice loud enough so Mike would hear her, and she couldn't help but smile when she heard him laugh in the other room.

"Well, tell you what. The next time I see a pig, I will buy it and the two of you girls can share it," Mike jested.

"Always a gentleman. You are good, sir. How was your day out?" Alexia asked as she watched Misty head back into the main room. She felt him sit next to her more then she heard him. She felt his hand find its way under the back of her shirt causing her cheeks to turn a bright shade of red.

"It was really good. I showed her the town and we ate at a fancy little place on the boardwalk. She stuffed her face with more food then I would have thought possible for a little girl, and then we got her some new gear."

"And you didn't pick a fight with anyone?"

"You almost sound surprised by that."

"Well, I know you that well already," Alexia added, still teasing him and trying to forget about the chills he was giving her as he ran his fingers along her lower back.

"I had a little girl by my side the whole time, which might have made fighting a little bit more of a challenge."

They were both interrupted from their teasing of each other when Misty came back on to the deck, gone was the black metal armor and it was replaced by a blue shirt and skirt. Alexia couldn't help but wonder if Mike picked out those colors more for his own love of the color blue than anything else. Again she handed over a note. *Can I go swimming?* It said, and she couldn't think of any reason why it would be a bad idea.

"Do you know how to swim?" she asked. Misty offered a nod and a smile and Alexia nodded in return to say it was okay. She watched the little girl walk to the end of the deck and look down into the water.

"The water isn't very deep and it doesn't get deep until you are really far out, so you should be able to stand in it." Mike said.

Alexia watched as Mike got up and followed Misty to the end of the deck. She almost missed his touch on her back right away and that is when she knew she was going to be in trouble with this man. She knew she had to have had feeling for him but wasn't sure how deep those feelings were yet.

She watched him pick Misty up under her arms and lift her off her feet with ease before placing her gently over the side of the deck and into the water. She watched as he laid on the end of the deck with his hand hanging over the side, within easy reach of Misty, she figured in case something went wrong. She knew then and there that their mission was in big trouble as she watched him play with the little girl in the water. She knew there was no way he would hand her over if he felt like there was something wrong.

It was her turn to sit beside him at the end of the deck and run her hand under his shirt. She felt the handle of one of his daggers as her hand passed his belt, and she wondered if he could ever go a few days without a weapon close by. The thought quickly disappeared though as she got a fair bit of water to the face and looked down to see a girl full of laughter looking back up at her.

"You should be lucky that she isn't wearing a bathing suit or else she would be in there right now after you."

Alexia smiled as Misty stuck her tongue out at her, teasing her a little bit more or maybe the girl just wanted someone to join her in the water. The idea did slightly cross her mind, but she figured loose fitting sweats wouldn't be the most comfortable swimming gear in the world.

Mike changed the way he was on the deck and she found him now sitting in front of her. She wrapped her arms around him and pulled him close to her chest. Again, she could feel something stir within herself but figured it was better to think about the here and now and deal with everything else once they had made it home.

She ran her hands from his chest around to his back and began running them up a little higher till they came to rest on his shoulders, right where she wanted them to be. She leaned forward to give him a gentle kiss on the back of his neck, knowing that would be enough to distract him from what she was about to do and just as he started to turn to face her, she pushed forward with all her strength, pushing him cleanly off of the deck and into the water below.

She couldn't help but laugh as he came up from under the water, spitting out a mouthful of salt water, which she guessed also covered a few select swear words he let out. She couldn't help but laugh even harder as he looked towards her with a very stern look on his face.

"Do you have any clue how much these shoes cost me and now you have helped me ruin two pairs in less than a week."

"I guess it is a good thing you have like ten more pairs waiting for you inside."

She watched as he turned all of his attention towards Misty, who now found an easier target to splash with water. She noticed the smile he had on his face, and she knew he wasn't mad at her nor was he even upset with the little girl splashing him with the salty water.

She wondered if this was what it was like to be a normal person with a normal life as she watched the two of them play in the water. She couldn't help but wonder if this is what her life could have been if she chose a different path, a path that led her to a husband and a daughter of her own.

"You owe me a kiss."

"How do you figure that?" Alexia asked smiling down at Mike as he pulled himself towards her on the deck.

"You pushed me into the water, so the least you can do is kiss me for it."

She didn't even think about the smile on his face when she leaned towards his waiting lips. It wasn't till the very last second that she realized what he was doing and by that time it was too late. With a speed she had no chance of matching and skills she didn't see coming he pulled her into his awaiting arms as he fell backwards into the water, pulling her with him.

She tried her best not to laugh as she began coughing the water out of her mouth as soon as she emerged from the water. She felt a very small wave of irritation wash over her, but it passed as soon as she saw the two people swimming next to her, both with very wide smiles on their faces.

Again, Misty wrapped her little arms around her neck and she couldn't help but enjoy the feeling as she felt the girl's touch, the touch of a very innocent child. This was something she thought she would never feel again, and she quickly lost herself in the water splashing and laughing, which seemed to carry on for hours. It was like the three of them were the only people left in the world, and none of them seemed to have a single worry. She was having so much fun that she didn't even think about the mission. She truly was living in the moment and even more so when she finally got her kiss from Mike, which was followed by him quickly dunking her head under water let again.

Chapter 18

Later that night, well after Misty was fast asleep in the bed, Mike found his way into the shower, a shower he needed more than anything else. He needed to get the nasty feeling of the salt water off of his skin. He let the ladies use the shower first, and it seemed like he waited a lifetime for his turn and then shortly after Misty was done she wanted him to tell her a story to help her fall asleep. He figured the story about how he fought and beat forty armed men would be a fitting bedtime story, until she kept asking him how he beat each person and it took at least a good two hours to get through the whole story.

So now it was his turn in the shower, and he loved the feeling of the very warm water running all over his naked body. He started thinking about everything that happened throughout day and he smiled as he did. He didn't know what it was, but he figured he was meant to be here now with these two girls, like fate needed him here. He wasn't a big fan of believing in destiny, but he knew something was happening now, which was out of his control.

"So what is the plan?"

"What do you mean?" Mike asked as he turned to see Alexia open the shower door, fully naked. He tried his best not to stare at her.

"I mean what is our next step?"

"I sent word to Jason today to swing by at sunset tomorrow to pick the three of us up in one of the life boats, and we will head out the following morning," Mike said as he turned to face her, the water now running down both of their naked bodies.

"And you plan on just handing her over to this man?"

"For all we know, Count Drake could be her father, and if that is the case, who are we to do anything other than hand her over to where she rightfully belongs."

"And what if that isn't where she rightful belongs, Mike?"

"Then we take her with us and leave," Mike said, reaching out finally and running his index finger along her cheek, her very soft cheek.

"This all seems very wrong to me, all of it, this whole mission. You and I finding her and having to give her back to a man who will do god knows what to her, and we don't even have a say in the matter."

He pulled her towards him as she began to cry and held her tightly against his chest as she rested her head on his shoulder. He could feel her naked body against his but his thoughts were too mixed at that moment to think too much about it. He knew she was right about all of this. He had the same bad feeling about the mission and about handing the girl over but that was his job and he had done a lot worse in his lifetime, but something about this multicolored eyed girl stood out to him. Something inside of his heart was yelling at him to stop, to run as far away as he could with these two girls and never look back. "Everything is going to be okay," he whispered into her ear.

"Do you promise?"

He lifted her head up so he could look into her tear filled blue eyes. "I promise you, I will do everything I can to keep that little girl and you safe no matter what, and if Count Drake gives me a bad vibe, I will up and leave with her, and we all know he won't be able to stop me."

She kissed him then with enough force that he stumbled backwards until his back came to rest against the wall of the shower. He felt her arms wrap around his neck as she kissed him more deeply. His hands found their way to her back and he couldn't help but run his fingers from the top of her neck all the way down to her butt.

He lifted her up with both hands under her butt, and she wrapped her legs around him as he spun in the shower and placed her back against the walls. The whole time they kept kissing each other, never once did their lips part. He could feel the hot water on his face and the back of his neck, he could feel her finger nails dig into his back as he pushed himself closer to her. He pulled away then and looked into her beautiful blue eyes and he couldn't help but smile. This girl was really beginning to grow on him, and he wasn't sure yet if he was fully ready for that.

"What are you thinking about?"

"I am thinking about how beautiful you are right now," Mike answered as he felt her squeeze her legs a little tighter around his waist. She leaned back a little more against the wall and he knew she did it so she could look him fully in his eyes.

He couldn't help but fully notice her naked now as she leaned back against the wall, revealing her entire upper half. His eyes wander from her belly button up her perfect abs, past her amazing breasts, and right back into her eyes. He knew she was watching him just as closely as he was watching her, and neither one of them seemed overly bothered with being this close together and fully naked.

"You are so going to make me take another rain check aren't you?"

"I swear one day we will be alone and we can spend a hundred days indoors and naked," Mike said, and almost as if on cue, they both heard a slight cough from the other room.

"And I can't wait for the day to get you alone and naked."

"Maybe one night we can convince Jason to babysit for us."

"If we are lucky that will be tomorrow night."

His response was cut short as her lips found his again. It was only a gentle kiss, but served as a purpose he figured as she grabbed his two hands and placed them on her breasts. He could feel her moan softly while they continual to kiss. He felt her slowly release her legs from his waist and stand on her own two feet again, and their lips parted once again.

They finished the rest of their shower in peace, their bodies gently touching from time to time, his lips would find hers and hers would find his. He didn't want it to end but knew that it would have to as he felt the warm water slowly begin to run out. He reached behind her and pushed the handle down and the water slowly turned off and he quickly handed her a towel before grabbing his own.

He watched her dry off her naked body more then he focused on drying his own off and he wondered if he had made a mistake by pulling away from her in the shower, by forcing it to not go any farther. He knew he made the right call though as he heard yet another soft cough from the other room but as he looked at her one last time still naked beside the towels, he figured the two of them would come to have a lot of fun in the future whether it be in the shower or anywhere else.

He found the pair of shorts he left on the counter and quickly put them on before he got two distracted with her naked body that he would be forced to kiss her again with no intentions of stopping. She too got dressed in a pair of cotton pants and another of his shirts and he couldn't help but smile at her. Maybe she would be that one girl who could change his entire life.

She took his hands in hers and pulled him out of the bathroom and towards the bed and he found himself laughing as he noticed Misty was fast asleep and laying completely sideways in the bed. The two of them stood there for a few minutes watching the little girl sleep, lost in their own thoughts.

He couldn't help but wonder when it was that he last saw someone so innocent fast asleep at night, without a care in the world. As he looked towards Alexia, he figured she must have been thinking something close to the same thing because she had a smile on her face as well. He watched her crawl into bed and gently move Misty to the far side, and she got under the covers right in the middle and he laughed again as he looked at her.

"What are you laughing at?"

"I would have never thought I would be crawling into bed with both a very attractive women and a cute little girl," Mike said as he got into the bed right beside Alexia.

"Join the club."

Mike rolled over and wrapped his left arm under the pillow and Alexia's head and used his right to pull her closer to him. She took his right hand in hers and rolled over softly so her back was against his chest and pulled his arm tightly around her, and he pulled her a little bit closer to him as well. He kissed her on the back of the neck and soon the two of them were fast asleep.

Mike could smell the food cooking before he even opened his eyes, and for a minute he was slightly confused because he could still feel someone sleeping on him. He laughed when he realized that someone was literally sleeping on him. When he opened his eyes he found Misty fast asleep on his chest, hands and head on his left shoulder, and her legs hanging off his right side.

He wrapped his arms around her slightly as he pulled himself up a little on the pillows under him and it was then that he saw Alexia busy away at making them food in the small kitchen. He noticed that a lot of light was coming in through the opened deck door and he realized then that he must have slept through a good portion of the day, which was very odd for him. He also found it odd that Misty was able to crawl onto him in his sleep without him noticing it and even odder that Alexia was able to get out of bed without him feeling it.

He cracked his neck as he watched her flip some pancakes over in a frying pan and smiled at her when she turned to face him, a smile appearing on her face as well. It was something he was getting used to seeing and he hoped she wouldn't stop doing it anytime soon.

"So you finally decided to wake up, sleepy head."

"You're calling me a sleepy head?" Mike said, pointing towards Misty who was now fully on him with her arms wrapped around his neck. "Look at this one fast asleep without a care in the world."

"The two of you looked far too cute this morning to wake up, so I started the day without you."

Mike noticed then the new bags sitting on the floor in the kitchen, and figured they must have slept away a good portion of the day if she had enough time to make it to town and back, let alone start making them food. "I take it you found some money then?" he asked, fully teasing her again.

"Yeah your hiding spot in the wall isn't that good of hiding spot, and do you really need that much gold, after all you are only one person."

"Remind me to never let you look under the floor in my cottage then."

"She can sure sleep, eh."

"Yeah, I don't think she would make a very good assassin," Mike said, gently poking Misty's back and the little girl didn't even stir.

"Maybe she just isn't used to sleeping on a nice bed with warm sheets."

"Maybe that or maybe she isn't used to sleeping on a bed with someone in it to sprawl out on."

"Or both maybe, I know for a fact that I am not used to it yet."

"Neither am I, but I am certainly starting to like the company in my life," Mike said as he watched Alexia smile at him, her cheeks turning a slight shade of red.

"Are you hungry? I made pancakes, eggs, and bacon."

It was then that Misty decided to wake up, as if she had just started to smell the food or something, and he watched as she sat up and began rubbing her eyes trying to get the sleep out of them. He was about to tell her that there was food ready when she turned to face him with her tongue out and eyes wide, which caused his words to be blocked out by his laughter. He found himself still laughing even after she got out of bed and took her seat at the table beside Alexia.

He struggled to pull himself out of bed knowing that this would be there last morning in the small bungalow but knowing he had already slept away most of the day. "So what did you buy today?" he asked, taking his seat at the table across from the two girls.

"Nothing overly awesome, just some warmer sleep wear for Misty and myself for when we are on the boat, and I got you a new pair of runners since I am so nice. I also bought some food and what not for the trip, plus I went to the post office and bought out all of their spare note pads."

"I am glad you did because that totally slipped my mind yesterday," Mike said, knowing that the note pads would be the only way that Misty would be able to talk to them.

"She can sure eat a lot."

"Like I said, yesterday she puts away food like there is no tomorrow," Mike continued as he watched Misty finish her first plate of food before he even started on his. She just shrugged her shoulders at him and hopped off the chair and grabbed another plateful from the counter.

"You slept well for a change I noticed."

"Yeah, and I think I needed it. I can't even remember the last time I slept that well."

"Does Jason know about our little friend here?"

"Not yet, but I am sure he will figure it out as soon as he picks us up," Mike answered in between bites.

"And do you think he is going to say anything?"

"I have known him for so long now, I doubt it will even surprise him, although this is the first time I have brought a kid on board before, so who knows maybe he will have a heart attack."

"Guess we will have to find her a nice job or something to do once we get on board, so she can earn her way."

They both laughed as Misty turned to face them one at a time with her cheeks fully puffed out and her eyes wide. Clearly, the idea wasn't a good one in her young mind. Again, he found himself lost in the moment as he sat at the table eating his afternoon breakfast with the two girls. He even tried to enjoy himself for a little while before he had to remind himself that in a week's time they would be on the Drake's family island facing the Count himself.

He spent the rest of the afternoon getting packed and changed and he couldn't help but feel like this could be one of the last times he ever saw his small little bungalow. He didn't know why, but he couldn't shake the feeling, the feeling of losing everything he used to love as he found a lot of new things to love.

He knew that Jason would be there soon because he could see the bottom of the sun begin to touch the ocean's surface, and again he looked around the small room and felt sad. He grabbed a large backpack and walked over to the wall right beside the fridge, and kicked a small opening right in the bottom of it. He held the bag under and watched as all the gold coins began to slide out from the inside of the wall.

As he waited for the gold to run out, he turned to face Alexia who was watching him with a puzzled look on her face. All he could do was offer her a shrug of his shoulders for an explanation as to what he was doing, a part of him didn't even know why he was doing it.

Misty came and knelt down right beside him watching the coins fall into to backpack and she kept reaching her little hands in and grabbing a coin or two and placing them in the bag herself. He couldn't help but laugh as he watched her doing this, her innocents, everything she was, he knew he could never be again. He gave that kind of happiness up so many years ago.

The sound of a boat approaching bought him back to the situation at hand and he knew this was going to be a long night, for that matter a long week, even and he was glad he managed to get one night of really good sleep in before they got back on his ship and headed out to the Drake family island.

He lifted the backpack onto his shoulders and he couldn't believe how heavy it was. He must have been hording gold in there for a lot longer then he realized. He grabbed a few of the bigger bags as well and passed them over the side of the smaller lifeboat to the waiting Jason on the other side, who was stacking them neatly towards the front.

It took them only a few minutes to get loaded, and Mike found himself standing on the end of the deck looking back towards the small place, his place, a place he knew he may not see again and he felt his eyes begin to moisten at the thought. He was holding Misty in his arms and she too was watching both the place and him and couldn't help but notice. He focused on her multicolored eyes and smiled and received a smile in return.

He jumped over the side of the boat with Misty still in his arms and he landed perfectly beside a now sitting Alexia, who was glaring at him like he suddenly did something wrong. He knew it was because he jumped on to the boat holding Misty, but the odds of him falling were slim to none, so he offered her a smile in return.

He sat right next to her, their sides touching, and he wrapped his right arm around her lower back while still holding Misty in his left. She was sitting on his lap now watching Jason get the boat back out into deeper water. She had a look of joy on her face, and he hoped she would keep it there no matter what happened to her in her life. He didn't want to be the one to ruin this little kid's innocence by bringing her into the bloodthirsty world of the assassins.

"The crew is all set and ready for our trip to the Drake Isles."

"Thank you again for coming to pick us up. It would have made for a long trip walking back to the boat with all of our gear."

"It would seem like you are leaving with a lot more then you came with, my old assassin friend."

"I will explain everything to you, my old friend, once we are safely aboard the ship and on our way," Mike said as the boat slowly began heading off into the sunset. He dared to turn one more time and he watched his small bungalow slowly fade away into the distance behind them.

They all remained silent for the rest of the short trip, and he figured that everyone was lost in their own personal thoughts about what the future might hold for them, well almost everyone. Misty was now leaning over the side of the boat looking into the clear water below. It was so clear and clean he knew she could see right to the bottom of ocean and all the many water creatures that dwelled within it.

He made out the outline of his ship in the distance. It was already out of port and waiting for them on the open waters and his heart began racing as they got closer and closer to it. He wanted to turn back then and there and take these two very interesting girls back with him, back to the small bungalow that they might learn to call home. He didn't need to work anymore. He already made enough money for ten life times, so he figured the three of them could live there, on his little island paradise quite peacefully.

But he had to let that thought leave his mind, as he felt the smaller lifeboat they were in begin to be lifted out of the water by the main crane on his ship. Soon it was gently placed back onto its resting area, and the four of them quickly unloaded.

The crew met them on the main deck and helped carry most of the bags up and into their main chambers, but he found himself staying behind as the sun finished it dip fully into the ocean. Even after the ship was fast on its way, he found himself watching the island now slowly begin to grow smaller and smaller. He reached into the pocket of his leather assassin's jacket and pulled out three gold coins and tossed them over the railing, into the water far below. He didn't believe in luck or fate, but he asked for strength to help him get through this week, a week he knew would be one of the worst weeks he had ever gone through.

He walked the narrow hallways with ease like he had done over a thousand times since he bought the ship so many years ago. He knew he could find his way around the whole thing even with his eyes closed and never walking into a single thing. He hesitated at the blue door, which would lead him into his chambers and a part of him wanted to keep walking while another part told him to enter. Never before had he ever felt so unsure about himself like he did now, never before had questioned his own life.

He walked through the door and a smile found his lips almost instantly as he watched Misty jumping on the big bed with Alexia right beside her. They both turned to face him as he walked in, and they both offered him a heartfelt smile, something he was truly trying his best to return. The sight of them having so much fun and so full of joy made him smile, but he knew it would all be different in a week's time, it would all go back to how it was and he would be alone once again.

He dropped the bag of gold coins onto the floor and they hit with a louder thud then he thought it would. He found himself laughing out loud. He figured he would forget about everything else and just enjoy the last few days he had before everything changed. He figured he would live his life for the moment and see where it took him. He walked closer to the bed and just as he got to the edge, Misty jumped towards him mid-bounce and he scooped her up in the air, spinning her around as he held her just under her shoulders. He laughed again as she kept crossing her eyes at him and sticking her tongue out as he spun her around, but that the look on her face changed pretty quick as he let her go and sent her sailing through the air and right into the waiting arms of Alexia.

"You know if you ever drop her, she won't heal as quickly as you and I will."

"Do you honestly believe I would ever drop her?" Mike asked as he lay on his back on the bed, which was a tricky task seeing as the two girls still continued to jump all around him.

"Honestly I believe a pig would have a better chance at flying then you ever have in dropping her."

The two girls quickly wore themselves out and settled in the bed next to him and all three of them starred up through the clear ceiling, watching as all the stars slowly began to glow so many miles above them.

Misty was in the middle of them, and now fast at work with a note pad. He could tell by the way she was moving the pencil that she was drawing something and not writing, so he looked past her to Alexia. Even as she starred up at the ceiling he could tell she had a lot on her mind. He knew something was bothering her but didn't know if it was his right to ask her not.

He sat up and quickly pulled the two blue glowing swords free from his back harness and leaned them against the side table by the bed and within easy reached, not that he feared anything on his own ship but it was another one of his bad habits. Next where the two daggers that he placed on the top of the side table and he quickly placed his head on the pillow and was a lot more comfortable now that he didn't have his weapons digging into him.

"Do you think it is a good idea to leave your weapons just lying around and within easy reach of Misty?"

"I am pretty sure Misty has no plans of playing with my weapons. Do you now?" Mike asked as he looked towards Misty who nodded her agreement.

"But I guess they will make a very good night light none the less."

"That they will and I know how much you are afraid of the dark." Mike said as he turned to face Alexia, with a smile on his lips.

"Well if I get too afraid I can always yell out for the master assassin to come and sweep me off of my feet."

"Unless the master assassin is far too busy enjoying his holiday to come and save you."

They both started laughing as Misty began mocking them with her hands using her fingers and thumbs to make little mouths and had each taking it turns at talking to the other one. He figured this little girl was very smart even though he had only spent such a short time with her. How she managed to express herself with words on paper or even with her actions made up for her lack of being able of speak. She might not be cut out to be an assassin but he knew she had greatness in her to exceed at anything she wanted to do.

Soon it was only the two of them awake and staring up and out at the stars, Misty had found her way into Alexia's arms and soon she began to gently snore, so he pulled himself closer to her as well and she accepted his arm under her head and he pulled them two of them a little but closer to him.

"What are you thinking about?" Mike finally dared to ask.

"I am trying to think about nothing but the more I try that the more I seem to think about things."

"I agree this is going to be a very long week indeed."

"Are you not worried at all? We hold the future of this little girl in our hands and if we make a mistake we can ruin her life forever."

"Even as the lifeboat was pulling away from my place tonight I started thinking about how much easier my life would be if the three of us just stayed there forever. We could all live together for the rest of our life and not have a worry in the world."

"You really thought about the three of us staying there together?"

"Yes I did but I also knew that if we did that we wouldn't be able to live care free because we would be turning our backs on the temple and the mission we are currently undertaking. They would consider that a breach in our agreement and we would be hunted down and brought in for justice and she would be taken to him anyways."

"And you would allow them to just take her away from you like that."

"I may be the best at what we do and have skills that cannot be matched but if every assassin came at us at once I would be hard pressed to defeat them all wouldn't I."

"So what do you think we should do then?"

Mike took a few deep breaths before he answered, he didn't even know if he had an honest answer or not but he knew what was in his heart. "We will take her to the Count's and if everything seems normal you and I will return home and live a life together if that works for you and if there seems like something is amiss with our Count friend then I will take the girl and leave and the three of us will start out lives together on the run and trust me we would always be on the run."

"I am thinking along the same lines as you myself, either way I think this will be the start of a new beginning, whether it is just the two of us or if our little friend here comes along for the ride as well."

"But as for now I am going to enjoy what time the three of us may have left together. Starting with this," Mike said as he leaned over and kissed her gently, just a short kiss but he knew there was more behind it then that and so he figured she would know it too.

"Well if we are going to enjoy moment how about we go and take a shower together and you can help me wash my back."

Mike didn't even have time to answer as he watched her left Misty up out of the big bed and placed her gently on the couch bed and covered her up in a ton of layers of blankets. He watched as she grabbed a change of clothes out of her bag and headed off towards the bathroom and just as she got to the door he watched her unzip her leather jacket and let it full to the floor leaving her upper body full exposed.

He couldn't help but smile as he walked to the main door of the chambers and locked the many locks on it and then grabbed a pair of pj pants and followed her into the bathroom to join her in the shower, the whole time he couldn't stop thinking about kissing her as soon as he got into the hot water.

Chapter 19

Mike found himself wide awake for the third night in a row as he leaned over the side of the railing watching the wave's crash into the side of the ship. Just an hour or so ago, he watched a strange set of big fish swimming along the side of the ship but even they were gone now. It seemed like the closer they got to Count Drake's island the more everything living seemed to disappear. Even the water tonight didn't seem as lively as it had been the last few nights. It was certainly a lot darker in color, he noticed.

He knew he should be back in his bed cuddled up against Alexia, but his mind wouldn't allow him to sleep, so he figured he would give the girls a chance to sleep well without him tossing and turning all night.

He could feel the weight of the world sitting perfectly on his two shoulders, and he knew it would only take one mistake to dislodge it, a mistake he figured he was only days away from making. The last few days on the ship he found himself getting more and more attached to Misty, which he knew wasn't fair for himself or for the little girl and the more he thought about it now that harder he knew it was going to be to just hand her over.

"What have you gotten yourself into this time?" He thought out loud as he watched a fair sized wave crash into the ship.

"I was just on my way here to ask you that very thing."

"What do you mean?" Mike said, turning to face Jason.

"In all my years sailing the open seas with you, never once have I seen you this lost boy, never once did I see you so trapped within yourself that you didn't know which side of the grey line you were walking on, not even when you and Candice broke up."

"Never before have I struggled with a mission like I am now."

"The girl is your mission, isn't she?"

"Yes, she is the reason why we had to go to the Merchant Island," Mike said, figuring there was no point in lying to his old friend.

"Does she belong to Count Drake then?"

"It would seem to be that way, yes."

"Is he the girl's father?"

"That is what I am hoping to find out," Mike replied, finally turning to face the captain.

"I have heard many tales about the business that happens on the Count's Island and for your sake boy I hope they are only tales but if the man is paying you for the girl he has to have a good reason to be doing so."

"Do you trust me, my oldest of mortal friends?" Mike asked, and it was his turn to watch the captain stare at him for a change.

"You gave me a life by allowing me to be the captain of this fine ship, and in all of our years sailing together I have grown old indeed, and let I had to watch you remain young. Others would be jealous of such a thing, but I was honored to be by your side all of these years. I have watched you go through great journeys and heartbreak, and I love you like a father would love a son. I am proud of the man who stands in front of me today."

Jason's words cut into his very soul like a hot knife. He too had enjoyed the life the two of them had shared over the many years of sailing the seas, and he too often looked upon the man now standing in front of him as a son might look upon his own father. This is why he knew he would regret the words he was about to ask, knowing that they would change this man's life as much as they would change his own. "If I fail in turning the girl over to the Count, I will be forced to run and bring the two of them with me, and I could use a captain with your skills to help aid us on our escape," he said, fearing how his old friend would react.

"If it comes to that, my boy, I know the perfect place to be running to, and there isn't another ship in these waters that will catch us. But I need you to promise me one thing before I agree to aid you."

"What's that?"

"I need you to promise me that no matter what happens on that island, you will keep yourself and those two girls safe and make it back to my boat or for the love of god, I will come to your aid with my men."

"I promise you I will die trying to keep them protected."

"Then it is a good thing you cannot die, I would think."

"I am just so confused about what I should do."

"Then go with your heart, boy, and trust me when I tell you it will never steer you wrong."

"Yeah I am sure you are right about that."

"And tell that beautiful blonde girl that you love her already before I have to do it and steal her away from you."

"Well, you are a lot wiser when it comes to the women folk, so who am I to stand in your way of trying to fall in love with Alexia. But I will warn you, old man, she is a crazy one," Mike said, laughing as he spoke.

"She is all yours, boy, don't you worry."

"Haven't you ever wanted to meet a woman of your own?" Mike asked, changing the subject around on his old friend. "Maybe have a family one day?"

"I have all I need here on this ship and all the family I will ever need in my crew and in you, boy. What else could an old man want?"

"What do you think I should do?"

"Live to be free and love like it could be your last day on earth. Never fear heartache, and never cry over a lost love because you might miss the one perfectly great blonde haired, blue eyed girl standing right in front of you if you're too busy looking back. And when it comes to you and this little girl, I am sure you have already got that one figured out on your own. The crew and I will always be willing to sail by your side no matter where are course is or who is chasing us."

"I owe you a debt I don't think I will ever be able to repay, my friend."

"It is a debt which you repaid in full the moment you named me captain of this ship, the moment you walked into my life and allowed me to live the way I always wanted to live. I will die an old man with little regrets and a long happy life behind me."

Mike turned back to face the waters once more, too filled with emotion to be able to come up with a response to his old friend. When he felt a gentle hand rest on his shoulder, he knew he didn't need to say anything at all. He could hear his friend walking away and yet it still felt like he was standing next to him, watching the waves like they had done so many times together over the years. He knew they would keep watching them, all the way up until the point that Jason passed away, as a very old man.

The man's words did the job and found their way into his very heart, into his very being, and he knew he would do right by the two girls he was traveling with, even if that meant breaking the contract and running. He didn't fear anyone Candice would send after them but only felt pain knowing that if he killed any of them, it would be like killing an old friend.

Sure, he only knew a handful of their names, but he had met each and every one of them over his lifetime. To kill any of them, would bring him no joy at all. He forced himself not to even think about the fact that Shelby and Eric could be the ones to come for him or even Candice herself.

He truly felt torn as he stood there leaning against the side rail, between who he was now in life and who he once was. He knew that a time would come and most likely very soon, where he would have to decide who the man was that he was going to be in the future.

But was he really ready for that life, the life of a husband or even a father, or even a life of both but on the run. How long would he be able to run before his past finally caught up to him? He never thought about having kids or getting married, not even when he was with Candice. He knew that he loved her, but he also knew a lot of that love was lust. She was the one thing he wasn't allowed to have, so he enjoyed the feeling of being with her even more so because of that. But was he good enough of a man now to be both a husband and a father figure to these two girls in his life, or was he still too scared to admit anything about any of it to himself.

"Are you going to come back to bed, or are you going to just stand out here all night again and pretend like I don't notice."

"I am just thinking that's all," Mike answered as he turned to face Alexia, who looked very cute wrapped up in her wool robe and her fuzzy slippers.

"You can always lie in bed and do your thinking with me beside you, you know."

"I know I can, but I didn't want to keep you awake. I figured at least one of us should be well rested before we got to the Count's Island." Mike said as he leaned against the rail of the ship wrapping his arms around Alexia as she got as close to him as possible.

"I often wonder about you a lot Mike. Did you know that?"

"And what is it you are wondering about when it comes to me?"

"You are a great man in my mind even if you are having a hard time seeing it in *your* mind. This life we have and the job we do is enough to eat away at anyone's soul. It is enough to leave a person empty inside and I want you to know I was empty. I was broken to the point that I didn't think I would pull myself back together, and then you fell from that beam and ended up in my bed. You started finding the pieces I lost so long ago, and then you brought me way out here and now I have Misty in my life: a little girl I thought I would never have the right to have, and here she is, but I don't think you see all of that do you?"

"That is the problem, really. I do see all of that and more," Mike said, pulling her a little closer to him, close enough he could feel her heart beating against his chest. "You have given me back something I thought I lost as well. My heart and I know you might not understand it, but this mission has shown me a side of myself I have never seen before, a side I never needed to know until now. I am more worried about the two of you now, than I have ever been about anything else in my long life. I am so confused about what is right and what is wrong. I feel like I am going to lose my mind, like I am going to wake up one morning and neither of you will be there."

"Well then let us figure this out together, side by side to the end if we have too."

"And what are we going to do about Misty?"

"For now, let's leave that in fate's hands until we feel like we need to intervene and take action on our own."

He lifted her chin up, and kissed her. He could feel her cold lips against his and knew she must have been freezing, but didn't say anything. So, he wrapped his arms around her even tighter and kissed her a little more deeply knowing that if her body started to react to his kiss, it would begin to warm itself up. "How about we go and get some sleep while we still can," he whispered as his lips parted hers and they both made their way back to their chambers in each other's arms.

"What do you know of the Count's Island and of his manor?" Mike asked as he watched Jason give over the main wheel of the ship to Misty.

"I have been there once before, but that was before I even met you. It is of simple design from what I remember. There is one long dock, which leads to a single walkway, which takes you to his main doors. The manor is about four stories high and is surrounded by thick trees and walls, so really there is only one way in, and one way out. That is unless you plan of burning the whole island to the ground."

"I plan on walking right through the front doors and back out the same way," Mike replied as he looked out the main window. "No matter what happens in there, that is what I plan on doing."

"From the best that I have heard, he keeps the place crawling with armed guards, lots of them."

"That doesn't really change anything."

"He could have an army waiting for you, boy."

"Then they will not be disappointed."

"I will tell the crew to get ready for a fight, and we will watch your back."

"I will not risk a life for my own. I am sure Alexia and I can handle anything the Count has in store for us," Mike assured him as he turned to face Alexia. She stood off to the corner, her head down facing her feet, but he figured she was listening to every word that was said.

He was forced to look away as Misty began pulling on his sleeve, clearly trying to get his attention. When he looked at the girl, she was pointing out the window. His eyes shifted again from her to the window, and he noticed a few glowing lights off in the distance, about forty of them or so. "What are those?" he asked, turning to face Jason.

"They are the torches that run along the dock, which means we have arrived at your destination. Welcome to the Drake family island."

He suddenly felt nervous, something he hadn't felt in a very long time. His hands found their way to the hilts of his blue glowing daggers. He wanted to feel some sense of calm, but he knew he wouldn't feel anything but nervous until this whole messed up situation was done and over with. He looked again towards Misty and then back to Alexia, both of them looking towards him. He couldn't help but wonder if this whole thing was a mistake. "Time to get yourselves ready, we have a long night ahead of us," he said walking out of the captain's cabin.

Mike realized the island was just as Jason described it, as soon as the three of them got off the ship and began making their way along the dock. He could feel Misty's left hand in his right as they walked side by side and he knew Alexia was only a few steps away from him, but they both agreed that they wouldn't show any kind of contact with each other until they were back on the boat. He didn't want the Count to see it as a weakness.

The walkway leading to the manor was wide enough for a group of people to walk ten at a time side by side and the three of them barely took up a quarter of it. He could see the many guards lining the walkway and could tell they were all watching him, hands on the hilts of their weapons, he figured. The closer they got the manor the narrower the walkway got until they were only enough room for the three of them to walk side by side.

The manor was a plain, four-story building, he noticed, and nothing really stood out about the place besides the guards with crossbows lining the main deck and all of the other decks on the front of the house. All in all, he counted close to fifty guards outside of the house, and he figured there would be more waiting for them inside. The door leading into the manor was nothing more than a simple wooden door with a cross engraved into the wood, a cross that matched the one on the back of Misty's neck.

He reached his free hand up to knock on the door, when it opened inwards before his hand ever made contact with it, he figured it was the Count's way of trying to through him off his game, but he just shook his head and walked through the door. The entryway was no different from the rest of the house, it seemed, and again he was met by a handful of guards, who freely led the three of them into the main chambers. He noticed that the rest of the guards from the outside slowly began to filter in through the door behind them and figured that maybe the Count truly was a paranoid man. The footsteps on the floor above him made him realize that the crossbowmen must have also switched their location.

He was finally glad to see some fancy furniture and items as he walked into the main chambers on the lower level of the room. This room even had an assortment of bright colors, from the chairs to the paintings and even the curtains. He noticed as well that the square room they now stood in had a square balcony, which ran all around it, now filled with all the men holding their crossbows.

He walked towards the almost bald man sitting on a giant chair, which was made up of more cushions then wood, and he couldn't help but notice the man's clothes. He was wearing a nice suit and tie and dress shoes but it all seemed very much outdated. It looked like the same kind of suit his father would have worn all those years ago when he was still alive.

"Welcome to my house, my fine assassin, and I am glad to see your mission went so well."

"It would seem that way. Do you have my payment?" Mike asked as he looked around the room and smiled at all the guards who now had the three of them very much surrounded.

"Yes, it is over there in the wooden chests, and since you brought the girl to me faster than I could have hoped for, I will be doubling your payment, assassin."

"Who is she to you?"

"Who is who to me?"

"The little girl you had me bring here," Mike asked, turning his gaze from the chest in the corner back towards the Count. He noticed now that he was close enough that the man's eyes were a pale shade of blue, almost as if the life had been drained out of them.

"That does not concern you, assassin, but now if you hand her over, I will get a few of my guards to carry the chest to your ship, and you can be on your way."

"Why did you ask for me by name when you contacted the temple with your contract?"

"Because everyone knows your name, assassin, and everyone knows you are the best at what you do."

"And what is it you think I do, Count?" Mike asked as he felt his nervousness begin to act up again. Something wasn't right here, and he could feel it all the way to his core.

"You are the world's top killer and they say there is nothing you can't find once you start looking for it. Now why are you still in my house? Leave the girl, and be on your way."

"I would rather not, if that is alright with you," Mike said as he pushed Misty behind him and towards the awaiting Alexia. "Until you tell me what is so important about this girl you want so badly."

"You would dare try to defy me in my own house. Do you not know who I am? How much I am worth?"

"I don't care who you are, and judging by your house here, I am worth far more then you will ever be, so do me the favor of answering my

173

question and then me and my friend will be on our way."

"Do you give me your word that if I tell you the importance of this girl you will leave my house and my land?"

"You have my word, Count Drake, and if I were you I would talk quickly before I get annoyed."

"The girl is perfect in every way, don't you see? She has eyes that do not match and she in unable to talk, thanks to a surgery I had my house doctor perform on her when she was baby, and she is branded with my house logo. So, isn't it easy to see the importance of this girl, assassin?"

"So, she is your daughter?" Mike asked, even though something told him he was going in the wrong direction.

"No, she is a toy, really. She isn't old enough to be of any use to me and my men yet, but one day she will be. Those thieves stole her from me when she was two years old, and it took me six years to track her down. One day she will bare my children and then I will kill her, and her importance to this world will be at an end. Her innocents will grant me a child of my own to rule on the day I decided to die."

"That day might be closer than you think," Mike said, his hands reaching for his daggers.

"You will attack me in my own house, assassin?"

"That will be in your hands, but I have no plans on leaving Misty here with the likes of such a sick person."

"I have close to twenty crossbows aimed at you right now, and even more men surrounding you and yet you think you can give me orders in my own house."

"Yes, because I have something you do not have."

"And what is that, assassin?"

"I have a surprise for you and your men."

Chapter 20

"Follow me, men," Jason said as he watched the rest of the guards follow Mike and Alexia into the front door.

He was leading his now fully armed and fully armored crew down the long dock leading towards the walkway and the manor in front of them. Even though there were thirty of them, they moved without a sound. After all, how could they have traveled so long with Mike without picking up a thing or two? They all had excellent armor and weapons paid for by the money that Mike paid them for manning his ship, and they all agreed they owed the assassin much.

Mike came to him just before they left the boat and told him of his master plan and about how he might indeed need the help of the crew. So they suited up right away and headed out as soon as it was safe. They approached the manor and Jason turned and pointed to the many decks leading to the upper levels. Fifteen of his finest archers began to scale the walls and found their way to the many opened windows and unlocked doors. He turned to face the last fifteen or so men still standing by his side and pointed towards the main door. He drew out his golden captain's sword, which was also a gift from Mike, and crept his way to the front door. He turned the doorknob and slowly pushed the wooden door open, without making a sound.

He walked into the entryway and signaled for his men to circle around the many rooms he knew would lead them to the main chambers. He had only been to the island once, but he had been inside the place a few times so he knew the lay out well. He walked on his heels to limit his footfalls and since he was barefooted, he made even less noise. They were all barefoot and moved through the house with ease.

He approached an open doorway, which he knew would lead into the main chamber and leaned against the frame listing to the debate going on inside the room. He could hear Mike and the Count talking back and forth, and he slowly leaned his head over to peek into the room. He knew he had lucked out right away when he saw only two guards blocking the doorway, their backs to him and right in front of them he saw Alexia and the little girl. He pointed towards one of his own men flanking him and watched as he headed out back down the doorway to give the order to attack.

He pulled a slender dagger from his belt with his left hand and got into position for attack, right behind the two guards.

Mike could feel it all the way to his very core. He could sense that his men were in place. He knew the call for attack would be coming very soon and a smile crept to his lips then and there as he watched the Count stand up out of his chair and take a few steps towards him, his hands on the handle of the sword he had leaning against the chair. "Like I said, Count, I will be taking the girl and leaving. If you wish to remain alive you will sit back down and let us leave," He said, pulling his two blue glowing daggers free of their harnesses, something that seemed to make the Count take a few steps back and the color in his face to quickly drain.

"I may not be able to kill you and your friend there, but I have enough men around me to put you down long enough for me to lock you away in the deep pit under my house, and mark my words, assassin, you will be down there till the end of time."

"I think you have fewer men then you think you have," Mike said, and he laughed at the timing of his words because just as he finished talking, fifteen of the Count's crossbowmen fell off of the balcony and into the middle of the main chamber, each with an arrow sticking out of their neck.

He knew the time for words was at an end and he could feel the guards behind him close in on him. It was then that the four doors leading into the main chambers flew open and in came the rest of his men, swords in hand and each killing a guard or two before they even knew it.

He turned quickly behind him just in time to witness Jason come through the last door. He watched his old captain friend quickly stab both his golden sword and his dagger into the two guards blocking their escape.

He watched Alexia hand Misty to the captain and he quickly turned to make his escape, just as they planned.

He turned his attention back to the fight at hand and quickly swatted away a sword that was heading towards his midsection with one of her daggers. He swung out with his other dagger with a speed and accuracy that only an assassin could do and sliced his attacker's throat.

Two more came at him at once, one on each side of him, and he felt his hands take over for him, doing what they do best with ease. It was like he didn't even need to think about his actions anymore, they were a part of his very being now. He quickly parried a weak slash from the man from the right as he jabbed out with his dagger and caught the man on the left right on the forearm, causing him to drop his sword. A sideways spin brought his left dagger into the neck of the man on his right as his right dagger embedded deep into the side of the man on his left, puncturing his lung and they both fell to the ground dead.

He felt the kick before he even noticed the Count was in front of him, and the man's foot impacted his chest with such force it shot him backwards before he came to a sudden stop as he slammed into one of the wooden walls. The back of his head whipped backwards and into the wall and the white spots came back to his sight again. He felt the daggers slip from his now numb hands as he tried his best to blink his eyes back into full focus.

This time he saw the Count coming in fast for a second attack with his sword. He noted the man's swift speed and movement and knew again something wasn't right with this whole situation. He got to his feet just in time to deflect the Count's sword thrust with his upraised left arm. Even with the thick armor he wore, he heard his left forearm crack under the blow, a blow far too powerful for a normal man.

His blue glowing sword was in his right hand then, but he couldn't even feel his left anymore so he knew that duel wielding both swords was out of the question. Instead, he went on the offensive for the first time since the Count had engaged him in combat. His right hand worked like a blur with a series of thrusts and jabs and he quickly had the Count out matched as he forced him to step backwards over and over again.

It was all too weird though because with each attack he lunched towards the Count he could feel the man blocking his powerful blows with strength of his own, strength that matched even his. Back and forth the two of them went, each waiting for an opening to make a solid attack.

Mike cursed himself for being so carless by losing the ability of his left arm, knowing that with both swords working away at the Count, it would have made for a quick fight. He looked away from the count and his eyes found Alexia right away. She was covered in blood, but it didn't look like hers and she was in a triangle with two other members of the crew. They worked as a team killing off the guards with ease.

His big break came as he heard a single click of a crossbow sending it dart free, even in the hustle of the fight, and all the shouting and death he still heard that single click and dropped to his knees. Just as he felt the floor on his knees he saw the dart fly past the side of his head and right into the Count's chest, causing the man to stagger backwards and trip over the corpse of one of his own men to land on his back.

He slowly walked over to the Count and watched as the man pulled the dart free of his chest and his eyes opened wide in surprise as he watched the wound slowly begin to heal right away. The Count slowly began to rise back up off the ground but this time Mike was ready for him with a kick of his own, right to the side of the man's unprotected face.

Again he watched the small cut on the side of the Count's face slowly begin to heal as the man looked up towards him. "So, assassin, do you really plan on killing one of your own and breaking the most important law of them all."

"The likes of you would never be called an assassin because you are nothing more than a sick freak," Mike said as the tip of his blue glowing sword came to rest right against the Count's throat.

"Kill me now assassin and learn what it is like to live a life on the run, like I have since the day that Candice took over as leader of the Temple of Legends. I planned your downfall from the moment that boy let his metal arrow fly free on her wedding day. So, like I said, boy, kill me now and know what it is like to be hunted."

"And you think I'm afraid of Candice and the other assassins?" Mike asked, already starting to feel his left arm again. "You think I am afraid to die for something I believe in?"

"Why do you believe so much in this girl? Why couldn't you have just let it be and left?"

"Because she is the innocents that we could never be. She is the answer to a free life that was taken from us at such an early age," Mike said, flexing the finger in his left hand, glad that they moved without too much pain. He could tell right away his arm wasn't broken. "You might have been one of us once, but you are no longer and I break no laws by killing you here and now."

Mike could feel everyone watching him now and he quickly looked around to see the death that was around him. Almost all of the Count's men were dead on the floor and pools of blood were everywhere. It looked like the surprise had worked for the most part, and he only saw a few of his own men dead. He looked up to see his archers all around him on the balcony looking down at him. He saw Alexia staring at him then from the other side of the Count, holding both of his blue glowing daggers. They were all watching to see if this moment would be the moment that would lead them all into a life of exile, a life on the run.

He couldn't help but ease on his right arm and the tip of his sword slowly pulled away from the Count's very exposed neck. The sight of Alexia amongst all of this death just didn't seem right to him. He knew that a lot of the dead bodies around him were there because of her, but he couldn't help but smile at her now as she smiled at him.

It was that split second of distraction that he knew had cost him the quick kill. He felt the Count slap his sword off to the right as he thrusts forward with his own sword aimed perfectly for his heart but was held back as the blade bounded harmlessly off of his black leather armor. The Count's foot to his midsection however, forced him to take a few steps back and give the Count time to regain his footing.

"You allow yourself the joy of another, and it will cost you the joy of killing me, you fool."

"You speak as if you think you are going to walk out of this place alive," Mike said as he watched the Count's eyes bulge open in a state of shock.

It wasn't until the Count turned his back to him that he saw the two hilts of his blue glowing daggers sticking out of his back. Neither would have been enough to kill the man, and he realized that too late as the Count thrust forward with what was left of his strength, and scored a solid hit right under Alexia's breasts, his sword going all the way through to the hilt.

The sight of Alexia dropping to her knees, holding the hilt of the Count's swords in her now blood covered hands, released something in Mike that he didn't know was there, some sort of rage and he reached back with his left hand a fought through the pain and pulled his second sword free. He went to work on the now weaponless Count with a series of attacks that the man couldn't have defended in his prime. To all those left in the room watching, all they saw was a blur of glowing blue and red blood flying everywhere.

The Count dropped to his knees trying to hold all of the many finely slashed cuts he now had all over his body. His fine suit was shredded all over, and blood ran out from every part of the man's body but still he lived. The smile founds it way back to Mike's lips as he thrust both blades into the man's shoulders, the tip of each entered his heart from the different angles at the same time.

He watched as the blades changed from a glowing blue into a bright red as the life drained from the Count's face, as he took his last haggard breath before letting it out. He watched as the man's head bobbed forward limp before he pulled his swords free, causing the Count's lifeless body to fall forward.

A quick kick sent the man's dead body across the floor as he dropped to his knees in front of Alexia who was still somewhat holding herself upright. He could see the blood running out of her wound from all around the sword's blade and he gripped the hilt of the sword.

Just like she did to him on the ship after he got shot with an arrow, his lips found hers, his left hand found the spot just under where the sword's blade was and he planted it there firmly readying himself to pull the sword free of her body.

Alexia couldn't help but lose herself in the kiss, even though she could still feel the blinding pain in her chest. She knew her ribs must have been broken and she could feel the blade sticking out of her back. Everything around her was slowly slipping away until his lips found hers. She knew she wouldn't die from this wound, she knew her body would heal and nothing but a nasty scar would remain, but a part of her wondered whether it was truly worth it after everything that had just taken place.

The Count was dead now, and by Mike's own hands he fell and that would mean together they had broken the main law of the Temple of Legends. An assassin could never kill another assassin unless the temple first agreed upon it and acted on their own accord with their own means, means to which she now knew would be aimed towards Mike and herself and even innocent little Misty. "Wait," She found herself saying as she felt his hand on her chest.

"I have to remove the sword so you can begin to heal."

"I need to ask you my question of the day."

Mike couldn't believe how strong Alexia truly was, even though she had a sword embedded right through her chest she still had the strength in her to want to ask him her question of the day. He relaxed the hold on the hilt of the sword and leaned back slightly so he could look her in the eyes better. It was then he noticed how bloodshot her normally bright blue eyes were. He could see the moisture in them as she struggled to hold back her tears. "Well, what are you waiting for?" he asked as he ran his blood-covered fingers through her blonde hair before he realized that by doing so he left a stain of blood behind.

"Together we killed that man and by doing so, we broke a law that will damn us both once word gets out. We will both be hunted down by assassins and even if Candice seems it to be fit by the Nameless Ones which will lead to a fight the both of us cannot win unless we stick together."

"Is that your question?" Mike asked, confused about where she was going and he felt a chill run up his spine when he thought about what she had just said.

"Do you love me?"

Her question shocked him once again to the core, but he couldn't help but match her desperate look as she stared into his eyes. He wondered if she was able to see past all of the dead body and blood that was him and see right into his very soul. He had only known her for such a short time, over the scale of his long life but he knew she would be by his side for many years to come. Was it love that he was feeling for her at that moment, or was it something else? He knew it wasn't love he shared with Candice but what he now had with Alexia felt so much more real. "Yes I love you, Alexia," He answered as he leaned forwards and kissed her lips again. The taste of blood in his mouth made him realize he had to get the sword out of her right away.

"I love you too."

He gripped the hilt of the sword with his right hand and put his left against her chest. He pulled with the speed only he had and the strength like no other and he still couldn't help but feel sick as he felt the sword slide out of her body. He dropped it to the floor just in time to catch her as she fell forward into his arms, her eyes rolling into the back of her head and he knew she was out cold as soon as her head his shoulder.

Alexia forced her eyes open when she realized she was no longer kneeling in the middle of a blood- covered room. She could feel herself laying on something soft, and when her eyes finally adjusted, she didn't have any clue where she was.

She knew right away she was in a bed, but it was a bed she had never slept in before, and it smelled oddly like dust and something that smelt like a cross between mildew and mold. She propped herself up on her elbows and felt a sudden wave of pain from her chest area. She looked down to see her upper part of her stomach was wrapped all the way to her breasts and she knew right away it was Mike who took care of her wound. Only he could wrap a bandage this nicely from all of his years of doing it to himself.

But still the fact that she didn't know where she was worried her a little bit. That was until she felt something move beside her. The sudden jerk she had from realizing that she wasn't alone in the bed caused another very painful jolt to shoot through her body, and after carefully adjusting the blankets, she found the sleeping form of Misty curled up in a ball right next to her.

She took that as a good sign because she knew in her heart that Mike would never leave the little girl alone unless he felt she was truly safe. She also knew in her heart that he wouldn't have left her alone unless she was safe as well.

She reached out and grabbed the dark blue tank top that was on the bedpost beside her and sat up enough to pull it over her head, the painful part happened when she tried to get her arms through the holes, and after struggling for a few very long and painful moments she finally managed it. She noticed her belt was hanging from the bedpost as well with both of her weapons attached to it and this time she slowly pulled her legs out from under the blankets, and let them hang over the side of the bed, thankful for the fact that at least she had pants on.

She figured she must have been out for a couple of days because she was able to stand up without too much pain and knew her wound had already begun to heal. She had to fight hard though to fight the temptation to remove the bandage and see how bad the injury really was. Some things were meant to be left unseen, she figured, and she began to walk out of the bedroom.

She knew as soon as she walked out into the plain looking wooden hallway, which was perfectly square in shape that she was still in the Count's Manor and she made her way over to the railing in front of her to get a better look at what was going on. She could tell right away that she was on the fourth floor of the house as soon as she looked over, and she could see the blood stained floor far below her but the bodies were all gone.

Every once in while she would see someone pass by under her, but she couldn't make out who it was. She knew none of them were Mike because she could suddenly sense him behind her. She didn't know how long he was standing there watching her or if he had just shown up but either way she smiled to herself as she continued to watch the people below her.

"How are you feeling?"

"Not as bad as I thought I would be for just having a sword ripped out of my chest," Alexia answered, turning to face him. It was then she noticed the look of sadness on his face. "But I am feeling better, and I can already feel my body healing."

"I'm glad that you're doing much better. When I first started applying your bandages, I honestly didn't think the blood would stop coming out of you. It wasn't until the third day that your wound began to heal."

"How many days has it been?"

"Today is the fifth day, so all in all, not a long time."

"Why are we still here?"

"Follow me and I will show you."

So she did just that and followed Mike as he led her towards one of the staircases, which lead them down to the second floor. They made their way around the square and came to another doorway, which she followed him into without missing a step.

She suddenly felt way too exposed as she stood in the middle of the room wearing only her pants and a loose fitting tank top as everyone in the room turned to face them. She was only met with quick looks and smiles as they all went about their own business. Which she quickly realized was unloading the contents to a very large walk in safe, which was built right into one of the walls in the room.

She followed Mike as he walked right into the safe, and she couldn't believe what she saw, all around her was money, not gold coins, just paper money. Even though it wasn't worth as much as gold, the entire safe was still half full with stacks and stacks of it. Some stacks reaching from the floor to the ceiling, which was about ten feet in height. "I can see why you guys stayed around here after all," she said as she grabbed a few of the crisp yellow bills, all clearly marked with 1000$ symbol on them.

"I figured since you three outlaws will be staying on my boat and what not, we would need all the money we can get our hands on, and Mike here found the safe when he did a solid search of the house looking for a safe place for you to rest in peace."

"There in more money in here then I have seen in my entire life," Alexia admitted, turning to face Jason who was now standing beside her.

"It would seem our very dead Count friend was a big fan of collecting it over his life time, which by the amount of money we found in this safe was a very long time."

"Well guess one good thing turned out from us coming here," Alexia said, looking towards Mike now who was leaning against one of the walls of the safe, his eyes almost fully closed. "When was the last time you've gotten any sleep?"

"The night I slept away most of the morning at my beach house."

"You should go and get some sleep," she said, taking his hand in hers. "I am sure these fine men can handle this job without you for a few hours.

"At the rate we are going, I give it a day and half maybe two days before my men have this safe picked clean, so rest up while you can."

"Maybe you guys are right about me getting some rest. It is after all, only a two week trip back to the main land and I am not looking forward to that."

"You plan on going back?" Alexia asked, looking into his eyes for any signs that he was joking.

"Yes I have a lot of gold there as well and I guarantee you that we will need my gold as well as this money here if we stand any chance of disappearing, and I plan on bringing the events of the last few days to Candice and seeing how far up this plot really goes."

She wanted to yell at him and tell him how stupid it all sounded to her, but she knew in her heart that he needed to do this for himself, to prove that the path they walked now would be a long one and they would have to go forth without any help or aid from the temple, something they took for granted until now. She knew he was hurting inside over everything that had changed between them. She knew that he loved the temple and being an assassin. She knew that he was aware that as soon as he killed the Count, who was a fellow assassin, he would never be able to return to his old life.

She led him back to the weird bedroom this time, and it wasn't till she had him alone and sitting on the edge of the bed that she truly saw the pain in his hazel eyes. For the first time since she had met him she didn't see anything behind his eyes. It was like he was lost and very far away from her. "What are you thinking about?" she asked as her hands found a side of his face.

"I think we were set up from the start. I think someone planned all of this to happen and we walked right into it."

"It does seem kind of odd that we were drawn all the way out here with a girl, only to find a long lost assassin that neither of us had ever heard of before."

"I am sure if we had the time and resources, we could search the temples libraries and find the answers we seek about Count Drake, but I fear we are no longer welcomed there. I fear we are no longer welcomed in our own homes anymore."

"Then we will make a new home," Alexia said, pulling him close to her. "The three of us will start fresh, start a new life together."

"You know the cost of this new freedom you talk of, and yet you feel it is the right course of action for us?"

"If Candice wishes to hunt us down then let her, but we both know that she has nothing that can match you."

"Almost nothing, you mean."

"Never once has a leader of the Temple of Legends relied on the Nameless Ones and I believe Candice will be no different," Alexia said, and she could feel him stiffen as she mentions them again. "She would do more harm than good by setting them free."

"Never once has a leader gone up against the likes of me and you, and everything we have. I stole the prized weapons that can kill an assassin, and my armor will keep me protected against almost all other types of weapons. She will fear me as soon as she realizes I am no longer on her side. They will be her only weapon against me."

"They are more of a legend than we are, Mike."

"And yet here we are, alive and real as we sit here and talk about us being legends."

"Let us get some sleep and we will figure everything out in the morning and on the trip back home."

She pulled him into bed with her and within minutes felt his breathing change. She knew he was out cold, fast asleep, and even more so as she watched Misty cuddle right into his side. She smiled as he lay there with her so close to him. She knew then that the world was going to be a very interesting place for the three of them; she knew then that despite everything, she might find a true meaning in her life with this master assassin and multicolor-eyed girl. She too quickly lost herself in their soft breathing, and sleep took her before she even realized it.

Chapter 21

Mike woke up in the middle of the night covered in sweat and he tried his best not to wake either of the sleeping girls as he got out of bed. The boat ride home was turning out to be more of a nightmare then he had though it would be, and the closer they got, the more he found himself having nightmares while he slept.

It had been over a week and half since they left the Count's island, burning his manor to the ground before leaving and still he found little peace in his dreams. He kept thinking about them, the Nameless Ones and now every time he closed his eyes he would see them, or at least what he thought they would look like.

They were in fact like Alexia had said, nothing more than legends that no one had ever seen, but he knew the stories were real about them. He knew it because the stories about him were real as well. They say for every immortal assassin in the world, there lies his or her counterpart, locked away in the deepest pits under the temple itself. The legend says that as an assassin learns and grows so does their counterpart learns and grows the same way and those counterparts are called the Nameless Ones because they truly have no names, but rather are an extension of oneself.

The part about the legends that made most assassins truly fear them was the fact that even after an assassin gives up the immortal life and goes out and dies, the nameless one that was their shadow in so many ways stays alive and locked away. If this was the case, there would be over a thousand of them locked away down there. They say they fight with weapons that can destroy an assassin and in many ways they were just like the weapons that he now possessed himself.

He laughed out loud as he climbed into the hot shower at the fact that he was even thinking about them in the first place. He knew in his heart that they were real or as real as any other living being was, but he didn't believe in the legends that they were as powerful as it said they were to be.

He didn't fear them for his own safety and would in fact welcome a fight with his counterpart if one truly existed, but he feared more for the safety of Alexia and Misty.

He let those thoughts slip out of his mind and he lost himself to the hot water covering his whole body. He leaned his head against the side wall and closed his eyes. He was tried but he knew he wouldn't be able to get any real sleep until they were far away from the mainland. North seemed like the most fitting destination, and he knew the farther they went that way, the safer they would be. Candice's power could only reach so far, and with his money, they would be able to find safe places to hide while being out of her reach.

He was surprised a little bit when he heard the shower door slide up, but he still remained with his head against the wall. However, a slight smile did find its way to his lips, which seemed to be very rare nowadays. He was hoping to make it to the mainland and back out to sea without a fight, but he knew it wouldn't be that easy. He just hoped that Eric and Shelby were out of town so they wouldn't have to get involved in any way.

He didn't even move as Alexia wrapped her arms under his and pulled her naked body against him, but he could tell she was in the same kind of mood that he was just by how stiff her body felt against him. He didn't want to drag her through all of this, and he even thought about taking the full blame and allowing her to go back her old life, a life she didn't seem to want to go back to but a safer life. He also knew that they still had Misty to think about, and he knew the three of them were in this mess together till the end now.

"Do you ever stay in bed for the entire night?"

"It is hard to stay in bed when you can't sleep."

"That's why I'm there, you know, so you can cuddle me so I can keep sleeping peacefully."

"The little one was there for you to cuddle with," Mike said, smiling as she teased him.

"What is really bothering you?"

"Do you think we made a mistake by bringing the girl with us and killing the Count?" Mike asked, finally turning to face Alexia. He was glad to see that her blue eyes finally had some life back in them.

"I think we did what any good hearted person would have done if they had the skills and the power to do so."

188

He thought about her words for a few minutes knowing that she was right. He knew deep down inside there was no way he was going to leave Misty with the Count, but maybe there was a way they could have made it out of there without killing the man. If they left him alive, then their punishment would be far less. They would still become outlaws and be exiled from their homes, but maybe they wouldn't be hunted down afterwards. "I know you are right, I'm just having a hard time getting used to it, that is all," He said, running his finger down her naked and wet chest, until they stop on her new scar.

"I know it isn't a very pretty looking scar."

"Is there really such a thing as a pretty scar?" Mike asked, holding up his right hand which had the two very ugly looking scars on it.

He watched as she reached out and took his hand and pulled it close to her face before giving it a gentle kiss right on the palm, and again he found himself smiling. He knew that in just over two weeks' time they would be on the run, and maybe then he would be able to finally relax and get some rest.

There shower seemed to last forever, and finally he started to feel cooler water begin to hit his back before he finally reached behind him and turned the water off. He didn't want to get out of the safety of the shower but he knew he had to, knew he couldn't keep hiding from his life, his new life as an outlaw. He watched her get out of the shower first, and a part of him felt sad when she started to cover herself up with the large thick towel. He was really getting used to having this beautiful, mostly naked girl around him all the time. His feelings for her were changing and growing every day, and even though he wasn't sure what that meant, he knew it was a good thing.

She smiled at him as she tossed one of the towels his way and he caught it with ease. He began to dry himself off, the whole time he kept his eyes on her. Her towel covered all of the important areas but the wet skin that was still showing kept his eyes very much interested. He walked towards her and his lips found hers as he pushed her gently against the counter behind where she was standing. His hands on both side of her keeping her locked in place, not that she was trying to go anywhere.

He lifted her up with ease, so she was now sitting on the counter, and she wrapped her legs around him and pulled him closer. They both lost track of time, and for once neither of them thought about the future, but instead just focused on each other. He could feel her kissing him more deeply now, more intimate and he couldn't help but kiss her back. At that moment, there was nothing else in the world but her and that kiss. That was until they both heard a slight knock on the bathroom door, which ended their very intimate kiss.

He pulled away from her and they both quickly got dressed even thought they were both still mostly wet, and he pulled open the locked bathroom door to find Misty standing there. He could tell right away that she wasn't fully awake yet by the way she half walked, half stumbled towards him. He leaned down and picked her up in his arms, as she almost immediately placed her head on his shoulders. He could feel her soft breaths on the side of his neck.

He carried her out of the bathroom and he couldn't help but notice the smile Alexia had on her face. He knew right away she was smiling at him because of how he was with Misty and because of their very passionate kiss they had just shared. He wondered if they would ever have a night alone so they could truly begin to explore each other's bodies. "Are you thirsty?" he asked Misty as he sat her down on the end of the bed and watched her nod at him as she struggled to sit up right.

He could tell right away that the ship would need to stock up on full supplies when they were on the main land, something that could take an hour or so to do but would be fully necessary if they planned on making it to the far north without starving to death. He reached in and pulled out a can of pop and quickly replaced it when he noticed Alexia rolling her eyes at him. He then pulled out a bottle of water instead.

He turned around to see his two girls, so to speak, sitting on the edge of the bed. Alexia was wearing flannel pajama pants and a long sleeved shirt. Misty was wearing almost a matching outfit, and he smiled at the sight. What an odd group they made. He opened the bottle of water, handed it to her, and she began drinking it right away. Over half of it was gone before she handed it back to him, and he watched her crawl into Alexia arms this time, and soon he could tell she was fast asleep again.

"Interesting girl we have here," he said, while quickly changing into a pair of jeans and sweater figuring he wouldn't be getting any more sleep that night.

"I think she gets it all from you."

"She is almost too big to get away with that," Mike said, laughing as he watched Misty curled up in Alexia arms.

190

"Well you can be the one to tell her that then."

"The two of you look cute together, so who am I to question that."

"I take it you are going somewhere?"

"I was planning on going for a walk. Did you want to come?" Mike asked as he grabbed his weapons belt.

"I could so go for a nice cold walk after someone found it necessary to get me all hot and bothered after our shower. Just let me get her back into bed and find my jacket."

He watched as she went about brining Misty back to the couch-bed, a bed that was hers even though she spent more time sleeping with them then by herself, but he figured the girl had been through a long rough time, and who was he to complain too much. He watched Alexia pull a thick fur lined jacket over top of her long sleeved shirt. She kissed him one more time before they headed out of the room.

The night air was crisp and even he felt a slight chill as he walked out onto the exposed deck. Even in the early morning before the sun had even shown its face, he could see the snowflakes falling towards them from the sky, a sign that they were getting closer and closer to the mainland.

That thought sent another chill up his spine, but he didn't let it worry him. How could he, after all. For the first time in his life he felt truly happy, a hundred percent confused but happy. As they reached the front of the ship, Alexia managed to get in front of him and he wrapped his arms around her shoulders pulling her close to him. He couldn't help but wrinkle his nose as her hair brushed against his face in the cold chilled air.

"The two of you are going to get sicker than a dog if you keep coming out into this cold with your hair all wet."

"We would have to be able to get sick in the first place in order for that to affect us," Mike said as he turned to face Jason as he approached them.

"We are making good time, and I figure we will reach the main land in about five days."

"Once we are there, we will need to stock up fully on winter gear and supplies. As well as send most of the men back and forth from my place to the ship carrying as much of my gold as then can in the time we are docked."

"Don't you worry about it boy, my men and I will clean your house dry of your gold and whatever else we see laying around, which could be of value."

"I want to dock just after the sun goes down. It will give you and the men a chance to get from the docks to my house with out to many people noticing. If we dock at the pier where you picked us up, that will be even better since no one uses it much anymore."

"How long will the three of you need on land before we have to leave again?"

"I figure we can buy you five maybe six hours to get everything done," Mike said as he ran his cold hand under Alexia's jacket and shirt causing her to jump at his side.

"More than enough time to clean your house up and resupply I would think."

"Will you be in need of an armed escort through the city to the temple?"

"No I have a way to get through town unnoticed. Just focus on the gold and the supplies and I will handle everything else."

"Then it should all go by without any problems."

"If you see us running, you know it's time to go," Mike said, smiling again as he tried to joke around with his friends.

"I am sure everything will be just fine with us."

"I believe Alexia is right as well, Mike. So. Maybe you shouldn't worry so much about it. Anyway I have captain stuff to do now, so take care you two."

Mike watched his old captain friend walk away, and again he felt guilty asking the man to get involved with all of his problems, to risk his life for him. He knew Jason would follow him anywhere he wished to go, but he didn't feel right forcing him and his crew into exile with them. He could feel Alexia lean back into him, and again he pulled her close. They both stood there for a very long time watching the sun slowly rise up into the sky.

Eric couldn't help but curse the snow as it fell harder than he had ever seen before. He was watching it fall from the window of the small room he was currently staying at. He couldn't remember the name of the inn or if it even had one, then again, he wasn't even sure of the name of the town he was in. He was only here because he was helping Candice with her stack of unfinished contracts, and he was kicking himself now as he watched the snow falling outside the house.

The job was very simple, and he completed it without even trying. He now held the item to which he needed to return home with, but he couldn't bring himself to start that journey home in the snow. At this rate, it would take him about five days before they even made it there. He turned to face his bed and he couldn't help but slightly stare at Shelby's naked body as she slept above the covers. She was lying on her stomach and he really wanted to open the window and grab a handful of snow and throw it at her. His eyes found the raging fire next as it burned away in the fireplace, which was centered in the middle of their room, and even though it was a small inn, it had amazingly nice rooms in it.

So, he stood there starring out the window, dressed fully in his bulky silver and blue armor with his crystal clear sword on his hip and his shield on his back. He also wore a bulky wolf-lined fur cloak to help stay warm in this winter wonder land he currently found himself in. He knew they needed to head out but he couldn't bring himself to take that first step out into the snowfall.

"Look at you all dressed up with nowhere to go," Shelby stated.

"I am thinking the snow isn't going to pass, and it would be best to get on the move before we get trapped in this little backwoods town. Plus, I want to leave before someone realizes what it is we have taken from them," Eric said, turning to face Shelby once again. He couldn't help but stare even more as he watched her slowly get dressed.

"This is true. I would hate for the town folks to come after us with their sticks and little rocks. One of us might get injured."

"You always know how to look on the bright side don't you."

"Is something bothering you?"

"Something just doesn't seem right. Something terrible has happened and I have a bad feeling about it," Eric said, and he saw that Shelby was about to say something but instead grabbed her mouth and ran off towards the bathroom.

He followed her and knelt down beside her as she began to throw up. He took off one of his bulky gloves and gently pulled her hair back. This was the third morning in a row that she had done this, and they were both starting to think that something was wrong. Neither of them said anything though, and when she finished getting sick, he pulled her towards him. He knew she couldn't have felt overly comfortable against his bulky armor but she didn't seem to complain at all. "Maybe it is best we get on the road today," He said, kissing her gently on the forehead.

"Maybe you're right."

Candice smiled as she walked around the courtyard in the quickly falling snow. She couldn't help but smile even harder when her husband came to join her, something that seemed to be happening more and more as of late.

The snow was falling so fast that her footprints didn't last long before being covered in fresh snow. She was wearing her normal people clothes today, and still she couldn't help but feel a chill, even with a fur jacket and sweater on, thick snow pants, and fur and leather boots she could still feel it.

She felt so out of place without her weapons on, but she figured she wouldn't need them out here this day. She looked around and saw seven of her fellow assassins also playing around in the snow and she knew she was perfectly safe. Kevin however still felt the need to bring his sword along and even though it was snowing out, he still wore a fancy three button dark grey suit with dress shoes on, shoes she knew would be ruined by the time they made it inside but he seemed happy for a change so she left it at that.

She found her way to one of the picnic tables. That were set around the courtyard and she quickly wiped off the snow before taking a seat. She began watching the others play around in the snow. Some of them made snowmen, and other were sparring, but she couldn't help but smile at it all. No matter how old they all got, none of them seemed to lose the joy of life, well almost none of them as she thought about Mike and his downward spiral since the two of them broke up.

She couldn't help but laugh as Kevin sat at the picnic table beside her, clearly risking the safety of his fine dress pants on the wet and snow cover seat. She noticed he didn't even take the time to wipe away the new snow that had fallen on it. She felt him wrap his arm around her and she didn't even fight it as he pulled her close to his side.

"So how many of them do you think you could take in a fight?"

"Right now not very many since I have no weapons, and I'm not wearing my armor."

"But what if you did have all of that?"

"Maybe four of them, but if Eric and Shelby where here I bet I would only be able to take on one," Candice said, carefully avoiding Mike's name.

"If Mike was here, how many of them do you think he could take?"

"All of them."

"What about if Eric and Shelby were here, do you think he could still take them all?"

"I believe he could take them all. Yes. But I also don't think he would ever go up against Eric or Shelby, nor do I think they would go up against him."

"Not even if you ordered them too?"

"Honestly, no I don't think even then," Candice said, turning to face Kevin to see that he still had a smile on his face, and that he was clearly only asking the questions because he was curious. "The three of them have fused a bond over the years, and I don't think it could ever be broken, no matter what happens."

"Does that not worry you?"

"Not at all. I trust all three of them to do what is right, and I believe by doing this they have all grown into great people, overconfident but great."

"Do you think I could take any of them in a fight?"

Candice didn't know how to answer his question without hurting his feeling, but he too must have already known the answer. He was, after all, just a mortal man and these were immortal assassins. "I believe you are talented with your swordsmanship, but even if you scored a hundred fatal hits you would not kill any of them, where as they would only need to score one on you."

The two of them sat in silence then, but she knew she didn't hurt his feeling and that he understood where she was coming from with her answer. She still couldn't help but wonder if her husband would ever be as rash as to challenge one of the assassins and if he did, then she would have no choice but to let the fight happen. She also knew that if that day ever came, it would most likely be with Mike, and that match truly would not be one for the record books.

"Have you heard any word from them?"

"Yes, it turns out they found the item and are in the middle of returning it to the owner, but he didn't mention who that was. He said he would be home in a month's time to give a full report on the mission."

"I never doubted his skills once."

"You doubt his skills every day, but I don't blame you at all. You had a lot riding on this mission, and I am glad it is finally behind us."

"So what are your plans for tonight and please don't say working?"

"Tonight I cancelled all work so people can enjoy the day in the snow. So, as far as I know, I am free all night."

"Then I look forward to spending the evening with you for a change. Maybe we can start with a dinner?"

"A dinner sounds perfect," Candice said, leaning a little closer towards her husband.

"God, I am really starting to hate the snow," Shelby said as she continued to walk along the road, which would lead them home.

"See it is a good thing that we didn't stay at the inn or else we could have been trapped there for months."

She agreed with Eric on the fact that they had to leave, but she wasn't really into this walking home in snow as deep as her ankles and quickly getting deeper. She was wearing her winter gear now and even with the thick fur jacket and pants and many layers under each of those, she still felt a chill creep up her spine every once in a while.

She knew why she was getting sick every morning and she knew that Eric knew it as well, but neither of them had brought it up yet. Neither of them had the courage to admit it out loud. Clearly she was pregnant and clearly this was her having morning sickness, something she was starting to get very annoyed about. The part that worried her the most was that as far as she knew, she wasn't able to get pregnant and yet here she was, very much still an immortal and very much with a child growing inside of her.

She tested the theory earlier that morning when she cut her arm slightly and watched as it healed right away. So she needed answers and she needed them now.

The two of them had already been walking for most of the day and she knew it would be another two days before they would arrive at home and as far as she could tell in the dead of night at the pace they were making. They covered at lot of ground since they left the inn. Unfortunately, the snow kept falling, granted not as badly as it was earlier, but it was still there none the less. "Are you not cold in your armor?" she asked, knowing that Eric's armor was both thick and bulky, but didn't offer much insulation.

"I'm fine, I promise, and it isn't that cold really."

"You are a bad liar."

"Thank you and I love you too."

"First thing I am doing once we get home is stripping naked and having the world's longest shower," Shelby said, facing Eric who was matching her steps beside her. His cheeks were now a bright pink color because of the soft winter breeze. "I don't expect you to join me since you are all nice and warm and all."

"You have always been the world's biggest tease."

"Isn't that the reason why you love me?"

"That is one of the reasons but also for so many more."

"We will be home before we know it, and this time we are going to take a break from traveling around and finally get some rest."

"At least nine months' worth of rest would be my guess."

"You honestly don't think I can be pregnant, do you?" Shelby asked, placing both of her hands over her stomach.

"I have lived this life long enough to know that anything can be possible, and that you and I will make it through anything together."

"Okay, then first thing we are going to do is have a very long and very hot shower. Then, I am going to Candice and try to figure this whole thing out."

"If only Mike was back in town."

"You think Mike would have answers for us about this?" Shelby asked, turning to see a smile on Eric's face, and she didn't fully understand his statement.

"No I think he would be just as clueless as we are on the subject, but he would be good at teasing us to get our minds off of everything, and I look forward to hearing about the adventures he and Alexia got themselves into."

"It would be nice to see him happy for a change because depression doesn't really suit him well."

The two of them walked the rest of the day side by side in the deep snow, each lost in their own thoughts of the future and everything it had in store for them. She knew she had to be pregnant no matter if it was impossible or not, she could just tell. She too hoped that Mike was returning in a far better place than when he had left. She knew he would always be reckless but if he found love then maybe that would be enough to get him to slow down a little in life. Maybe one day he would have a baby of his own and forget all about the assassin life. Maybe.

Chapter 22

Mike could see the outline of the dock as it grew closer and closer to the ship. He had a million different things going through his mind at that very moment, none of them seemed to come with a happy ending for them though, and that made his heart sink even lower in his chest. He truly wanted to just turn around and run, but he knew he had to figure this whole thing out, and get behind who was really involved with setting him up.

He knew that this was going to be one of the more challenging things for him to do in his life, but he also couldn't help but feel whole again. His life felt like nothing for so many years after he broke up with Candice, and he fell into a sadness he didn't think he would get out of once she got engaged to Kevin. But things were different now. He wasn't feeling the weight of that sadness as much anymore. Now he was feeling something else inside of him.

His serious look changed as he felt Alexia wrap her arm around his waist and he found his arm going around her shoulders without even thinking about it, as if that is where his arm was truly meant to be all of his life. He turned slightly to face her and even in the dead of night he could see the bright blue of her eyes glowing with life, he could also see the fear mixed in as well but he could also tell that she was trying her best to hide it from him.

The snow was still coming down and he could see the little white flakes land softly onto her blonde hair and remain there. He wanted to run his fingers through her hair, wanted to say so many things to her at that very moment, but he couldn't do any of it. He just pulled her closer to him, their bodies side by side and he couldn't help but wonder if they were meant to be here this cold winters day.

"The crew is ready, they know their jobs, and will start off right away once we are tied to the dock." Jason pointed out as he walked back towards the assassins.

"Thank you my friend, and like I said, we should be able to give you guys an easy five hours to get everything done," Mike said, turning to face the captain.

"I will leave two people on the ship to keep it running in case we need a quick getaway."

"I am hoping to avoid any bloodshed today."

"As are we all, but you can never be too careful when dealing with the temple and its assassins."

Misty was at their side as if she too could sense the coming struggle of power which was about to happen, he wanted to leave her behind on the ship where she would be safe but at the same time she was the reason why all of this was happening and he figured if she came with them maybe he would finally learn some real answers.

The three of them were on the dock and heading towards one of the snow covered side-streets within minutes of docking, and Mike couldn't help but watch almost all of the crew head off in the direction of his house as Jason and two other headed deeper into town for the supplies. He felt like he should be with the crew at his house helping them with the gold, but he knew his place was in the temple and so that was where he needed to go. Plus, he knew the crew would remain hidden in the dead of night, and he told them about the secret door at the back of his cottage that would lead them into the gold filled cellar below.

He led the two girls along one of the side streets before heading down an abandoned alleyway, which led them straight into the tree line of the older part of the forest around the city. They made their way slowly through the trees and were easily hidden by the amount of snow covering them, more snow then he had ever seen before. He came to a fair sized boulder, which looked like it could easily weigh five or six hundred pounds. He pushed it off the side like it was nothing, which it was, mostly nothing, since he made it so many years ago out of plastic and small weights. Underneath it was a hole in the ground with a ladder leading downwards.

"What is this?"

"It is the entrance to a tunnel, which will lead us right into the middle of the temple," Mike said as he began to climb down the dark tunnel.

He pulled out one of his blue glowing swords and it lit the small passageway up without a problem. The three of them made their way along it in silence, even though he could feel Alexia's question gaze upon the back of his neck. He knew she would figure out the reason for this tunnel soon enough.

The tunnel was straight and they covered ground a lot quicker down there than they would have above ground. He knew this would be the safer way for them to travel without being seen with Misty. "Is something bothering you?" he asked, finally turning to face Alexia, who was holding Misty's hand. Both of the girls turned to face him.

"No I am just trying to keep myself calm that's all. I have never done well with tight underground spaces."

"We will be out of this tunnel in a few minutes and inside the middle of the temple. We will still be enclosed but in a much wider space."

And it was true enough because soon they walked out of their current tunnel and right into the main foundation of the temple itself. He watched as Alexia turned in a full circle to take it all in, much the same way that he did the first time he discovered this place. They now stood in a dome like area, which would have been perfectly black if it wasn't for his blue glowing sword. There was only three ways out of this room: back the way they came, up the ladder in the middle of the room, or down the ladder in the middle of the room.

"Where do they go?"

"The one going up will take us to a secret door, which will lead us to Candice's personal bed chambers where I am hoping to find her," Mike said, and he couldn't help but notice the sour look appeared on Alexia's face before disappearing a moment later. "And the lower ladder will lead you down into the basement and whatever hell lies within."

"You have never gone down there before?"

"I have been tempted many times just too see if the legends are true, but I believe some things should be left a secret, and whatever lies below us is one of those things."

"Whatever it is we are about to do now we do it together."

Before Mike could say anything, her lips found his and he returned the kiss right away. It only lasted for a second or two before she pulled away with a smile on her face. He couldn't help but laugh when he saw the look on Misty's face as she silently made fun of them for kissing. He picked her up into his arms and she wrapped her arms around his neck. He quickly began climbing the ladder leading up hundreds of feet to the secret door he knew would be awaiting them at the top of it.

"Can we go for a walk along the boardwalk for a bit before we head home?" Eric asked as they entered the main gate leading into town. "I just need some more fresh air I think."

"I am in no hurry to return home so if you want to walk around for a while I am fine with it."

That was one of the many reasons why he loved Shelby, even if she was truly exhausted and wanted to head home right away, she would keep walking beside him if he needed more time alone with her. This was something he knew he wouldn't have, once they returned home. Plus, he wasn't quite sure if he was ready to figure out if she was truly pregnant or not, and if she was, what that would mean for their lives.

"What is on your mind?"

"I am just worried about Mike that is all. Never has he gone so long without sending word to us or even checking in."

"I'm sure he's fine. From what we have both been told about the mission he is on, it could take him months to complete and I am sure when he can, he will get word to us."

"I think we should tell him before we tell anyone else and see how he reacts," Eric said as he turned to face a smiling Shelby.

"We don't even know if there is anything to really tell yet."

He grabbed her then and quickly pulled her towards him, well as close to him as he could since he was still wearing his bulky armor, and he leaned down and kissed her. She stepped on her toes to raise herself up to his lips, and they both lost themselves in that very kiss, so much so that they didn't even notice the three hooded figures running past them, heading into one of the main shops which was always open.

Mike slowly pushed the secret door open and poked his head out. He wanted to make sure it was all clear before he walked out onto the small ledge where he jumped the two-foot gap onto Candice's balcony. He could tell by the lack of footprints in the fresh snow on the balcony that no one had been out on it for at least an hour or so. He placed Misty back onto the ground. He watched as Alexia made the jump as well and came to land right beside him. Neither of them made the slightest of noise.

He placed his hand on the handle of the sliding glass door, which would lead him into the main chambers, a place he used to enter all the time using this secret path. He looked at Alexia one last time before slipping into the unlock door, leaving the door open behind him. He knew Alexia would be waiting close by, listening for her cue to enter with Misty.

The room was mostly dark besides the two candles burning on each end table next to the king sized bed, a bed that currently had two bodies in it, very much awake and very much in the middle of kissing very intimately. He felt his stomach turn at the sight of his former lover in the mist of kissing her new husband very passionately and he had to hold himself back from killing the man that very moment. He turned to see Alexia still standing on the balcony and she gave him a slight shrug, most likely wondering why he was hesitating because she couldn't see the bed from her.

Mike found his way to one of the chairs a few feet from the bed, and he was quite disappointed that the leader of the Temple of Legends would leave herself so exposed and unaware of the fact that someone had so easily walked into her room. "I hope I'm not interrupting anything, but I have returned from my mission and I figured I would come check in," he said, while taking a seat as he watched the pair scramble around in the bed, trying to keep their mostly naked bodies from revealing anything.

He couldn't help but laugh as he watches the two of them try their best to get dressed as quickly as possible and he smiled even more so when Kevin fixed him with the deadliest of looks. He finally had his pants on as he climbed out of bed and grabbed his sword from it harness and began taking a few steps closer to him.

"Kevin, enough already, and sit your ass back down on the bed before he is forced to kill you if you make a move against him."

"He comes into our room unannounced and in the middle of the night, and now you're telling me you are not going to do anything about it."

"I am going to get to the bottom of it and quickly and he will be punished for his actions tonight, I can promise you that much."

"If you two are done talking, I would like to say what I came here to say and be done with it," Mike said, looking at the pair once again, no emotions at all showing on his face this time, even as he looked at Candice wearing nothing more than a very revealing night robe.

"Why couldn't this wait until the morning, Mike?"

"Because you set me up to fail and I want to know why?"

"What are you talking about?"

"You sent me to find an item, this item," Mike said, pointing towards the sliding door as Alexia and Misty walked into the room.

He watched as Candice looked at both girls with surprise, but noticed that Kevin was looking right at the girl, as if he knew who she was.

"Why did you bring her here and not back to Count Drake where she belongs?"

"Kevin, what does the Count have to do with this little girl?" Candace asked.

"So you honestly had no clue about the girl?" Mike asked, turning to face Candice who was once again staring at Misty.

"She belongs with the Count so why did you bring her here instead?" Kevin asked.

"What do you know about all of this, Kevin?" Candice asked. As she looked back and forth from the little girl in her room and Kevin.

"I brought her here because Count Drake is dead," Mike said, which shut them both up as they turned to face him.

Candice noticed his armor right away but she couldn't bring herself to believe it was the same armor she had locked away all those years ago, and it wasn't until Mike said that Count Drake was dead that she noticed the hilts of the two swords strapped to his back, hilts she figured would lead to two blue glowing blades. "Did you kill him, Mike?" she asked, watching him for any sigh of emotions.

"Yes," was all he offered for an answer and before she could say anything in return, Kevin launched himself at him with his sword drawn and ready, but Mike didn't even make a move to stop him, didn't even take his eyes of hers. He didn't have to, though, because it was Alexia who grabbed Kevin's exposed arm with speed he couldn't have countered and it sent him flying, head first, into the wall, leaving him very still on the floor.

Candace found her hands reaching for her axes as her anger began to flare inside of her at the sight of her husband being handled in such a way, even if he had it coming.

"I wouldn't do that if I were you," Mike said as he watched Candice go for her weapons.

"I am the leader of the Temple of Legends, and you think you can give me orders in my own room."

"Call for help if you wish, but I warn you now if anyone tries to harm us as we leave, I will kill them."

"Why did you come here, Mike?"

"I needed to know how deep this scandal went. I want you to know I only killed him because he planned to do horrible things to this little girl, planned to use her as a play thing until she became pregnant and offered him a child and then he was planning on killing her," Mike said, and this time he watched all of the anger wash away from Candice's face as she regarded the little girl once again. "Promise me you knew nothing about this, and I will leave now in peace with the girl and you will never see or hear of me again."

"I promise you that I would have never accepted this contract if I knew it involved a little girl and not some foolish item."

"That is all I needed to know," Mike said, getting up from the chair. "You might want to get him some medical aid."

"You are forgetting something very important though, Mike."

"And what is that, Candice?"

"You killed one of us, and I cannot let that go unpunished."

"You would call that sick and twisted person one of us?"

"If your blades turned red when you killed him, then he was still one of us."

"Then I will leave the next move in your hands, but I am warning you to choose carefully the path you wish to go down."

"Hand over your weapons and allow yourself and Alexia to be arrested and face the penalty of killing an assassin."

"You want to take our lives because we took his life?" Mike asked, turning to face Candice once again, this time she had both of her axes in hand.

"If you two leave now with that little girl, I will label you both outcasts and you will be hunted down by the full might of the temple, and trust me, I will supply them all with weapons that will kill the both of you."

"I want you to listen to what I have to say. Listen and understand that every word I am about to say is the truth," Mike said, drawing one of his blue glowing daggers from his belt. "If you send anyone after us, I will send their dead bodies back to you, everything single one of them and their deaths will be on your hands, not mine. You and I both know there are none who will freely come against me once you tell them who they are hunting. Their fear will be the weakness I need to win every time. So, hunt me if you must, but know you will never find me and know in your heart that if you push too hard, I will return and find you. Do you truly believe you can stop me from killing you?"

He watched her come back to life with both rage and fear. He could see it written all over her face as he turned his back on her, and the three of them began heading out of the room, back onto the balcony. He sensed the attack coming before he made the door, but he knew she was attacking out of anger and that she would be sloppy in doing so. He turned around in a flash and caught both of her arms in mid- swing, the edges of her axes resting on his black armor. He looked her in the eyes and all he saw was regret. She knew she had just made a mistake, one that could likely cost her life.

He smiled at her then as he brought his knee up into her fully exposed stomach. The force of the blow caused the air to shoot out from her lungs. He placed her gently to the floor, close to where her husband was and again she tried to rise, this time though he landed an attack to the side of her head with the hilt of his dagger, sending her falling sideways. He felt sick to his stomach but he knew this was a much better way to leave her. He knew he couldn't kill her, but they needed time to get away.

"Remember my words and know that they are true." He sighed as he ran out of the room, and onto the balcony where the three of them made their quick escape through the secret door.

Candice could hear someone talking to her before she was able to force her eyes open. She couldn't make out the words he was saying, but she knew it was Kevin. It was that thought that made her wonder how hard Mike had hit her if Kevin came to before she did. She opened her eyes to find her room was full of assassins and she quickly scanned the group of ten to realize that Eric or Shelby weren't among them. She needed them more now than ever, but she knew they were out of town on a mission.

"Where are they?"

"They were gone when I came to, and we found you on the ground. I feared you were dead."

"I don't think he would have ever thought about killing me," Candice said as she sat up or tried her best to with the help of her husband, she didn't realize Mike could hit that hard.

"You have to send people after them."

"I can't send anyone after him right now," Candice said as she looked at the fear on all of the assassin's faces. None of them wanted to go after Mike. "He has four weapons that will give him the edge over them. He will kill them all before they could even wound him."

"So we are to do nothing then?"

"I didn't say that, did I?"

"I don't understand."

"Send word to the basement to release the Nameless Ones," Candice said, and every single person in the room let out sounds of fear. "There is one down there who knows Mike the best, and he will find him before he can get away and if he fails, then the rest will finish the job."

"How many do you want to release, my lady?"

"All of them."

Eric and Shelby found their way into the more deserted part of the boardwalk, which very few people used nowadays but was their normal meeting area whenever they hung out with Mike. He was always trying his best to stay away from the rest of the world. The two walked side by side, hand in hand, with the ocean to the right of them and the thick tree line to the left. The snow was still falling and Eric knew he would have to head home and soon to change into something warming, but something inside of him told him to keep walking. "Do they really taste good?" he asked as he turned to face Shelby who had her tongue out catching the falling snowflakes on it."

"I could so go for a nice juicy burger right now but they will do."

"You have to be the oddest person I know."

"No, the oddest person we know is Mike, but I am the cutest person you know."

"Oh I knew it was something along those lines," Eric said, making them both laugh.

"I don't think I have ever seen it snow this much before."

"I am starting to think it might be a bad sign."

"Having another of your bad feelings again, are we?"

"Are you telling me you don't sense something is off tonight, that something just doesn't feel right?"

"You are just worried about the fact that I am pregnant and we have no real way to explain as to how it happened."

"You are most likely right," Eric said, even though he couldn't help but feel like something was very wrong.

"What are you truly thinking about, my love?"

"Isn't that Mike's ship?" Eric said, pointing towards the big ship docked across the road from them.

"Is that Mike and Alexia?"

Eric followed Shelby's pointing finger towards the three figures coming out of the back ally, and heading towards the ship. He noticed Mike and Alexia right away, but had no clue as to why they were running towards his ship with a little girl but something didn't feel right to him. He was about to call out to his friend when an alarm sounded so loudly all around them, coming from the temple itself. He had never heard the alarm before, but it brought true fear to his heart. He knew it was the alarm to clear the streets and head inside because they were let free, the Nameless Ones were let free.

"What have you done, my friend?" he said to himself as he watched Mike stop mid-step in the middle of the dock drawing out two glowing blue swords.

It was then he noticed the ground under his feet slightly shake. It was then he noticed the form moving towards his friend in the dead of the night. A form of a monster of a man, easily ten feet in height and well over four hundred pounds, most of which Eric guessed was pure muscle. The form paid him no attention as he began running past him to get to Mike, a mistake it should not have made.

He placed his silver helmet on his head and rushed forward as fast as he could. He barreled into the side of the monster of a man with a very rough tackle. He could barely get his arms all the way around its massive body and even at his six and half foot tall height, the thing still looked down at him. The two of them slammed into the snow covered ground and he was still holding onto it when he pushed the little button on his left glove, which triggered the hundreds of hidden spikes to shoot out of his silver armor, each one finding it marks in the thing's body.

Chapter 23

Mike almost tripped mid-step when he heard the alarm go off, something he had never done before, but that sound was something he thought he would never hear because it was a sound that signaled the start of a war.

He turned around to face the single road that led to the boardwalk and he almost didn't believe his own eyes at what he saw fast approaching them. It was a person but it wasn't like anything he had ever seen before. It stood about ten-feet in height, and he didn't even want to try to guess its weight. "Take her and get to the boat," he shouted, turning slightly to see Alexia and Misty, who were also watching the thing approach.

"I won't leave you here to fight that thing alone."

"I'll be right behind you, I promise. If I don't slow that thing down, none of us will be getting out of this mess alive and that would mean everything we have done up to this point to save Misty would have been a waste," Mike said, turning to kiss Misty on the forehead and Alexia on the lips before turning back to face the monster in front of him. He could hear to two girls running behind him and he reached up and drew out both of his swords. This thing was too big for him to use his daggers. The swords lit the area around him with a faint blue glow, and he found himself smile as he took a step forward to meet this monster of a thing head one.

But someone beat him to the punch as he watched a form wearing bulky silver and blue armor come out of nowhere and tackle the thing right to the ground. A second later, he watched as a hundred little spikes shot out of the armor, each one finding its mark on the thing. He couldn't help but be thankful that his friend had showed up when he did, but at the same time he couldn't afford for anyone to find out he had helped in this fight.

He watched as the thing forced its way back onto its feet and he couldn't help but notice how small Eric seemed standing in front of it, even in his bulky armor. It moved with a speed that Mike thought he was the only one who had, and swatted Eric aside like he was nothing. He watched as his friend went flying backwards until he came to land just inside the tree line with a crash. The thing was once again fast approaching him and he knew it was time to fight.

He began running towards the thing just as the thing began running towards him, he watched the beast pull out two giant swords from its own back harness and each of them looked like it was almost as long as he was tall, again he found himself smiling when an arrow shot right into the things neck causing it to slightly lose it momentum and giving him the chance he needed to get the first real strike in.

He dropped to his knees and the speed of his run allowed him to slide right in between the giant's legs. Just as he reached the other side, he spun as quickly as he could, both blades of his swords slashing across the back of both of the things knees. He was back on his feet as the thing dropped to the ground onto its knees, and he began running back towards it, hoping to score a few more quick slashes.

He was almost at the back of the thing's neck, and he had his right sword coming down at a perfect arch as his left came upwards and he smiled at the thought of scoring two more perfect strikes. That was until the things turned around with great speed and reached forward, accepting both of his slashes like they were nothing, and it reach out and grabbed him by the neck. He suddenly felt his feet lifting from the snow covered ground and he tried his best to keep a solid grip on the hilts of his swords as the thing gripped his neck even tighter. He looked into its cold white eyes for the first time and he didn't see anything behind them. This thing was nothing more than a tool for killing and it seemed to be living up to it name so far.

He kicked out with both his feet with all of his might and still the thing held him off the ground by his neck. He even brought both hilts of his swords flying towards each side of its head, and still it didn't let up its grip. He could feel his lungs trying hard to get air, and he didn't know how long he could last before he blacked out.

Two more arrows to the side of its chest finally made it let up a little, and then it took a third to the arm, which was holding him off the ground, and he felt its grip loosen. He planted both of his feet on its chest and pushed backwards, launching himself a few feet in the air. He landed in a roll coming back up to his own two feet, swords glowing in front of him. He watched the thing smile at him as it again began to approach him and again was cut off by a flying tackle of bulky silver armor. This time Eric came to a stop right beside him, and he drew his mighty shield from his back, pulling free his crystal clear sword.

"You two just out for a friendly walk or something?" Mike asked as he quickly turned to see Shelby take a few steps behind them, bow already aimed at the things chest.

"I knew you two have been fighting a lot lately, but what did you do this time to get her to release him," Eric asked.

"Long story and I would love to fill you in once it's dead or we have made it to my boat."

"Are we on the run now?"

"I am on the run along with Alexia, but I beg you and Shelby to return home once this is done and live out your life. I don't want you caught up in this."

Mike didn't have time to hear Eric's answer before the thing charged in again, but this time it was three against one and these three spent a lot of time training and fighting together. Eric moved in front of it at the very last second and stopped the creature's rushing attack with a single shield bash. This sent the both of them backwards slightly, giving him the perfect angle to swing around to the right and score two more slashes along the things leg, this time causing it once again to stagger but not fall. Just as it was about to swing its own right sword towards Eric, it caught two more arrows in the shoulder causing it to howl out in pain and drop one of its massive swords.

He moved in again from behind as Eric lunched another shield bash this time catching the thing on its right arm as Eric swung out his sword catching it squarely on the left arm, leaving a wicked gash on its forearm. Once regaining its composure, the thing managed to get one foot out and scored a solid kick to Eric's midsection, once again sending the man flying slightly backwards, leaving a dent in his bulky breastplate.

Mike was there in a second both of his swords glowing bright in his hands as he slashed out over and over again at the creature's exposed back. He watched as splashes of blood flew through the air all around him as he hacked and slashed but again the thing turned to face him. This time he was ready, and he jumped backwards, nearly missing a nasty left hook.

Shelby kept reaching back and grabbing arrow after arrow making sure every shot counted, but quickly realizing that she would be fresh out of arrows before this thing was dead. She knew about the legends of the

Nameless Ones, but she didn't believe any of them till now.

She couldn't help but focus on the dance Mike was doing as he moved and wielded both of his glowing swords with ease, never missing a step and always scoring a solid hit on the thing, but even his attacks didn't seem to slow it down.

She noticed Eric slowly getting back to his feet and she watched him run his right hand along the new dent in his bulky suit of armor, armor she knew was made to be indestructible. She knew they were all in trouble if this thing scored any kind of attack with it remaining sword, but she didn't want to think about that as she watched Eric rush right back into the fight, his crystal sword gleaming in the moonlight.

She used the last of her five arrows each of them finding their mark on the thing before she dropped her bow to the ground and pulled free her sword from its harness. She took a step forward to join in the fight like she had done a thousand times before beside the man she loved and Mike, but she suddenly pulled up short, her left hand finding its way to her stomach. She knew right away she couldn't risk the life of her baby and she found herself taking a few steps back.

It was then she noticed a figure running past her, a green sword in one hand, and an orange dagger in the other. All she noticed after that was a flash of blonde hair and a new quiver of arrows falling to her feet.

Alexia had seen enough of the fight to know that she was needed, and after leaving Misty safely on the deck of the ship, she rushed off towards Mike and the others. It took her no time to run back towards the end of the dock and past Shelby, who seemed at a loss standing still holding her sword in one hand and her stomach with the other. She dropped a quiver of arrows at her feet as she rushed by knowing that she would still be in need of her bow.

The thing was so distracted by Mike and his attacks that it didn't even notice her fast approaching until it was far too late. She jumped towards it with all of her strength and scored a solid thrust right into the thing's upper

213

chest driving her sword straight to its hilt. As her left hand brought her dagger around in a perfect semi-circle, she couldn't help but watch as it slid right through the flesh of its neck. Her dagger too was buried to the hilt, but before she could pull both weapon free she found herself flying backwards as her eyes began to blur, and the world started spinning under her as she slammed into the snow covered ground hard.

Mike watched the thing put all of its strength into a powerful head butt, which hit Alexia just above her eyes with enough force behind it to send the assassin flying backwards to the ground, in a bloody mess. He wanted to run to her, but he knew if he did, her two powerful attacks would have been for nothing.

As he watched the thing bleed out of so many different wounds, he knew it had to be slowly running out of life. It had so many arrow shafts sticking out of it and so many deep gashes all over its body and yet it was still willing to fight on and so was he.

At that moment he felt all of his strength come back to him knowing that they had almost won, that they had almost beat the unbeatable and so he moved forward once again, his swords going on the offensive so quickly the thing didn't have time to bring up any real defense. He slashed its chest twice and his blade dug in deep and again he hopped back just in time to avoid a massive strike from it last sword. Finally, he watched Eric's crystal sword arch downwards with all of the man's strength and sever the things wrist right off. He watched as the sword and hand fell to the ground and winched as the thing hollered in pain.

It was that howl that cost the thing dearly when a flying arrow blew right into its mouth with enough force that it shot right out the back of its head. As it reached its hands behind its head to cover its newest wound, Mike moved in with his great speed and thrust forward with both of his swords and they shattered the things ribs caged as they entered into its chest. He felt his own wrists jerk back painfully, he even heard the bone in his left wrist crack and he suddenly lost all feeling in it.

But the fight was over and he knew it as both of the tips of sword sliced perfectly into the things heart. He watched as its eyes bulged open wide in the few seconds it took him to realize he was dead before it landed once again on its knees. It remained upright still, but that only lasted as long as it took Eric to smash the side of the thing's head with his mighty shield causing it to fall to its side, very dead.

He was on his own knees before he knew it, kneeling beside Alexia, her forehead was bruised pretty badly but she opened her eyes slightly at his touch. He found a smile on his face as he lifted her up into his arms just in time to see Eric and Shelby walking towards him.

"So, do you want to fill us in on what that was all about, my friend?"

"It is a long story but to make it as short as possible, I am an outcast now, and clearly Candice is resorting to the Nameless Ones to hunt me down," Mike said as he watched his two friends in front of him, trying his best to read their emotions.

"What did you do?"

"I killed a fellow assassin."

"If you killed him, then I am sure you had your reasons," Shelby started, "and Eric and I would love to hear them, but we should probably wait until we are on the boat and safely away from here to talk."

"I agree with you more than you think right now," Mike said as he watched three more figures rushing down the road. They were the size of normal people, but even from so far away he could see the whiteness of their gleaming eyes, he could sense their hunger for death. "Take her my friend and get her to the ship."

"I will not allow you to fight them alone."

It was almost as if Eric's word were heard from the entire crew of his ship as all thirty of them walked towards them, each of them with a bow and arrow ready. They all let the arrows fly free and all thirty of them found their mark on the three approaching enemies.

Mike handed Alexia to Eric and he ran towards the wounded things with only one sword in hand, he was fueled by rage or maybe it was love, but he felt like he was invincible at that very moment. He reached the three of them shortly after a second wave of arrows slammed into them and he used that as his starting point of attack.

He lunged forward at the closest one and thrust his sword right through the poor things neck and he pulled it out without slowing, without even looking back at the thing as it fell to the ground dead.

It was Eric's turn to watch his friend in action as Mike struck down the first of the three with a single blow. He watched his friend take a nasty stab to his ribs with a dagger of the second but that only seemed to fuel him on more. "Take her to the ship," he said, handing Alexia to the captain.

He ran as fast as he could towards his longtime friend, and he turned at the last second and jumped as high as he could into the air. An arrow whistle by just under his legs and slammed into the third thing's chest causing it to lean forward in pain, a move that cost the thing its life. As he began descending back to the ground, he gripped the hilt of his sword in both hands and jammed it down as hard as he could. It cut through the things flesh with ease, shattering its spinal cord before it exploded out of its chest, impaling the poor thing to the ground.

Mike took the jab to his chest in stride, even as he heard a few of his ribs crack under the blow. He slashed down at the same time with an attack of his own and just like Eric had done to the first one, he cut right through this one's arm causing it to stumble backwards as it grips its wrist with it free hand.

He reached down and painfully pulled the dagger from his chest, its jagged edge cutting even worse on the way out as it did on the way in. He dropped the dagger to the ground just in time to witness Eric's epic flying attack, killing the third of the attacking group. There was one, or at least he thought there was one left, but when he turned back to face it, he noticed it laying on the ground with close to twenty if not more new arrows sticking out of it.

"Now I think it is best we get to your ship."

"I couldn't agree more," Mike said as he removed his second blue sword from the first of the dead things lying on the ground. "Grab the other swords and daggers, my friend, I only have the use of one of my hands."

With that done, the two of them headed off towards the ship and quickly boarded it. The ship was quickly moving before they even fell to their knees on the dock and he looked up to see all of the archers including Shelby were standing on the side of the ship, letting arrow after arrow fly through the sky.

"Stop shooting already or you are going to hit her by mistake," Mike said, pointing in between to two new Nameless Ones standing on the dock facing the fast leaving ship. "She will only hunt us down even more if you wound her now."

With one final look at Candice standing on the end of the dock staring back at him, he turned away and headed towards Alexia who was slightly sitting upright now against one of the side rails of the deck.

Candice couldn't believe the carnage that was laid out in front of her when she finally took her sights off the ship, which was quickly disappearing into the dark horizon. She figured that Mike was good but not this good, three of the lesser things laid dead and mangled on the ground and one of the bigger brutes was dead as well, with hundreds of wounds to it. She knew right away by the amount of arrows everywhere that he must have had helped, but she still couldn't believe he managed to kill four of them.

She turned back to the ocean once again and felt a deep sadness in her heart. She knew that she had over- reacted by calling forth the Nameless Ones, but she didn't know what else to do. She honestly thought they would have been able to stop him from getting away, if only she was a little bit faster in getting there.

She knew Mike was gone and out of her life now, and this time she figured he was gone for good. She didn't quite know how to handle that. She thought she loved him the whole time they were together, but she was starting to realize it wasn't real love. What she and Mike had was more like a love two people would share when they feared being alone, so they stayed together for just that reason.

She watched her husband as he searched over the dead bodies as if he would find something that she didn't already know, as if he could fix all of the problems he seemed to play such a role in. She had figured it out as she was laying on the ground in her room after Mike's attack that Kevin might have set the man up with help from the Count, causing the massacre in front of her now.

"Where do you think they are heading?"

"It doesn't matter really. Wherever they are going, we will never find them again."

"So you are going to give up your search for him before it even starts?"

"You are more than welcome to go after him, my dear husband, but you might want to take a couple handfuls of them," Candice said, pointing towards the two Nameless Ones standing by her husband. "Keep in mind that he killed four of them already, one of which was the most powerful of the group."

"It would seem he has friends still in the temple."

"If he had any friends left here they are now sailing away with him as we speak, but like I said, feel free to hunt him down and take with you anyone else who is willing to go. Somehow I doubt you will find many who are willing to go up against that outcast."

Candice turned away from her husband then because she was getting tired of talking in circles. She knew that very few of her fellow assassins would be willing to take up the cause of hunting Mike down. Hell she didn't even know if she had the heart to go after him herself. "Send word out to any assassin willing to hunt down and kill the outcast that I am offering a reward of over a million gold coins for him and more so if he is bought in alive. However, any assassin who leaves here after him has to take four if not more of the Nameless Ones with them. At least that way they might make it back home alive," she said, and once she finished she gave a nod to the one of her assistants who ran off to deliver the word.

"And what are you going to do, my wife?"

"I am going to go and search his cottage and then burn it to the ground. Then head out to the Merchant Islands and find his hiding place there and do the same," Candice said, turning to face her husband. "And you are going to take three of them and head to Count Drake's manor and see what clues Mike left behind there, and don't bother returning until you find something useful."

With that she walked off into the still snowing early morning, and headed off to a place she knew very well.

Chapter 24

They were four days out of port and still Mike was having a hard time relaxing. He knew if Candice planned on following them, she wouldn't be able to catch up to his fast moving ship so easily, but he just couldn't shake the feeling of unease. Maybe it was something in his heart finally telling him his old life was over, or maybe it was something else. Maybe he had finally taken that last step to getting over Candice, and now he was free to move on.

It was sunny out for the first time since they left port and even the snow on the ship was slowly melting away under his feet. He turned and rested his back against the railing, and he watched his friends, Eric and Shelby playing some sort of game with Misty. He was surprised at how quickly the two of them took to the little girl. Alexia was off to the side reading one of her books, but he could tell by the look on her face that she was lost more in her own thoughts than in the words of the book in front of her. Most of the crew were along the railings of the ship fishing and trying their best to enjoy the sun.

The thing that made him smile the most was the fact that everyone seemed so free and not a single person on the deck of the ship had a single weapon on them, well he had his two blue daggers tucked into the back of his belt, hidden under his jacket. Maybe the outcast life was a life he could learn to love, he thought, or maybe it was the fact that he was finally free.

He made his way over to the bench Alexia was sitting on and placed his legs on either side of her pulling her back into his chest. She didn't even fight it as she sunk into him. They hadn't spent very much time together since their run-in with the Nameless Ones, and even though she didn't think she played a big role in the fight, she had indeed.

He felt her take his still broken hand in hers as she turned her head slightly to kiss him on the cheek. He could feel his hand throb at the contact, but he didn't pull it away from her touch. It was after all, a reminder of what it was he could have lost if he had died fighting those nasty things. Something that could have just as easily happened if Eric and Shelby weren't passing by when they had been.

"Look at you all full of thoughts," Alexia stated.

"I'm just happy to finally be free."

"Are you happy enough to maybe find your way into our bed tonight?"

"I had a lot of planning to do and I had to figure out a lot of stuff on my own but I wasn't avoiding you in anyway," Mike said, stealing a quick kiss from her. "Eric and Shelby needed to know the truth about everything."

"And are they okay with everything that has happened."

"Yes, they seem to be. Eric was mad that I didn't invite him along to the Count's manor and all the fun we had there."

"True. Getting stabbed through the chest was one hell of a time."

"Hey now, no complaining. It only happened to you once now, while I have been stabbed in the chest twice in the last few months."

"Do you think you would have been able to defeat it alone?"

"I am sure I would have won sooner or later, but I would have been hard pressed to kill it before the other three had arrived," Mike admitted, trying his best to ease the sadness in Alexia's blue eyes. She still had slight bruising on her forehead and he leaned in and gently kissed her on it.

"I don't mean to interrupt you two love birds, but where is it your captain planning on taking us?"

"He says he has the perfect place far to the north where we can both hide the ship and find places to live. He says the land is frozen year round but the people are nice, and there are no real cities or towns, just small outcrops of houses or villages from place to place," Mike said as he watched Eric sit across from them.

"Sounds like a place fitting for us, then."

"You are not happy, my friend?"

"It just sounds like we are going to be on this boat for a long time, and you know how much I love boats."

"I am sure we will be there in about three months," Mike said, teasing his friend but he did figure it would take about three months to get there.

"Do you think she will come after us?"

"We were the best she had and now we are on the run. She has no one left to send after us who would even stand a chance."

"She could send a thousand more of them if she has that many. She could send them all."

"And then the four of us will kill them all. Once we reach land we will find a few places close together with a great view of our surroundings. If they come, we will see them coming from miles away."

"And how do you plan on buying all of this stuff. You might remember that Shelby and I left home without knowing we would ever be going back and have little with us."

"Come with me, my friend, and I will show you," Mike said, giving Alexia one last kiss before heading off towards one of the back stairways with his longtime friend.

The two of them walked in silence down the stairs and around a bunch of twists and turns in the hallway before coming to a small elevator, which was only meant to hold two people which you could tell by just looking at its small size. The two of them took the short trip down and when the doors opened they were in a single hallway, which led to a single metal door, which was about as thick as it was wide. He placed his right palm on the scanner, which was placed on the front of the door and it read his palm print perfectly, including his two oddly shaped scares.

The door slid to the left reveling a massive square room, which was the front of the ship and inside that room was all of the money they had stolen from the Count's place and all of the gold from his own house, some stacked up neatly but most of it was tossed all over from the waves and the rocking of the ship. "This, my friend, is how we are going to start our new lives," He offered, giving Eric a slap on the back.

"You have been holding out on me, my friend."

"The gold is mine but the money we stole from Count Drake since I figured he didn't need it anymore."

"So you are an outcast and a thief then." Eric pointed out as he made his way into the money filled room.

"It seems like a fitting life from what I used to be."

"You have a girl and a kid now. Who would have ever thought the great master assassin would have come this far."

"I am still unsure what it is that I am trying to find in my life, but I knew in my heart that I couldn't leave Misty there with that sick man, so that left me with only one choice to make," Mike confessed leaning against the left wall as he watched his friend dig through the piles of gold and money.

"You did what you had to do, and what anyone else would have done in your position."

"So you and Shelby aren't mad that I forced you into joining me into the outcast life?"

"You forced us into nothing. I saw an enemy about to attack one of my best friends and I made the first move. Plus, I think we were looking for a way to get out anyway, and it just happened you had a boat full of money to help us."

"At least you should be happy that the two of you didn't have to face off against me one day," Mike said, teasing his friend as he watched him stick a thick stack of money into his back pocket.

"Maybe I would have liked to face off against the master assassin."

"And if you ever decided to, I will have to remember not to hug you and those nasty little spikes you got hidden in your armor."

"You are the one with the glowing weapons, and that would just mean it would be an unfair fight."

"I would fight you with just my fists and nothing else."

"That would be interesting to see, since you currently only have one hand."

"Want to know what the hardest part of this new life is going to be?"

"What is that, my friend?"

"The fact that we will have to find real jobs so we can fit in with the rest of the world," Mike said, making them both laugh.

"That will be the easy part. I think it is going to be a lot harder to convince the women to find real jobs."

"Speaking of women, let's get back to them and see if we have missed anything important while you were busy stuffing your pockets with my money," Mike said, once again making them both laugh as they headed out of the room.

"So is this the life you thought you would be living?" Alexia asked Shelby, shortly after the boys went off to look at all the money.

"It is the life I am living and I have no regrets, so I am happy with the outcome. Are you?"

"I felt like I was walking alone in a dark place for a very long time, but all of that changed when I had that first dance with Mike. It was like something inside of me came back to life, so I don't regret meeting him or where we are now, but I figure the two of us will have our hands full for a while though," Alexia said as she watched Misty fishing over the side of the boat with a few members of the crew.

"She seems like a really good kid."

"She is the best of kids, but I still think it is going to be a bit of a struggle going from what we were to living this simple life raising a girl who isn't even our own."

"But who better to raise her then the two of you."

"You mean two people who are struggling every day with their feelings for each other, even though we both clearly love one and another? I do get what you mean, though. It just doesn't seem right brining her into our outcast lifestyle."

"If it helps any, I am pretty sure Eric and I are bringing a child into our outcast life as well."

"You're pregnant?" Alexia asked, a little louder then she planned on, but she was taken fully by surprise.

"I have been having morning sickness and all of the other signs, so I am starting to think that I am in fact pregnant."

"How is that possible if you are still immortal?"

"I am not sure and it was something I planned on asking Candice about, but we never got the chance to before we ran into the three of you fleeing the city."

"So that is why you hesitated on the battlefield."

"I was hoping no one noticed that."

"You played you role during that fight perfectly."

"So I guess we can both figure out how to raise our kids in our new life together then."

Alexia agreed fully with Shelby's words, but she found herself not saying anything as she watched Mike and Eric returning from the side doorway. She didn't know if Eric had told Mike yet about the baby and she didn't want to ruin the surprise. She watched him as he walked with his old friend as if he didn't have a care in the world. She smiled back at him as he made his way across the deck towards Misty.

Mike snuck right up behind Misty before lifting her into the air and catching her in his arms. He couldn't help but laugh as she fixed him with the world's cutest evil stare, but even she couldn't keep it up for long before she was smiling back at him.

The two of them spent hours fishing together and sharing in each other's company, and soon even Alexia was there with a rod of her own. To Mike, it seemed like he had finally found a purpose in his long life, and he looked forward to seeing where and what would come of it.

Candice awoke early in the morning like she had every morning since Mike left the main land, only this time she was staying in his old beach house, a beach house he seemed to have left in a hurry she figured by the amount of stuff he left behind. She found the hole in the wall as soon as she got there realizing it must have been where he had his gold hidden, but if it was, it was long gone.

She had been there now for over a month, and she had five of her top assassins searching the entire island for any clue as to where Mike and his crew had run off to, but so far no one was talking. It didn't bother her much though; she didn't really want to find him. She knew, however, that she had to make it look like she was trying or else she could have more problems on her hands than just a single powerful outlaw and his friends.

She was also very hurt at the fact that out of all the years they were together, he had never once brought her to this place, but in the short time he had known Alexia, they spend how many nights alone in the very bed she now slept in.

She took the time to replace the entire bedding set but she couldn't bring herself to burn the place to ground like she originally planned. She was really beginning to fall in love with its beauty and she could tell why Mike kept it as a secret all of these years. She couldn't help but wonder how many more hidden places he had all over the world. She figured that would be her main goal in her search for him, hunt down his old hiding places, and see what she could learn from them. She honestly didn't think she would find him held up in any of them, but she had to keep herself busy.

The sound of a boat approaching snapped her out of her thoughts, but it didn't worry her at all because it was either someone going by a little too close to the deck, or it was her husband returning from the mission she sent him on over two months ago. Either way, she was finding it hard to get out of bed and find out. She had grown to love Kevin, but since finding out that he had played a role in Mike's downfall, she was having a hard time finding a way to forgive him. She was beginning to even question their marriage.

She could hear the sound of footfalls on the deck and since the Nameless Ones she had posted outside didn't kill the person right away, she figured it had to be her husband. She sat up in the bed and quickly pulled a shirt on so she wasn't topless, but she did it to slow and he smiled as he walked in on her getter dressed.

"So, the Count's manor or at least what was left of it, gave me no clues whatsoever about what happened there, well besides the countless burnt bodies and the fact that his massive safe was empty. Your friend has effectively covered his tracks."

"He is the best assassin in the world, did you expect anything less from him?" Candice asked, trying to keep the anger out of her voice because she didn't want to start a fight this early in the morning.

"What have you come to learn while staying here?"

"That he had a better taste in life than I would have ever thought."

"It would seem he had you all tricked in the end."

"And yet he would still be on my side if you didn't get involved with this Count Drake, and force Mike into a situation you knew he couldn't go through with," Candice reminded him, staring hard at her husband. "You set him up to fail, and I am still not sure how well that sits with me."

"I did what I was paid to do. No different than what your assassins do on any given day."

Candice didn't even bother to respond to that or anything else Kevin had to say as she made her way across the room to grab a bottle of water out of the fridge. She could feel his eyes on her the whole time, and she knew it was because she was only in a pair of tight shorts and a small shirt but she wasn't going to allow herself to be distracted by that. After all, he did nothing to deserve being able to sleep with her as of late. She couldn't bring herself to think about having sex with her husband while her mind was still favoring the thoughts about killing him. "I am going to stay on the islands for a while longer, so you can either book yourself a room at one of the inns or return home," she told him, turning just in time to catch Kevin frown at either idea.

"And what are you planning on doing about Mike?"

"I will find him sooner or later, but until then, let him enjoy his freedom."

Again Candice didn't wait for Kevin to respond before walking into the bathroom and locking the door behind her. She needed a shower to clear her thoughts and knew that if he joined her, she would be forced to forgive him sooner then he deserved. She was meaning to make him suffer this time. She also figured that there would be no harm at all in letting Mike get some much needed time to relax before the two of them met again, face to face.

THE END...

ACKNOWLEDGEMENTS

First off I want to thank everyone for buying my book and I hope that you enjoy reading it as much as I enjoyed writing it. It has been a while now since *Dragonsbane, Spiron's Legacy* was released and I want everyone to know that I am working on starting it over and getting the last two books out as well. I know a lot of you are looking forward to reading more about Spiron and his life but for now I hoped you enjoyed learning about Mike as he makes his way through this book and the rest to come.

I want to start off by thanking my girlfriend Ashly for pushing me to get this book done and for not letting me give up on my writing after *Dragonsbane* didn't do as well as I wanted. You mean a lot to me and I am happy you came into my life when you did and I wouldn't change anything about us. I am looking forward to us moving into our first place together and I can't wait to see what our lives have in store for us. <3

I also want to thank my parents who never turned their backs on me no matter what I seemed to have put them through. Also for always believing in me and what I could do even when I didn't believe in myself. I will never forget that. I also want to say thank you to you both for putting up with me this whole year as we waited for our place to be built. I know it couldn't have been easy.

I also want to thank my two brother for always being there for me and for all the help and advice that you have shared with me over my life time. I am sure it hasn't always seemed like it but I have always loved you both.

For everyone who loved this book I want you to know that I am currently working on a second part to it and I am hoping to make it about 5 parts in totally. So bear with me as I work on this project because I have a lot of great thoughts as to where this story line will go and that means a lot of hard work and time.

Also for those of you who are waiting to read more about Mike and Spiron I am letting you know that hopefully it isn't that long till you can.

Thank you again for everyone who has supported me over the last few years of my writing and I am looking forward to a good year in 2015. I want to thank Reagan Rothe at Black Rose Writing for publishing my book and getting the printed copies out there for all of my friends, family and fans. I am looking forward to a great year working with everyone at Black Rose Writing in 2016.

I also want to dedicate this book to my Grandpa Long who passed away last year. You were a great man and I really looked up to you. I miss you more and more each day and life just isn't the same without you in it. I just hope that I made you proud and I wish you were still around. You are missed by a lot of people and it sucks you won't get to see your great grand kids growing up. Thank you very much for all the good memories of us at the cabin and everything you have thought me. I will miss you forever. I still remember the last time I saw you alive and well as I walked into your hospital room and saw you sitting there in your bed with your shirt off doing your puzzles. It is that moment I will keep with me for the rest of my life. You were gone too soon and will never be forgotten.

I still think about my Grandpa Salamon all the time as well and I miss having him around. Life has changed a lot since you left us and I still sit around thinking about you from time to time. Everyone misses you so much and I wished you were around to see the man I grew up to be. This will be my second published book and I am buying my first house this year as well. None of this wouldn't have be possible if you and grandma didn't bring my mom into your lives and I want to thank you for that.

Losing both of my grandpa's so close together has showed me how short life can be and I just want them to know that even though they are both gone I will try my best to keep their memories alive in my writing even if it is just a small write up at the end of my books. Even as I write this and think back to all of the camping adventures, cabin trips, Mexico trips, and just sitting around with you both it brings tears to my eyes and it seems like it was just yesterday. Those memories will go with me in my heart till the day I day and I will share the stories with kids so they can share it with theirs and so on and so on.

THANK YOU AGAIN EVERYONE... MY LIFE WOULDN'T BE THE SAME WITHOUT ANY OF YOU IN IT.

MICHAEL LONG   FEB 11/2016

Purchase other Black Rose Writing titles at <u>www.blackrosewriting.com/books</u>
and use promo code PRINT to receive a 20% discount.

BLACK ROSE
writing™

CPSIA information can be obtained at www.ICGtesting.com
Printed in the USA
LVOW07s0956150316

479150LV00002B/77/P